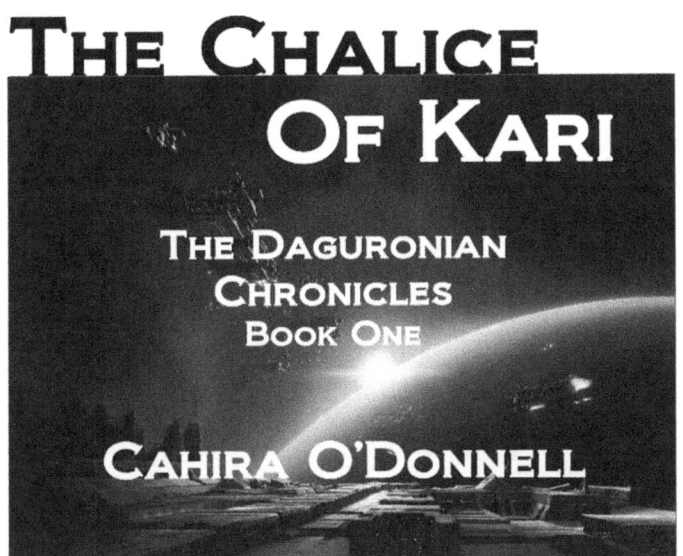

THE CHALICE OF KARI

THE DAGURONIAN CHRONICLES
BOOK ONE

CAHIRA O'DONNELL

I0685468

"I trust our love to gentle you," she whispered.

"Kahara, oh please lady, at least have Rom present to stop me if I cannot stop myself. I beg of you, for your safety, let me call my brother to be with us."

Rah's mental call had already reached Rom who quietly flowed into the dimly lit room. His beloved brother and mate sat before the fire, Kahara's beautiful naked body draped over his brother's lap. Rah shredded the leather seat in an attempt to keep his hands off of her.

"I am here."

"Hi Rom. Rah seems to have some misgivings," Kahara blushed. She was still unaccustomed to the unity of the brothers and the novelty of having two mates rather than one.

"I was trying to soften him to my wiles but he is proving rather resistant."

"I know you are trying to get used to us one at a time, but Rah feels it best that we are all here for this. Can you bring yourself to embrace us as a triad?" Rom wanted nothing more than to witness and support the bonding of the two most beloved people in his life.

"I trust your judgment and I trust both of you." Truth be told, she still felt a bit awkward. Yet the way Rom's eyes drank in the sight of them together, the silver depths full of passion and love, was one heck of a turn on.

"Rom, I am not sure what to do," Kahara confessed on her private link with him.

"Looks like you are doing fine. You have his full attention."

"Rom, if I start to harm her in any way, put me down," Rah pleaded on the private link with his brother.

Rom settled himself in the chair across from the couple, stretching out and crossing his booted feet at the ankles. He looked deceptively relaxed. Both regarded him with worried eyes.

"You might try undressing him, Kahara. As I recall, that was my undoing."

"You're actually enjoying this, Rom!" she admonished.

"You have no idea, lady. You have no idea," he winked at her.

The Chalice Of Kari
A Dark River Publishing Book / Jan 2015

Published by Dark River Publishing
A Division of Path Home LLC
Coaldale, Colorado

This is a work of Fiction. Names, characters, places, and incidents are either the product of the author's imagination or are used fictitiously, and any resemblance to actual persons, living or dead, events or locales is entirely coincidental.

All rights reserved.
Copyright © 2015 by Gwilda Wiyaka
Cover photos Shutter Stock
Cover design by Gwilda Wiyaka

No part of this book may be reproduced, scanned, or distributed in any printed or electronic form without permission. Please do not participate in or encourage piracy of copyrighted materials in violation of the author's rights. Purchase only authorized editions.

ISBN: 978-0692348888

For my Children
Whose undying faith and love
Make everything possible

With Deep Gratitude

To my editor, Cody Alexander, and to my proof reader, Terry Lamond, whose dedication and laborious attention to detail have made this work readable.

To my literary assistant, Trixie Phelps, whose "preparation for publication" magic has brought this story from the ethers into ordinary reality.

To my PR wizard, Rob McConnell, whose vision, artistry and mastery moves mountains.

The Chalice
Of Kari

Dark River Publishing
PO Box 271
Coaldale, CO 81222

~ *Chapter 1* ~

Joining the Special Forces had seemed like the right thing to do when Kahara had been approached that February of 2004. She was in her last year of college and had just undergone testing in her parapsychology class. Her scores were unusual, to say the least. She took the class hoping to delve into the mysteries of her "special gifts," as her mother had always called them. More like special curse, she decided, as once again she was on the run, leaving everything she'd known and built in order to stay one step ahead of those that would use her to harm others.

"Your precognitive abilities are running at ninety-four percent accuracy. Medical intuitive, backed up with X-ray, CAT scan, MRI and lab work score at ninety-eight percent accurate. Your animal communication skills are in the ninety-seventh percentile. Your emotional empathy scores are off the charts. You don't show any tendencies toward telekinesis or pyrokinesis, but your personality discernment and behavior projection scores are very high…" Dr. Allan, her parapsychology professor, droned on and on as he shared her evaluation. For him, it was quite the animated dissertation. His normal monotone had given way to an almost passionate accounting. She felt like a bug under glass. No, she'd felt like a bug under glass during the testing and then the follow-up tests. By the time the follow-up tests led to more tests, she had graduated to "prized bug under glass." Now she felt like a whole new species of bug running the risk of being preserved in formaldehyde.

1

Three months later, just before graduating, she was called into Dr. Allan's office to meet with a tall, fatherly man her professor had introduced as Master Sergeant Walker. He'd not been in uniform at the time, but his military bearing could not be missed. Well-toned and disciplined, he'd impressed her with his intelligence and seeming kindness. He appeared to be as altruistic as she, speaking of the greater good and using one's gifts to protect and serve her country.

Kahara had been alone and vulnerable at the time, unsure of what to do when she graduated. Both her parents and brother had been killed two months before in an automobile accident while vacationing in Canada. At least that's what she had been told. Now that she thought about it, the "accident" came just after her first barrage of parapsychology tests. Call her paranoid, but life had taught her not to trust surface appearances.

~

She looked both ways before slipping from between two buildings to cross the darkened street. Dressed in black with a hoodie pulled over her flaming red curls, Kahara blended into the shadows. She did that well. She'd been taught by the best. Her only possessions rested in the black pack she carried; weapons and special ops gear, rather than makeup and memorabilia. Not even a change of underwear was important enough to take up precious space. It was all about survival – survival or death – whichever it took to protect the innocent from the deadly weapon she had unwittingly become.

Her training, while exceedingly intense, had been exciting and she took to it like a fish to water. She'd become well versed in all forms of weaponry and martial arts. Her body, though slim and small, was honed to a fine instrument. Powerful and agile as a cat, she could run, jump, climb and roll with the best of them. She'd been trained to fly just about anything the military had, from helicopters to jet fighters. She even had flight-sim time in space shuttles.

Kahara could survive in any terrain with minimal gear. Her "gifts" had been honed to a razor sharp edge. She could conjure weather or communicate with animals. Her ability to forecast the future enabled her to read situations and discern the best tactics to reach a goal. Through empathy, she could read people and accurately judge their motives. Between her training and gifts, she was nearly unstoppable.

A black SUV unexpectedly rounded the corner with its lights off. Kahara dropped and rolled under a parked car, her diminutive size enabling her to fit under the Mustang. They were close on her tail this time. Fortunately, the Mustang had been recently driven, the engine still warm enough to mask her from heat sensing scanners.

~

Her first missions had been totally wonderful, everything she'd hoped. She'd been assigned as a consultant to a tight team of well-trained Seals specializing in hostage situations with no-kill orders. While at first, the men had balked at her gender and size – there were no female Seals – her hidden talents and tenacity had soon won her the position of a trusted and well respected teammate. Teammate – she later discovered, but not friend or lover. The very talents that made her invaluable on mission put the men off.

Kahara still felt the humiliation when she'd tried to develop a relationship with one of the members of her team. Sam had been tall, muscular and gorgeous. They worked well together and had pulled each other out of numerous jams. He'd even thrown his own body over hers to protect her from gunfire.

"I'm sorry, Kahara babe, but I like to spend my off time with a fluff bunny," Sam had informed her when she'd suggested they get together while on leave.

"What's a fluff bunny?" she wanted to know.

"You know, all boobs and no brain. No offense, honey, but I'm not comfortable knowing you can walk around in my head. It's okay on mission, but when I'm off, I just want to relax with something soft and have some good ol' mind blowing sex with no complications."

To say it hadn't been her finest moment was an understatement. After the humiliating conversation, she became aware that, while she was appreciated by her teammates on mission, they'd always held her at arm's length. When the men got together with each other for drinks, she'd never been invited along. Kahara had been careful not to "read" the other members of her team in order to respect their privacy. But when she reached out with her gift to see how they really felt, she found they were all secretly afraid of her. The men were glad they had her skills at their disposal, but, all said and done, she gave them the willies. It was a devastating realization.

~

After the SUV disappeared down the street, she rolled out from under the Mustang. Staying low to the ground, she slid between two high-rise buildings like the ghost she'd become. Drawing a grappling hook from her pack, she threw it up to lodge on the roof of a shorter building. After scaling the building's side, she traversed several city blocks from rooftop to rooftop.

Belaying down to a darkened alley, Kahara gathered her gear into the pack, stepped from between the buildings and onto a city bus just before it closed its doors and pulled away from the curb.

Slouching down in her seat, she activated her new prepaid cell and dialed a number she tried to never use.

"Sam here."

"Hi, I'm on the run. Can you set me up?"

"You bet. You know the place."

"Thanks, I owe you."

"No, babe, I owe you. My son would be dead if not for what you did. I'll never be able to repay that."

"Thanks, Sam."

"Be safe, babe."

"You bet, safe-R-us," she said, and ended the call. Opening the phone, she removed the sim-card and battery, ground them under her heel, and threw the remnants out the window. She got off the bus at the next stop and onto another heading in the opposite direction.

~

Sam had been assigned to another team for over two years when Kahara had received a panicked call from him. He'd married one of his "fluff bunnies" and they had a child together. His nineteen month old son had been abducted and was being held hostage. It was an attempt to coerce Sam to assassinate a prominent government official. Kahara and another old teammate had gone in with Sam on what had turned into a major blood bath.

They'd found the boy's abductors in a remote cabin in the Montana wilderness. Using her animal communications skills, she had rallied a team of cougars to aid them. Kahara and the cats took out several men, including the one holding a gun to the sobbing toddler's head. She'd silently dropped to the ground from a tree behind the abductor, deflected his gun hand and cut his throat.

It had been her first personal kill, something she swore she would not do. She'd never gotten over it. She had used her healing skills to remove the trauma and memories from the child. Sam's son had been retrieved relatively unscathed, but an essential part of Kahara had died that night.

Sam knew her well enough to know what saving his son had cost. He'd vowed to always be there for her, and he had. Sam had many special talents and skills, not the least of which was making people disappear. When her handler started insisting she go on questionable missions, requiring shady ethics often resulting in deaths, she submitted her resignation. It was firmly refused and she went AWOL. Sam had provided her with a way out and a new identity. He'd done so more than once over the following years. He always had a backup waiting for her at a pre-disclosed safety deposit box should she be tracked and need to run again, and run she had.

The honeymoon with special ops had ended when she was assigned to her new team. To call them "badass" would have been an understatement. No more no-kill hostage retrieval, they were straight up assassins sent in to "cleanse" situations. In and out with no trace, she was to be the star of the show.

At first, she'd been delighted when they gave her a team of three black German Shepherds. Her animal communication skills enabled her and the beautiful canines to become flawless in their collaboration. The dogs were totally loyal and would do absolutely anything for her. She'd been led to believe they would be used for search and rescue. At first they had, but only long enough to be field tested. Then they'd been put on "team badass" for a search and kill mission. When told she was expected to use the dogs to track and kill individuals deemed to have too much information, she'd outright refused.

"I will not exploit these animals, nor will I kill to protect dubious military secrets. I signed up to save people, not murder them," she'd informed her superior officer.

"You signed up to do what you're damn well told," was the response. She was threatened with court marshal and imprisonment if she did not comply. She'd pretended to acquiesce only long enough to be sent on another mission, giving her the opportunity to bolt, and her life on the run had begun. One by one, she had found good homes for her beloved dogs and continued on alone.

~

Kahara got off the bus four blocks from the bank, Sam's next prearranged pick up point. She pulled off the hoodie, revealing a royal blue, silk dress blouse, and fluffed her hair. With her black pants and boots, she was instantly transformed into a business woman. She stuffed the hoodie into the pack, pulled out a black leather clutch purse containing a safety deposit box key.

Heels clipping smartly on the tiled floor, she walked into the bank. After pressing her palm onto the reader, she punched in her security code and entered the vault. Taking the safety deposit box into a private booth, she opened it and closed the door on her last identity.

The box contained a new prepaid cell phone, new contact phone number, a safety deposit box key and address for the next pick up point, cash, passport, driver's license, credit cards, brown contact lenses, tanning cream, black hair dye and hair straightener. Most surprising of all was the business card of a cosmetic surgeon. Apparently, Sam had decided it was time for drastic measures.

Two weeks later, she'd recovered from surgery and put the dye, straightener and tanning cream to use. Looking in the mirror of the hotel bathroom, she didn't recognize herself, which she supposed was the point. Her hair was jet black and cut into a short, straight bob with blunt bangs. Her eyes were brown, almond shaped and slanted from the surgery. Tanning cream had turned her fair skin into a yellow copper shade. Riko Yamamoto, the American born daughter of deceased Japanese immigrants, looked back at her from the mirror. All signs and evidence of her former identity were gone.

~ Chapter 2 ~

Friday March 11, 2011

Takata, Japan

It had been a lifelong dream for both Riko and Rhiannon to visit Japan. The women had met and become fast friends while serving as hospice volunteers in Denver, Colorado. Kahara had settled there after taking on her latest identity as Riko Yamamoto. The two women had saved for over a year to fund the trip.

Upon arrival in Japan, they'd rented a car and had been working their way up the coast. After passing through rice paddies and pear orchards, they planned to stop in the rural Japanese port town of Takata, hoping to take in the museum of sea and shells. Suddenly, the car started to shudder and shake.

"Darn, I think we have a flat," Rhiannon, who was driving, complained, pulling over to the side of the narrow mountain road near a rice paddy. As the car came to a stop, the shaking did not. In fact, it seemed to increase.

"I think we're actually experiencing an earthquake," Riko told her friend in an amazed voice. While both women were widely traveled, neither had experienced the phenomenon.

"Wow! I think you're right! What do we do?" Rhiannon exclaimed.

"I haven't a clue."

"Well, there's nothing close that can fall on us. Maybe we should just stay in the car until it quits."

"Sounds as good an idea as any."

The women sat in the car for what seemed a long time while the shaking continued.

"It's still going on!" Rhiannon observed nervously.

"I feel that."

"How long do these things last?"

"No idea."

"Do you think it's safe to drive now?" Rhiannon asked as the quake finally subsided.

"We're almost to Takata and we can always pull over if it starts again," Riko stated after consulting the map. She had an uneasy feeling she couldn't put her finger on.

They arrived in the sleepy little town, found a place to park and were trying to find the museum on foot when sirens started going off.

"What in the heck?" Rhiannon wanted to know.

"I don't know, there are signs but they're in Japanese."

"Go figure, we must be in Japan. You look the part. Don't you read Japanese?"

"Sorry, American born and bred," Riko laughed at her friend.

People were calmly filing out of buildings and heading to some sort of center near the shore. No one seemed upset or in any big hurry, yet Riko's feeling of unease increased exponentially.

"Those people seem to know what they're doing, maybe we should follow them," Rhiannon suggested, just before a squealing pig dashed up the street in the opposite direction. Riko suddenly stood still and closed her eyes.

"Lemmings," she said in a distant, trance-like voice.

"What?" Rhiannon wanted to know.

"Like lemmings to the sea! To heck with the people, follow the pig!" Riko grabbed Rhiannon's hand and headed up the street at a dead run.

"What about the car, why don't we take the car?" Rhiannon shouted above the sirens, looking over her shoulder to where they had parked.

"No time. We have to find higher ground."

"What do you know that I don't?" Rhiannon asked, having witnessed some of Riko's abilities during their friendship.

"The sea is coming. I saw a midnight wave of death."

Riko opened up all of her senses and cast into the future. A ghost image of black water swallowing everything around them superimposed itself on the present. With her spirit vision, she searched desperately for a safe place they could reach in time. The mountainside was too far. She dragged her friend toward a building with an outside fire escape leading to a roof which seemed to be above the ghost wave from the imminent future. The ground started to tremble and shake under their feet while an unearthly noise built behind them.

"Holy shit! Would you look at that!" Rhiannon screamed, coming to a dead stop in shock. Rising up behind them, like an avenging black angel of death, the water approached in seeming slow motion, pushing boats, buildings and cars ahead of it like so much sea foam.

"Run!" Riko screamed at her friend, dragging her into motion and to the fire escape. "Here, give me your foot," Riko instructed, boosting her up to the bottom rung of the ladder suspended six feet off the ground. She gave Rhiannon time to scramble up a couple rungs before she jumped, swung her legs, wrapped them around the bottom rung and hoisted herself up.

"Climb all the way to the top. It's our only chance!" she screamed when Rhiannon showed signs of stopping to watch the horror of the approaching wave devouring everything in its path. Wailing sirens and terrified screams rent the air.

They'd barely gained the rooftop when the wave reached them. The neighboring two story buildings disappeared under the relentless groaning progression of the black wrath. The building they were on shuddered under them as the inky water climbed up its side, nearly reaching the flat roof where the two women stood watching in horror.

The four story structure shifted on its foundation under the incredible pressure. The roof where they stood buckled and gave way, sending the women crashing to the story below. Debris rained down on them with a thundering crash, a joist pinning them both to the floor.

Riko felt her ribs give way and lost all feeling in her legs. She could tell one of her lungs was filling with blood as breathing became a distant memory. Rhiannon lay motionless beside and slightly underneath her.

Unable to move, she reached out for Rhiannon with her gift. Her friend was unconscious from a blow to the head. As Riko scanned her body, she found Rhiannon's heart laboring under the pressure of the massive weight pressing down on them from the joist. She could also "see" Rhiannon's neck was broken.

The sirens gave up the ghost as, one by one, they disappeared under water. Screams and moans of the dead and dying faded. Riko realized she was drifting in and out of consciousness as the building groaned around her. She had worked in search and rescue enough to realize that, given the devastation she'd witnessed, there was absolutely no hope of a timely rescue. She knew that, without immediate medical attention, they were both going to die.

Riko lay quietly, preparing herself to cross over, as she had helped so many others during her hospice work. She felt badly for Rhiannon, who'd just begun to find some enjoyment in life, but for herself – there was neither fear nor regret. She was tired and ready to go home.

Her life and path had not been an easy one. As a shaman, born in a world that invalidated spirit, she had served the best she could only to be exploited. She knew too much, felt too much, to ever blend in. She'd been on the run too long to develop relationships, much less take a husband.

Most people sensed she saw into the shadows of their lives and were uncomfortable in her presence. Her walk had been solitary. She sought respite in nature, the wilderness her only true comfort. Now, that was disappearing under the wheels of ATVs and progress. She left no family behind, she would not be missed. It was time…

~ *Chapter 3* ~

"I have found her," Rah called to his twin brother on their mental link as he leaned over the petite feminine form nearly buried in rubble. Short, black, dust-coated hair was visible through the pile of debris engulfing the diminutive woman. The pressure of the weight had to be crushing her. He could see another female buried beneath her. Sleepy, dark-brown, pain filled eyes opened to look up at him, yet he could detect no fear or panic in their hazy depths.

Recognition slammed into his gut like a fist. This was her, this was their woman. There could be no mistaking his visceral reaction.

When Riko opened her eyes, a giant dressed in black leather, wearing a helmet with an opaque visor, was looming over her. The floor was shifting dangerously under their combined weight. He squatted, lifting rubble from her body with massive, but surprisingly gentle, black-gloved hands. Another identically dressed giant was holding a light on her prone form.

"How bad is it?" Rom asked his brother on their mental channel.

"Bad enough," Rah responded after running a small, hand held device above her body. Both men worked to unbury her until all that remained was the joist.

Riko would not have understood their language, even had she been aware of the telepathic communication. To her, the two men appeared to be working in silence.

"My friend, Rhiannon, see to her. I'm beyond saving," she whispered to the man closest to her.

"What did she say?" Rah, who did not speak English, wanted to know.

"She wants us to help her friend. What is the other woman's condition?" Rom responded.

"Alive, but she will die soon if we do not intercede," his brother informed him.

"Is she a fertile?"

"Yes," Rah confirmed after running the device over Rhiannon.

"Then we will take them both, but only if it does not endanger our lady to do so." He bent low over Riko. She could see her reflection in his visor. She was covered in dirt, bruised and blood caked – her face unrecognizable.

"We have come to get you out of here, little one, but we need your permission to do so. Will you come with us of your own free will?" Rom asked in thickly accented English from behind his visor.

"Not without Rhiannon."

"Rhiannon is the woman here with you?"

"Yes."

"If I promise to bring her, will you give your permission for us to take you both?"

"Yes, but be careful, her neck is broken."

"What is your name, little one?"

"Kahara," she unwittingly answered, then realized what she had said. Oh well, she wasn't going to make it anyway. It was fitting to die with her true name on her lips. She was so tired of living a lie. "Kahara Mitchell, my name is Kahara Mitchell."

"I am going to put you to sleep, Kahara, so you do not feel the pain of transport." It was the last thing she knew before all went as black as the wave that had washed away an entire community.

~

As soon as the woman lost consciousness under Rom's formidable will, Rah engaged an antigravity device to lift the joist, freeing both women.

"Marc," Rah addressed the leader of the landing team over his com. "We need you and Chief Medical Officer Saul. We have found our lady, but she is in critical condition. There is another fertile with her, so bring two life support chambers for transport."

Soon, the quiet hum of the surface cruiser could be heard as it hovered over the building. Rom could see the craft through the hole in the ceiling where the women must have fallen when the roof collapsed. Two men dressed in black recon gear appeared from the cruiser's bay door with the requested healing chambers. The men and the chambers were lowered through the opening to hover just above the floor.

"Put these on, my lords," Marc instructed the two brothers as he handed each of them an antigravity harness. "Scans of this structure show it to be unstable, inadequate to bear your weight for long."

Understandable, Rom realized, as each of the seven foot tall brothers weighed in at over three hundred pounds in full recon gear. Rom and Rah complied. The four males made short work of freeing the unconscious women.

When Rah lifted the child-sized woman in his arms, he suddenly froze. It was all he could do to release her to the life support chamber. Having found her, he did not want to let her out of his sight. His brother reached past his shoulder and gently brushed her cropped midnight hair from her face with a trembling, black-gloved hand.

"My lords, we need to seal her in. She has a punctured lung and will soon drown in her own blood," Saul informed the brothers.

The reminder from their medical officer forced the two men into action. Rah gently placed her in the life support chamber and Saul sealed it. Rah signaled Kev, who was piloting the surface cruiser, to bring the chamber on board.

The four males carefully loaded Rhiannon into the second life support chamber after securing her in a neck brace and sent her to the cruiser as well. A quick scan with their medical equipment indicated there were no other surviving fertile females in the ruined building. Rah signaled Kev to bring the landing crew on board the cruiser and they were quickly under way.

The operation had been shielded. No one would know they had been there. With the devastation of the entire area, the missing bodies of two women would not be cause for suspicion, even if it were noted. The operation had been a success. In the task of obtaining their mate, failure was not an option for the lords of Kari.

The surface cruiser rejoined the massive, shielded fleet and docked with the medical ship. Both brothers accompanied Kahara and Rhiannon's life support chambers as they were transported from the docking area, via antigravity gurneys, down the long corridor to the treatment rooms. Rom and Rah walked on either side of Kahara's chamber, unwilling to let her out of their sight.

"Saul, what is our lady's status?" Rom asked the chief medical officer as soon as they had entered the sealed medical deck.

"She has a broken back and a punctured lung in addition to various bruises and contusions. Her brainwaves are abnormal, though she doesn't appear to have a head injury," the chief medical officer responded while reading instrumentation on the life support chamber.

"What do you mean, abnormal?" Rah wanted to know.

"She has more brain activity than we have seen in others of her race and seems to be using more of her brain overall. Her IQ is unusually high. She is showing more consciousness than I would expect someone to maintain while under Lord Rom's compulsion. Given the level of physical trauma, the normal mental stress and shock levels are not present."

"So it is not necessarily something wrong?" Rom asked.

"No, 'abnormal' as in 'not typical,' but it may very well be normal for her. I don't think the unusual brain activity is a result of trauma," Saul assured him.

"How many females were gathered from the disaster?" Rah asked Command Central over his com as healing chambers continued to arrive in the medical wing.

"We were able to rescue thirty Fertiles destined to die before help could arrive," Marc responded.

"That seems a very small number, given the size of the disaster," Rah observed.

"With the small number of surface cruisers and limited time we were able to remain shielded, it was the best we could do, my lord."

Gathering Fertiles was not something their fleet normally did. Lords Rom and Rah Andor, the co-rulers of the entire Daguronian Sector, only embarked on this mission to retrieve their destined mate. The brothers had not been willing to trust the task to another.

There were fleets that specialized in the art of collecting Fertiles. Galactic law required the females be taken at the moment of death to not interfere with their life path. They had to be aware enough to give permission, yet facing actual death. Timing was everything. It was a true art form.

To have collected thirty other Fertiles while procuring their mate was an additional benefit. The females would be healed and transported to a Surrogate planet. There, they would be educated and given a second chance at life as the treasured mate to a worthy male from one of the planets in the Galactic Federation.

The availability of fertile females had dropped alarmingly in Daguronian and many other sectors of the Sagittarius Galaxy, threatening many races with extinction. Centuries ago, numerous planets in the sector had taken up the practice of collecting females from other galaxies in order to survive. Laws designed to prevent abduction and human rights abuse were in place to protect them.

"Marc informs me we have managed to collect thirty other females while on the surface. Make our lady an absolute priority, and after her, the one in the chamber next to hers. Then you may proceed with your normal triage protocol," Rah instructed Saul.

"Is the other female a destined soul mate?" Saul inquired.

"Not to our knowledge, but she is important to our mate and therefore important to us," Rah responded.

"Your lady has stabilized enough to be transferred to a healing chamber," Saul apprised the brothers after consulting the life support readouts.

"We will remain by her side," Rom informed the medical officer.

"Her clothing and anything artificial will need to be removed. Her body must also be bathed in preparation," Saul warned them.

Rah growled. "My brother and I will perform that task after everyone leaves the room."

"I thought that would be your preference," Saul said, trying and failing to hide his amusement.

Rom and Rah removed Kahara from the life support chamber and placed her unconscious form on a gurney. The condition of their mate was heartbreaking for the brothers. There was barely a hand width of space on her petite body that was not scraped or bruised.

Both warriors had chafed at the necessity of waiting until she had sustained fatal injury to obtain her. It went against everything in them to see her harmed in any way.

"She is so small, even for her race," Rah remarked as they lifted her from the chamber to the gurney. "How is it possible for her to be our mate?"

"Do you doubt it?" Rom met his brother's eyes in challenge before continuing to cut the tattered clothes from her body.

"No. How can I deny what the very sight and scent of her does to me? I fear harming her. Simply lifting her requires all of my care. She is not one third the weight of either of us. For the first time in my adult life, I fear failure. I have never been known as a gentle male, but she will require gentle handling. The thought of both of us mating her seems impossible."

Rom understood his brother's misgivings. He had many himself. Yet, there were no known cases of a predestined mating that proved to be physically impossible. He could only trust Spirit knew what it was doing in matching the two oversized Karinians with this small, delicate female. That she was their mate, he had no doubt. As the three of them touched while the brothers tended her, he felt complete in a way he never had. Everything in him responded to her. She was the heart of both gigantic warriors. There could be no other.

"Her hair and contact lenses will need to be removed," Saul said after running a scanner over her body. "I will also have to take out her fillings and earrings."

"Why do we need to remove her hair?" Rom wanted to know.

"It has been chemically treated. We cannot put her into the healing chamber with anything that is not her natural frequency or we run the risk of distortion," Saul answered.

The healing chamber would return her to perfect health according to her DNA. Even scarring would be healed. Had she had any plates or joint replacements, they would also have to be removed.

21

Saul felt fortunate that earrings, fillings and hair were all that would need to be taken from the lords' mate. He could only imagine the reaction if he had been forced to eliminate a hip or knee. To say the two warriors were protective of the female was a gross understatement.

~ Chapter 4 ~

Their lady was suspended in the healing chamber for nearly two months. While the damage from her near death had been extensive, there had been other complications they had not anticipated. Earth was a barbaric planet where pollution and programming ran deep. The food, water, air and electromagnetic frequency was so distorted that Earth females had to spend extended time in the healing chamber to correct the long term damage.

In Kahara's case, she had considerably more old injuries than expected for a woman her age, even in Earth's barbaric culture. From broken bones and scarred muscle tissue to gunshot wounds, their lady had been through the mill. She even had an electronic tracking device in her hip that, while no longer functional, had to be removed before she could enter the chamber.

~

Rom and Rah stood by the transparent, upright cylinder where she now floated. It was the final stage of her healing. She could be suspended indefinitely at this stage.

It was this state of suspension that enabled their race to manage long durations of space travel. Their lady, on the other hand, would be revived soon for retraining. The other females would be held in stasis until they reached a Surrogate planet. They would be revived by a facility specifically designed and equipped for the purpose of initiating and placing fertile women. It was considered less stressful to revive the women on planet, rather than in deep space, when they came from a world that did not have interstellar capabilities.

The lords had agonized long and hard about the proper handling of their mate, and finally decided to revive and train her en route. Neither wanted to trust her initiation to a Surrogate planet. They wanted to earn her trust as soon as possible in order to secure her commitment, rather than risk losing her to another male during the courting process. It might be considered taking unfair advantage, but she was far too important to the continuance of their dynasty and their line to risk her in any way.

"Are you sure this is the right thing to do? It doesn't seem fair to her," Rom asked his brother as he drank in the sight of their stunning, child sized mate floating in her chamber. Her hair had grown past her hips – a riot of flaming red floating around her beautiful ivory body like a veil.

"We have gone over this. We do not have the luxury of fairness. There are too many factions invested in keeping her from us or eliminating her altogether in order to destroy House Kari," Rah reminded his brother. What he did not mention was his fear that, if she were given choices, she would choose another rather than be shackled to two grossly oversized warriors, one of which was a perverted barbarian. Just looking at her tiny, unconscious form floating in the embryonic fluid had his cock screaming to sink into her. His massive, scarred hands shook with desire and she was not even conscious, much less in her season. Nothing had ever affected him so. What he viewed as his inappropriate reaction caused him deep shame.

"Saul informs me that we can revive her tomorrow. If we are committed to this course of action, I see no reason to wait," Rom decided.

"Agreed. I will see to securing the safety of the passenger ship and her new quarters there. I will set the day aside from my duties in order to be available, should you require me," Rah told his brother.

"We both need to be present when she first awakens, brother. Plan on not only being available, but being here," Rom insisted.

"Don't you think that may be a bit overwhelming? I am a hardened warrior. I know a thousand ways to kill, but I have no skills to gentle a lady,"

"We are a Triad and must start as we hope to finish. She will need to be exposed to both of us from the beginning."

Rah knew his brother was right, but still it terrified him. Never had his control been more threatened than by this tiny scrap of a female. He was bound to ruin it for them both.

~

The next time they saw her, she was lying on a treatment table, still unconscious, but bathed and wrapped in a soft blanket to warm her.

"She is still unable to maintain her own body heat, but her vitals are stabilized," Saul informed the brothers.

"Who bathed her?" Rah wanted to know, fully planning to cut the hands off of any male that dared touch her.

"The female clones you assigned. Amazon Zana, her tutor, and Lena, her lady's maid, attended her," Saul assured him.

Saul and Rom had witnessed the difficulty Rah was having and decided not to torture him further with having to tend her nude body. Rom was not unaffected himself, so he well understood the difficulty of touching their unconscious mate without suffering premature sexual responses.

"We are ready if you are," Saul told the brothers. At Rom's nod, he picked up the mask and placed it over their mate's face to administer the medication that would fully revive her from stasis.

When Kahara opened her eyes, both brothers were rendered speechless by the beauty of the emerald color. While a lovely

Japanese woman had entered the chamber, a breathtakingly beautiful Caucasian had emerged. Seeing her in her natural form instantly bonded the brothers to her on a deeper level. Nothing had prepared them for the intensity of their response.

"Hello, little one," Rom whispered, running the backs of his knuckles down her velvet cheek in a gentle caress as he looked into her dazed emerald eyes.

Rah, on the other hand, took a step back, not trusting himself to resist snatching her from the table, dragging her off to his lair and having his way with her. He was worse than an animal, he decided, as he took in her sweet scent, wanting to ravage her on the spot.

"So you found me," Kahara stated in a resigned whisper.

"Yes, little one, nothing could have kept us from you," Rom assured her.

"It changes nothing. You can torture or kill me, but I won't be your assassin," she vowed, turning her head away. She sank into unconsciousness, all systems crashing as medical alarms screeched a warning and Saul scrambled to revive her.

~

It was several days before Saul felt comfortable attempting to bring her out of stasis again.

"It had to have something to do with her unusual brain patterns. Apparently she is very refined and has an adverse reaction to most drugs," Saul shared with the brothers.

"What caused her to think I meant her harm?" Rom asked the question he had been agonizing over for the last two days.

"I am not sure. She appeared to be fully cognizant, but with her it is hard to tell," Saul responded.

"Maybe you should speak to her first," Rom suggested to his brother.

"Oh, by all means. If you, with all of your diplomatic skills, scared her, I will surely send her into cardiac arrest," Rah protested.

As she opened her eyes this time, she seemed more alert, looking around before settling her gaze on the brothers.

"I'm seeing double," she whispered, her voice raspy with disuse.

"No, there are two of us, little one," Rom assured her.

"Where am I?"

"In the medical facility. Do you remember the tsunami?"

Slowly, it came back to her; running with Rhiannon, the collapse of the roof, then the crushing pain.

"You're the ones that pulled us out?" she asked the brothers.

"Yes," one said as the other nodded silently.

"Where is my friend?"

"She is well, but we have not yet brought her out of stasis," Rom responded.

"Stasis?"

"Consider it a drug induced coma to help her heal," the third man spoke for the first time. He appeared to be a doctor, while the other two, much larger men in black uniforms, must be rescue workers or EMTs.

"Is this a military base?" she asked, suddenly alarmed and trying to sit up.

"No. You are safe here. No one will harm you," Rom assured her as he helped her lay back, instinctively knowing she feared whatever a military base was.

"Thank you," she whispered. She closed her eyes and drifted off to sleep.

"That seemed to go better. Is she well?" Rom asked the medical officer.

"Yes, she will be in and out of sleep for several days. We were unable to fully revive her due to her drug sensitivity. She will have to work it out of her system naturally,"

~

The next time Kahara regained consciousness, she found herself in a dimly lit, richly appointed, windowless bedroom. The walls were papered in soft sage and hung with paintings of surreal landscapes. The wainscoting, floors and furniture were dark hardwood, polished to a deep, rich shine. The canopied bed was dressed in silk sheets, a cashmere blanket and down comforter. A sculpted cream, rose, and sage area rug covered the floor next to the bed. A matching rug established a seating area across the room where a kind looking woman of indeterminate age was sitting in one of the chairs watching her.

"Where am I?" Kahara addressed the woman.

"You are in your quarters on the passenger ship of the Daguronian fleet, my lady," the woman responded.

They must be at sea, Kahara decided, which would explain the lack of windows if her room was mid ship.

"Why am I here?" Kahara asked, trying to figure out what she was doing at sea and who had taken her into custody. She could tell she had been drugged, her mind still foggy.

"It was where they brought you when you were released from the medical facility, my lady," the woman answered, clearly perplexed.

"So, she is awake. I told you to call me the moment she awoke," a massive woman accused as she thundered into the bedroom. Kahara had never seen a female the size of the one that had just entered. She had to be six foot four and built like a linebacker. Her cropped, platinum hair, thin mouth and hawk-like features lent her a cruel look. Her demeanor was in agreement with her appearance. She was dressed in a navy jumpsuit, knee high, black leather boots and wore a holster with what appeared to be a gun on one hip and a blade on the other. Both women's speech was heavily accented, but that's where the similarity ended. The first woman was respectful and soft spoken, while Broadzilla was coarse and demanding.

"I just woke," Kahara spoke in defense of the smaller woman. "Who are you?"

"I am Lieutenant Zana. I am to see to your training and safety. This is Lana, your lady's maid." It seemed to Kahara that the answers to her questions only raised more questions. What kind of training, protection from what, and why was she appointed a maid? "Bathe and dress her. I will return shortly," Zana ordered the maid, leaving as abruptly as she had come before Kahara could make another query.

Lana immediately approached the bed, reaching under it to pull out a dark wooden step stool. "Here you go, my lady, easy now. You may still be a little weak." Sitting up and looking over the edge of the bed, Kahara realized that not only was the bed of giant proportions, it was also quite elevated.

"A person could get lost in this thing," Kahara observed, drawing a smile from Lana.

"You are very petite, lady. Is your entire race so small?"

"My race?"

"Yes, the other Earthlings. You are from Earth, aren't you?"

"From Earth?" What in the hell was going on here?

"I am sorry, lady, I forget you have not yet been debriefed," Lana apologized at Kahara's alarmed expression. "Come, let's get you bathed and dressed so Lieutenant Zana can answer your questions." As Lana helped Kahara from the bed, she noted that the maid was small only in comparison to Zana. Standing next to the woman, Kahara realized Lana was probably a good six feet tall.

Lana escorted Kahara to a bathing chamber out of a fairytale. The room was dominated by a huge, sunken, white marble pool fed from a waterfall cascading down a marble wall. Steps were carved into the pool on one side, next to which was a rack of fluffy towels and an inset shelf full of soaps, lotions, potions and oils in blown glass bottles. One entire wall was mirrored. When Kahara caught sight of her reflection, she stopped dead in her tracks.

Looking back at her was the young woman she had been in college before joining Special Forces fifteen years earlier. Not only had the cosmetic surgery been reversed, but even her scars were gone. Her eyes were bright green and hair flaming red – longer than she had ever worn it. She glowed with youth and health. *WTF was going on here?*

Kahara was so shocked she couldn't even formulate a question. Lana drew her forward and pulled her gown over her head, directing her to the steps into the bath. The water was warm, fragrant and soothing.

After Kahara's bath, Lana offered her a thick robe and showed her to the dressing room just off the bathing chamber. At a soft spoken command in a language Kahara didn't recognize, the mirrored panel on one wall slid aside to expose a closet full of colorful, floor length gowns in rich fabrics.

Each one of these puppies is probably worth over a grand! Kahara noted. Lana pulled out a powder blue dress in silk brocade. *I'll bet that thing weighs a ton,* Kahara thought, eyeballing the elaborate gown complete with long belled sleeves and lengthy train. *Make that two ton,* she reevaluated once she was laced into it.

"Who do these dresses belong to?" Kahara asked.

"You, lady," Lana responded, clearly surprised by the question.

"Where did they come from?"

"Lords Rom and Rah Andor provided them, my lady."

"Who?"

"I do not want to misspeak. I am just a lady's maid with a limited command of your language. You will have to speak to Lieutenant Zana. She is much more fluent, and is responsible for your training," Lana apologized. "Come, she awaits you in the sitting room."

The sitting room was actually a large living room, with a nook that served as a study. Zana, aka Broadzilla, was pacing the expanse impatiently as Kahara arrived.

"Leave us," she barked at Lana, who exited the premises posthaste. "Sit," she ordered Kahara in the next breath, indicating an overstuffed chair in the living room. Kahara, in her haste to comply, stepped on the hem of her long dress, nearly falling. "Lana will educate you in the proper handling of a gown later," Broadzilla barked. She grabbed Kahara by the arm to prevent her falling, leaving bruises with her mammoth paw as she virtually lifted Kahara off her feet and slammed her into the chair.

"I don't suppose I could get an outfit like yours?" Kahara ventured when she had caught her breath.

"Absolutely not! My uniform is not for the likes of *you*."

"Hope springs eternal," Kahara muttered.

"Let's get to your debriefing."

"Yes, by all means, let's," Kahara replied, but her cynicism was lost on Broadzilla.

"Your life as you know it has ended. You were as good as dead when the lords of Dagur rescued you from your planet. You are now a homeless refugee, beholden to the lords for everything. You are of little value and viewed as chattel, a churl if you will. The best you can hope for is to be indentured on a remote planet for breeding purposes – the worst, to be exterminated should you fail to please. Your future and that of the woman rescued with you depends upon your compliance and your performance. Do you have any questions?"

"Where are we?"

"On a Daguronian intergalactic transport headed to the Sagittarius Galaxy."

"In outer space? On a space ship?" Kahara was incredulous.

"Did I not just say that?"

"Where is my friend Rhiannon?"

"She is being held in stasis pending your evaluation."

"What evaluation?"

"The evaluation that determines whether you and the other woman live or will be surplused."

"Surplused?"

"Euthanized, then jettisoned into space, is the usual method."

"And what do I need to do in order to pass this evaluation?"

"You must excel at your training, accurately and faithfully follow my instructions, speak only when spoken to and stay out of the notice of the lords."

"What will my training involve?"

"We will start with linguistics. The sooner I don't have to sully my palate with your barbaric language, the better. You will be hooked up to our accelerated learning unit. You can expect to learn several dialects a night while you sleep. By tomorrow morning, I don't want to hear another foul earthling word come out of your mouth. During the day you will study the history, politics, economics and customs of the major planets in the Daguronian Sector. Lana will see to training you in etiquette and, if you can manage them, some of the more basic social graces." Zana sneered in her face. She was leaning over Kahara with both hands braced on the arms of her chair, the air crackling with sexual intimidation and fouled with her bad breath.

I know several overbearing, macho, jackass men that could take lessons from this bitch, Kahara decided, careful not to let her thoughts show on her face. *If not for the threat to Rhiannon, I would kick her ass, consequences be damned.*

And so Kahara's training began. In the following weeks, she was careful not to let Zana know how quickly she learned or how much she absorbed. Having a photographic memory in addition to her formidable intellect and esoteric gifts, Kahara easily absorbed all the information Zana gave her.

When she was alone, having observed how Zana operated the educational port, she covertly learned all she could about her captors. She also reprogrammed the accelerated learning unit to feed her ten languages a night rather than two. At the end of two weeks, she probably knew more languages and had a better grasp of the various cultures than Zana herself. Kahara used her gift to "read" Zana's expectations and give her exactly what she expected, no more and no less. As far as Zana knew, Kahara was a primitive, dim witted, weak, helpless humanoid that posed no threat whatsoever.

Kahara's studies with her maid, Lana, were much more pleasant. Lana took great pride grooming her lady for a prominent position in society. Kahara was in possession of a natural refinement and grace that lent itself well to the demands of her future station. Kahara took care not to display her mastery of etiquette and grace in the presence of Zana, instinctively knowing it would not be well received.

~ Chapter 5 ~

Two weeks later, Kahara was absorbed in her studies when her stateroom door slid open following a quiet knock.

"May I enter?" a deeply accented, baritone voice inquired, sending chills up her spine.

Kahara looked from her educational screen on the desk to find a veritable giant standing in the doorway. The man was over seven feet tall and densely muscled. His skin was warm bronze, hair black as a raven's wing and pulled back from his forehead. It was secured at the neck, hanging to the middle of his back in a thick fall of midnight. Intelligent, silver eyes swept over her, leaving chills in their wake.

The memory of her first days out of stasis were hazy, but she was relatively sure this man had been there when she had been in recovery. He was not the sort one forgot.

Afraid to speak, she nodded, wary and fascinated at the same time.

As he stepped further into the room, she noticed he moved like a predator, silent and deadly, muscles rippling. He slowly lowered his impressive frame into one of the oversized chairs in the sitting area as if unwilling to move too quickly and frighten her. He was dressed in black leather, skin-tight pants and a black silk shirt with wide sleeves. Knee high boots encased larger-than-life feet. His waist was encircled with a fully loaded weapons belt.

For a while, Rom just sat across the room from her, drinking her in. What a lovely surprise she had turned out to be. He would have desired her no matter how she appeared, as her beautiful spirit was the perfect match. So perfect, it had drawn him and his twin across galaxies to obtain her. Yet, what had emerged from the healing chamber was beyond belief.

As he already knew, she was diminutive in height. Easily a foot and a half shorter than he, she stood no more than five and a half feet tall. That was the only part of her that was not a surprise. She was slender, but at the same time lushly curved with soft, ivory skin. Her straight, short black hair had been replaced with thick red curls. Her hair had grown long in the healing chamber, cascading across her finely boned shoulders and down her back to pool on the chair behind her.

She sat quietly, watching him with wary curiosity. Her long lashed, emerald eyes searched his, yet she said nothing. Her perfect features were composed, tiny hands folded in her lap, her back straight. And her scent! Dear gods, her scent was honey and ambrosia calling to him like no other.

MINE. Finally the one that is mine, his inner voice purred.

"Come, sit with me, little one."

Kahara started at his softly spoken request. God! That whisky and smoke voice was pure sin! She had heard that voice before. She hesitated.

"Do you fear me?" Rom had to ask at her apparent reluctance.

Fear? Not exactly. In awe, yes, in lust, absolutely. Lightning fast, the thoughts bombarded her overloaded mind. Rom watched expressions flit across her flawless face. What he would not give for a premature glimpse of her thoughts.

"Well, do you?"

"I'm sorry, what was the question?" Even her voice was unexpected. Deeper and richer than he would have thought, it was full, melodic and erotic.

MINE!

"Do you fear me?"

"I'm not sure, should I?"

An honest response, followed by a loaded question. What an enigma their little soul-mate was turning out to be.

"Upon my honor, I will never harm you, nor will I let you come to harm."

Kahara, extending her awareness, felt the honest vow as truth, backed by great integrity.

"Have we met before?" she asked.

"Yes, my brother and I were among the ones to take you from the planet."

"You were also with me in the hospital?"

"Yes, we spent time with you on the medical ship during your recovery from stasis."

"You are very large." Why, oh why did her every thought have to blurt out of her mouth at a time like this?

"Yes, even among my people, I am considered such. It is all the more to protect you with, rather than something to fear." He prayed that was entirely true as he took in her slight form and contemplated mating her. At the resulting surge in his groin, he quickly decided to think of other things, lest his body prove his words a lie.

Kahara, disgusted with her own uncharacteristic cowardice, stood carefully. Shaking out the lengths of her long sapphire gown and lifting the hem as her maid, Lena, had taught her, she took cautious steps toward the sitting area. Not accustomed to the formal dress, it would never do to step on her skirts and fall on her face in front of him.

Trying to remember all of the etiquette she had been recently studying, she carefully checked the insignia on the breast of his shirt in order to address him properly. No help there, she had not seen this one before. It appeared to be a Celtic knot embroidered in gold. Deciding to err on the side of caution, she stopped in front of him and lowered into a proper curtsy, her long hair falling over her shoulder to pool on the floor near his booted feet.

"You must forgive me, I am still learning your ways and have not seen your rank mark before. How do I address you?"

Rom's breath caught in his throat at her graceful movement and the beautiful sight of his woman's hair at his feet. She did not know, he reminded himself. To take such a stance in front of your prospective mate was the greatly coveted sign of submission and acceptance of his claim. In any other context, it was in deference to one of much greater rank. Who had taught her to take on the behavior of a commoner? She was the future queen! Gathering as much calm as he could muster, he reached out and gently took her arm, helping her into an upright position before him.

"You need bow to no one. It is beneath your rank. Who has taught you otherwise?"

"Zana is the name of my teacher, but I may have misunderstood her. I am still struggling with the language as well as all the protocol. I don't know my rank. I thought it was yet to be decided." Rom made a mental note to talk to the Amazon and clarify the desired focus of Kahara's education.

"True, but nonetheless, bow to no one. There is only one occasion for it. You will never err by not bowing until you are clear it is time to do so. Sit here next to me. We will talk a while, if you are willing, little one. When we took you from the debris, you told me your given name is Kahara?"

"Yes, my given name is Kahara."

"You may call me Rom. I know there has been much for you to adjust to and learn. Do you have any questions for me?"

"Have you come to tell me you're going to surplus me?" Kahara asked the question foremost in her mind while taking a seat next to him, careful not to let their bodies touch.

"As in send you back?"

"As in jettison me."

Rom searched his memory for a definition of the English word "jettison" and, coming up with "abandon" or "discard," decided she was asking if he would return her to Earth.

"Your life on Earth is over. The day we took you from your planet was the day you would have died there. You are dead to your old life and everything in it. Your new life is with us now. We will not jettison you," Rom replied honestly, fully expecting the hysterics to begin.

Saul had informed him that the newly acquired Fertiles needed time to mourn after being taken from all they knew. They were often so upset as to require sedation. Rom was fully prepared to use his will to tranquilize her. To his amazement, his answer seemed to calm her rather than cause upset.

Kahara reached out with her gift to read the giant man sitting next to her and felt brutal honesty laced with watchfulness. She could tell he had no intention of lying to her. This level of integrity was beyond her experience.

"What is your ranking, if I may ask? I haven't seen your crest before."

"It is no surprise you have not seen it before. There are only two of us that wear this crest, myself and my twin brother Rah. We are mirror twins and one in all things, but you can tell us apart as my crest is gold, while his is platinum. His is on the right, mine on the left. We also carry the mark on our wrists." Rom pulled back his cuff to show her the Celtic knot tattooed on the top of his right wrist.

"What do they mean?"

"We were tattooed at birth to discern who was the first born." Rom intentionally addressed the tattoos rather than rank.

"Who was first born?"

"I was, by five minutes."

"What is the ranking?"

Oh, not so easily deterred, his little mate.

"Lords of House Kari."

"Is Kari not the name of the planet that's our ultimate destination?"

"One and the same."

"So you are the lords of Kari?"

"Guilty as charged," he confirmed, deciding not to address the fact that they were also rulers of the entire Daguronian Sector. "We want you to get to know us. From now on, we will have time together each day. Soon, I will bring my brother to meet you and you will spend time with him as well."

"What possible interest would you have in a homeless refugee, and what possible rank would I have that did not require my bowing to you?" There she went again with the blurting.

"Because, little Kahara, you are under our protection and therefore a ranking member of the House Kari."

"What of the woman picked up with me?"

"I understand she is your friend. She is well, and still located on the medical ship. Because she is your friend, we have extended the protection of House Kari to her until she has found her place among our people. There were other females rescued who will eventually be taken under the protection of several fine houses under our rule."

Kahara's eyes misted over. Zana had stated her friend Rhiannon would be euthanized and jettisoned if she were to displease the powers that be. Kahara had been on her best behavior so not to offend anyone. She was not about to relax her guard, but was grateful he was willing to protect her friend.

"You are a kind man, Lord Rom. Thank you."

"I will endeavor to always be so to you, Kahara." Her gratitude stunned him. It also made him want to do anything he could to receive that look again. One hour in her presence and she was already becoming a major weakness, he thought wryly. He had been warned it was so with one's mate, but did not really believe it would apply to either he or Rah. They were, after all, nine hundred years old and hardened warriors.

~ Chapter 6 ~

"How did your meeting with our mate go?" Rah inquired as he entered the common room of the brothers' suite, the door sliding closed behind him. His tone was a bit harsh to cover his eagerness for news of their intended bride. He did not like such weakness in himself. As commander of all Daguronian forces, as well as co-ruler of the entire sector, he could not afford weakness.

"She is a remarkable female, even more beautiful and refined than we had first imagined. She seems to be adjusting well, but there are major gaps in her training. I have set a conference with Zana at first bell tomorrow to correct the oversights."

"What oversights?"

"The first thing she did was bow before me."

"And you did not jump her on the spot?" Rah could not imagine the restraint required not to do so.

"She did not even know who I was," Rom responded.

"She bows for any male that approaches?" Rah's tone was incredulous and filled with rage. He could barely contain the jealous possessiveness he was experiencing.

"No, it was an entirely innocent gesture. She is totally unaware of the significance and her ranking. She also did not recognize our crest or ascertain who I was."

"What is Zana teaching her, weapons and defense? I told you it was not a good idea to have an Amazonian clone train a lady."

Many of Rom and Rah's people were cloned in an attempt to forestall the extinction of their race, due to the lack of fertile females being born. While cloned individuals were considered equals, both males and females were sterile, unable to contribute to the continuation of the race as had been hoped. Most of the cloned females tended to be very masculine and aggressive, serving as the powerful warriors referred to as Amazons.

"As I said, I am meeting with her tomorrow to straighten her out on a few points. The advantage of the protection of an Amazon well outweighs her shortcomings as a lady's tutor. Would you prefer a male body guard?"

"Only if I get to castrate him first," Rah snarled. Thinking of a eunuch alone with their lady, he corrected himself, "No, not even then."

Rah seemed unaware he was pacing back and forth, the heels of his boots clicking smartly against the marble floor of the common room, weapons belt rattling at his side. For the normally silent warrior, the act was clear indication of his agitation.

"Rah, I told her she would meet you soon, but she is a delicate lady. You will have to soften some or you will frighten her."

"I am a blasted warrior, the head of defense, I do not do *soft*. I will leave that to you. Your diplomatic skills are far superior to mine."

Oh, great, all he needed to bolster his confidence was a shrinking violet. She would see him as an animal. Probably best to keep their time together to a minimum until Rom managed to woo her for them both. "Trust me – if she pools her hair at *my* feet, softening will not be the result." As if that would ever happen, he thought in self-disgust.

"I instructed her not to do so with anyone until she fully understood the meaning and ramifications of such an act," Rom replied, lips twitching to avoid a smile. He could well understand Rom's discomfort. The female had *him* on a bed of nails and his passions did not run as high as his berserker brother's.

~

It had been several days since her meeting with Lord Rom, but Kahara still couldn't get the giant Karinian off of her mind. He was, by far, the most provocative man she had ever encountered. She had asked Zana about him, but the woman had been evasive and discouraging. The Amazon told her that Rom was a diplomat and therefore unerringly polite, which could be easily be mistaken for being open to familiarity. She warned against speaking unless spoken to and instructed Kahara to never to ask questions of the man. Zana indicated that Kahara could be risking the tolerance of her presence and that of her friend.

"He may have indicated he will not jettison you, but he could easily choose to sell you both for a profit to slavers if you prove to be too high maintenance. Never forget, you are a lowly thrall and beneath his notice," Zana had advised. "If he contacts you at all, it is to test your progress in knowing your place and not trying to reach beyond your station. Do not act overly friendly or let down your guard. Remember, you are on probation."

~

"My lord captain, we are detecting a ghost effect that may indicate shrouded crafts shadowing the fleet," Kev, Head Tactical Officer, informed Rah as he entered the bridge of the flagship. "See, here and here," Kev pointed on his screen. Rah walked to the tactical station to take a look at the terminal over Kev's shoulder.

"How long has this been showing up?"

"Off and on for the last fifteen minutes, sir, but there was a moment yesterday when I thought I detected something as well."

"Send out a shrouded drone probe and see what it comes up with."

"Yes, my lord, right away."

"Rom, can you meet me back at our quarters?" Rah inquired over his throat com.

"I am en route from the passenger ship. I can be there in ten minutes," Rom replied.

If Rah was asking to meet in their quarters, he wanted to discuss something in total privacy. Open channels or telepathic communication ran the risk of being overheard, so he did not bother to ask what was on his brother's mind.

"Keep me updated," Rah instructed Kev as he headed out the door.

"Will do, sir."

Fifteen minutes later, the two brothers arrived in their suite. Rah set up a jamming frequency to protect their privacy as Rom sat down with him in the library.

"What's up?" Rom asked his brother, noting the unusual precaution.

"I think we are being tailed. Kev detected a ghost yesterday and again today, and I also picked something up last night. It is subtle, only showing for short periods of time, but my instincts tell me there is someone stalking us."

"We are in a friendly sector and not at war. What do you think it could be?"

"I find it suspicious that we are transporting not only our mate, but thirty unclaimed fertile females and suddenly have a shadow."

"Do you feel the Fertiles are at risk?"

"There has been an increase in slaver abductions and a few pirate attacks on legitimate gathering missions reported over the last year. It is not beyond the realm of possibility."

"We are not listed as a gathering mission. Where would they have gotten their information?"

"I have been researching our security. There is indication we may have a leak."

"What prompted your investigation?"

"When we left to get our lady, I wanted to be sure we could provide secure passage for her. As far as her safety is concerned, I do not think we can be too careful. Just the fact she is the only possible mate for House Kari puts her at great risk."

"Agreed. What action do you suggest?"

"I do not want to alert them to the fact that we are aware of their presence. Whatever we do needs to be subtle. I want our lady moved as soon as possible from the passenger ship to the flagship where we can better protect her, but I do not think that should be our first move. If they are watching, that is the very thing they will be looking for in order to locate her."

"How about making use of the regular supply transport from our freighters? Our lady could be smuggled onto the supply ship when it delivers to the passenger ship, and then moved to the flagship when it delivers here."

"I have always said your skills were wasted on being a diplomat, brother. You are by far our best tactician," Rah complimented as he pulled up the supply transport schedule on his terminal. "It looks like there is a scheduled run tomorrow."

"Put in an order for a Sandorian carpet to be crated, placed on the transport and delivered to our lady's quarters as a gift from us. I will go visit and present it to her. I can have Saul put her in a portable stasis chamber, secure it inside the crate and have her loaded onto the transport. I will return in my shuttle alone, as always. You can oversee the unloading of the supplies and have the crate delivered to her new quarters here where Saul and I will meet you to revive her."

"Perfect! Consider it done," Rah replied, scribing instructions on the pad of his terminal.

~

Saul appeared at Kahara's quarters with a healing chamber, a portable suspension chamber hidden inside. He activated the door chime and awaited the lady's permission to enter. Rom opened Kahara's door, inviting the doctor inside. The lady in question was sitting in the living room of the suite, dressed in a lavender day gown with a tea service on the table in front of her. Two half-filled cups evidenced that she and Lord Rom had been sharing refreshments. Kahara looked from one man to the other questioningly.

"We need to speak with you, little one," Rom said to her, indicating Saul take a chair with them in the seating area. "There is evidence the fleet is being followed. For your safety, we need to move you to the flagship without alerting anyone."

"Followed by whom, and why do you think I am at risk?"

"It may be nothing more than a sensor ghost, but fertile females are a rare commodity in our galaxy and there have been incidents of kidnapping. We want to be sure you are well guarded," Rom answered her in his forthright, honest manner.

"I appreciate your being candid with me. What do you have in mind?" she asked, eyeballing the healing chamber.

"Saul has hidden a portable suspension chamber inside the healing chamber. We will place you in the suspension chamber and put it in the carpet crate. Saul will take the empty healing chamber to the medical ship, giving the impression you are ill and being transported there. The crate will be loaded onto the transport and delivered to your new quarters on the flagship. Are you comfortable with the arrangements?"

"To be honest, no, I really dislike being in suspension. I feel so out of control. Can't I just go under my own power? I can be stealthy when necessary."

"You will be safer in the chamber. You will not require life-support as the chamber supplies all you need and you will also be undetectable. Anyone stalking us would scan my shuttle and be able to tell how many are onboard, or I would take you with me when I leave."

Kahara looked at the dreaded chamber, and back to Rom.

"Do you not yet trust me, little one?" he asked in a quiet voice.

Kahara reached out with her gift. He was telling the truth and had nothing but her best interest in mind. This much she could sense. He also knew much more than she about the technology and capabilities of anyone trying to kidnap her.

"Yes, I feel I can trust you. It's that thing I dislike." She glared at the chamber.

"With your permission, I can put you to sleep like I did when we took you from Earth," Rom offered. She would have to be undressed, and he felt it would be easier for her if he put her under compulsion.

"I don't do well with drugs."

"I would not drug you, lady. I simply use my will."

Gifted! He was gifted like her? She had sensed there was a lot to the man during his visits. That would explain what she had been feeling.

"How many times have you done that to me?" she asked suspiciously.

"Only once, after obtaining your permission, when taking you from your home world. I would never do anything without your consent unless there were an emergency and I had no choice," he assured her.

Again, she could sense the truth of his words.

"How long will I be out?"

"Three hours at most."

"Okay, I'll get in the darn thing on my own," she finally agreed.

"Lady, if I may make a suggestion," Chief Medical Officer Saul spoke for the first time. "When you initially get into the chamber, it is flooded. Your systems shut down, you are never at risk, but if you have not been brought up with the phenomena, you will feel as if you are drowning. It can be very uncomfortable. It is advisable that you accept Lord Rom's offer."

"I see your point. It sounds very unpleasant." Looking up at Rom, she said, "Okay, sand man, do your thing before I lose my nerve."

Rom immediately complied, catching her before she could fall from the chair. As he scooped her diminutive, limp body into his arms, he was deeply moved by her trust.

"She is a brave little thing, is she not?" Saul praised. "I have noted trust does not come easily to her, yet I have never seen her to panic. She shows uncommon logic and reasoning. Any other females we obtained would have required forcible sedation."

Rom nodded his agreement, never taking his eyes from the female in his arms. She felt so right there, it was difficult to relinquish her to the suspension chamber.

Saul stepped back a respectful distance, allowing Rom to undress his lady in privacy. After Rom managed to get her clothing removed, he looked down at his sleeping mate in the chamber. She was exquisite in her beauty. Unable to help himself, he leaned down and brushed a kiss over her already cooling lips and sealed the chamber. Saul filled it and checked all of the readouts before they secured it into the crate.

~

When Kahara woke, she was lying on a large bed wearing a soft dressing gown. As she looked around her, she found Rom sitting next to the bed, watching her carefully.

"Hi beauty," he said in the deep voice that never failed to give her goose bumps.

"Is it over?"

"Yes, you are in your new quarters on the flagship of the fleet."

"Who undressed me?" she asked, looking down at the dressing gown.

"I did, lady."

"Who bathed me?" she queried, noting her long hair was still damp.

"I did that as well," Rom confessed.

"Why?"

"The suspension chamber requires nudity and submerges you in embryonic fluid. The jell needed to be washed from your hair and skin before it dried."

"Why you and not the doctor or my maid?" she pressed, blushing to the roots of her red hair.

"Your maid was not to be informed of your move, and I cannot bring myself to let another man touch you, little one."

"I don't suppose you closed your eyes," she asked. He silently shook his head, his eyes never leaving hers and a smile forming on his sensual mouth.

"I am so embarrassed," Kahara agonized in a small voice, covering her face with her hands.

"There is never reason for shame or embarrassment between us, little one." Reaching up to pull her hands down, he gently forced her to look into his eyes. "It was my intent to protect you, not dishonor you." He wisely decided not to inform her that Rah had been present as well, helping him care for her.

Kahara could feel his sincerity and honest regret that she was embarrassed by his actions.

"You will have a new maid, her name is Shan. She will take over the next portion of your training," Rom shared, deciding a change of subject was in order. "She is well versed in the etiquette of our culture and will be your tutor as well. I hope you like her, but if you do not, let me know and she will be replaced. You will also have two security guards posted outside your door at all times for your safety."

He reached over and indicated a small control panel on her bedside table. "This is a com unit. Press this button and it will page me or my brother Rah. Do not hesitate to call if you have any needs or concerns."

"Oh, I would not want to bother you," she protested.

"You could never bother us, little one. You are our first priority. With your permission, I would like to bring my brother to meet you tomorrow."

"Yes, of course, I look forward to meeting him."

"Until then," he said, standing and silently gliding out of the room.

Kahara was still tired, feeling the aftereffects of stasis. She lay in bed for quite some time after Rom departed, going over some of what he had said. She remembered his statement, "I cannot bring myself to let another man touch you," and wondered what he meant by it.

Zana had indicated he had no interest in her, yet Rom told her she was a priority to both he and his brother. There was much that was not adding up. She also wondered that Zana had not been informed of her change of location and had been replaced by a new lady's maid. Zana had indicated that she should not trust Rom. Yet when she read him, he was always honest and sincere, while all her attempts to read Zana had been blocked or inconclusive. She had put that off to Zana being alien, but Rom was from the same race as Zana and his motives were always open to her.

~ Chapter 7 ~

"Kahara, I would like to present to you my twin brother Rah."

Rom was formal with the introduction, indicating a clear protocol. Both men waited expectantly as if there were a prescribed response required, but, searching her mind, she couldn't think what it might be. Standing, she remained silent.

Dear god, they were identical. She had not imagined such male perfection could be reproduced, but apparently she was wrong. Side by side, they were mirror images.

As Rom had informed her, their crests were on opposite lapels. Rom's was gold while Rah's was platinum, but that was the only discernible difference between the two. Well, that and the expressions - Rom's was warm, while Rah looked thunderous. The longer she remained silent, the more thunderous he seemed to become. Now she was sure they awaited a response.

"Forgive me, I don't know the proper reply to your kind introduction," she managed in a small, trembling voice. She could not remember ever feeling so off balance. The two men seemed to fill the room with masculine power and they were still standing in the doorway.

She thought she heard Rah mumble something about inept Amazons before Rom spoke over his grumbling.

"It is now your choice to welcome us and bid us enter or refuse us to cross your threshold, little one."

"Oh, sorry, please, come in. I mean, you are welcome to come in. Nice to meet you, Rah, please have a seat." Ugh, could she sound more gauche?

Both men glided into the room. Rom sat on a settee while Rah carefully lowered himself onto a wooden, upholstered chair that groaned under his weight. Seeming totally out of place, perched as he was on the edge of the dainty chair, he looked everywhere but at her.

Silence ensued.

Sitting, back straight with hands neatly folded in her lap, Kahara regarded Rah from under her lashes. He was dressed as his brother in a black silk shirt bearing their crest, black leather pants and knee high boots. They were indeed identical, but there were differences as well.

While Rom was unarmed, Rah had a fully loaded weapons belt. There was warmth and ease about Rom while an intense charge of almost violent energy radiated from Rah. This was a man not to be crossed. He would make a formidable enemy.

Rah could not look at her without remembering the beautiful sight of her naked body as he and Rom had bathed her the day before. Hell, it was all he saw every time he closed his eyes, and his raging hard-on had become a permanent affliction. He was an animal, he groaned inwardly, and not fit to be in her company.

Silence continued to scream in the room.

Although this was to be his brother's meeting with their mate, Rom determined he would have to bridge the gap. Traditionally, he would have stayed a short time until they seemed comfortable with each other before giving them time alone. Comfort was not a part of this picture.

Noticing Kahara eying Rah's weapons belt, he attempted to break the ice. "Rah is head of defense for House Kari," he boasted for his brother.

"What do you need defense from?"

Oh that was great, now she really sounded dense. Zana had told her all of the houses had military defense units. She had also cautioned her against questioning the lords. Her recent evacuation from the passenger to the flagship was also evidence that defense was definitely needed.

Rom backtracked, deciding that might not be the best place to start after all.

"That is only one of his many duties as Lord of Kari." He carefully sidestepped her question, not wanting to get into the dangers they faced. "Rah also manages all things pertaining to our transport fleets and is currently admiral of this fleet."

"That is most impressive, Rah. It appears to be a very large fleet." There, that didn't sound quite so dumb, or so she hoped.

"This is just one of many," Rah responded, falling silent as he studied the wall behind her head with great interest. Gods, being in her presence was heaven and hell. Her voice stroked his nerve endings and her scent filled the room, while her ethereal beauty nearly blinded him. Just being in the same room with her had him wanting to take her down and make her theirs.

She was no larger than a child. How could he hope to touch her, much less mate her, without breaking bones? He was doomed. His expression darkened further at his grim thoughts.

The silence stretched on.

Great! Now I've insulted him, Kahara agonized.

This is going well, Rom thought sardonically – *so much for leaving them alone. At this rate, we will need several epochs rather than a year to win her over.*

"Kahara, my brother and I have come to invite you to dine with us at the captain's table this evening," Rom tried again, earning a startled look from Rah.

"Thank you both, I would be delighted." Oh great, yet another opportunity to screw up and put herself and Rhiannon at risk. Yet, what could she say? Sorry, I'm all booked up this week, places to go, people to see and all of that?

"You honor us. We will pick you up at third bell." Both brothers rose and Kahara stood to see them out. As they reached the door, Rah turned smartly on his heel to face her. Placing his fist over his crest, he gave a stiff bow, saying, "My Lady," and he was gone.

Noting the worried look in her eyes, Rom hastened to reassure her.

"Your maid will help you dress and debrief you in all you need to know." To her surprise, Rom took her hand and lifted it to the crest at his lapel, bowing.

"I don't think he likes me much," she blurted, thrown off balance by the physical contact and the warmth of his large hand engulfing hers.

Retaining possession of her hand, Rom stepped back into the room and closed the door. Leading her to the love seat, he encouraged her to sit with him.

"While my brother and I are equal in rank and one in all things, we have been trained to very different purposes. I serve more as the head of state, requiring diplomacy, while he is the leader of men, requiring dominance. He has many skills, but few prepare him to deal with the gentler sex. Don't mistake discomfort for dislike, little one." After searching her eyes, he waited until she nodded her understanding, and returned to the door. "Until tonight," he said, and departed.

~

It was going to be a stretch going from quiet meals with Shan, her maid, instructing her on etiquette, to dining at the captain's table with the lords of Kari. She found herself going over all the table manners and customs she had been studying, directing the occasional question to her maid as Shan helped her with her bath.

"You have learned your lessons well, my lady. Even if you falter, all present will know you are not from our world and think nothing of it. Your manners were already impeccable before we began. When in doubt, fall back on what you know and none will think the worse of you."

"Okay, okay, I can do this, for Rhiannon, I can do this," Kahara assured herself.

After drying and applying scented oils, Kahara, wrapped in a silk robe, entered her dressing chamber to find some new additions. Hanging on a hook next to the full wall mirror was the most beautiful gown she had ever seen. She was sure it had not been among the other lovely dresses in the wardrobe provided. Layer upon layer of emerald green gossamer silk caught the light. Beneath it were matching silk slippers, trimmed in platinum and gold braid, inset with emerald gems and sparkling stones that looked suspiciously like diamonds.

"Where did this come from?"

"Your lords sent it, is it not lovely? It perfectly matches your eyes."

"I can't wear this. It's too much."

"Oh, but you must wear their gifts, my lady. To do otherwise would indicate your rejection of them. This would cause grievous injury to them both." Shan seemed extremely distressed at the very notion. "Come, let me help you into your gown. We still need to dress your hair before they arrive."

In a state of shock, Kahara complied. Everything fit beautifully, right down to the slippers.

After dressing Kahara's hair into an intricate upswept weave, Shan led her to the mirrored wall. The reflection that greeted Kahara was that of a complete stranger, straight out of a fairytale.

The dress had an empire waist and a low, square neckline that beautifully displayed her ample breasts. Gold and platinum braid, set in gemstones matching the slippers, encircled the high waist. The gown fell in clouds of emerald silk to the floor forming a small train in back. The long, wide sleeves were a single layer of gossamer silk that belled out to flow into her skirt. Her perfectly shaped arms were visible beneath the sheer fabric.

"You are lovely," Shan exclaimed, eyes misting over. "Come, your lords await you in the parlor."

"Oh no, they are already here?" Kahara was about to panic. She could feel it coming on.

"It is customary they come early. You are right on time. They will probably present you with other gifts. Whatever you do my lady, do not refuse them," Shan instructed in a whisper as she escorted Kahara through the dressing room door and into the parlor.

That's where her maid deserted her, the coward.

Kahara found herself standing alone in the arched doorway of the parlor with no place to hide when both men looked up at her with identical pewter eyes. As one, their gaze swept from the top of her coiffured head to the bejeweled slippers peeking out from under her hem. As one, their eyes turned from steely gray to molten silver.

At this point their behavior became divergent. Rom rose and glided toward her, holding out his hand, while Rah stood ramrod straight, finding extreme interest the arched doorway behind her.

Oh, for the ground to swallow her up. She was *so* not up to this. They were gorgeous in formal dress uniforms of heavy silk, so black as to absorb light. Tonight, instead of the crest on the lapel, they both wore signet rings on opposite hands, one set in gold, the other in platinum. Even without that clue, she still had no problem telling them apart, ice man and the diplomat. They left her completely breathless and off balance.

"You are a vision, little one. You honor us by wearing our gifts." Rom's voice seemed deeper than usual – his eyes brighter, his hand warmer as she placed hers into it.

"I thank you both. I have never worn anything so lovely."

"Will you sit with us for a time, and share a glass of wine?"

She allowed Rom to lead her to one of the three chairs arranged around a glass topped coffee table. Upon it sat two freshly opened bottles of wine, one white and one red, three exquisite crystal glasses and two purple velvet boxes. Both men waited until she took her seat before returning to theirs.

"Which do you prefer?" Rom asked, indicating the bottles.

"The red, please," Kahara responded. Both men froze.

Now what had she done?

Rom quickly recovered and picked up the bottle of red wine.

"A cabernet from the northern cluster, I trust you find it to your liking," Rom said as he poured. Rah took it from him and tasted it before handing it to her. Their eyes met briefly over the glass before he tensed, looking away. The wall became his next preoccupation.

He should have been an architect, as much time as he spends studying structures, she thought uncharitably.

Rom poured a glass for himself and one for his brother.

"This is to your new life, Kahara," Rom toasted in her direction. Again, Kahara could feel a strange formality to his words that seemed to carry hidden meaning. Both men waited expectantly.

She was supposed to drink first, she gathered, as the tension rose between them. Carefully, she sipped from her stemware. The men relaxed simultaneously before drinking from their own glasses.

"This is delicious, thank you." The brothers appeared pleased, if surprised, by her praise of the wine.

"Are you sure you would not like to try another? We have numerous choices on hand tonight," Rom asked.

"No, this one is quite lovely. Thank you, though." The men glanced briefly at one another. "I'm sorry? Did I do or say something wrong? It's just that I never met a cabernet I didn't like."

"Red wine is to your preference, then?" Rah asked, speaking for the first time as if he couldn't help himself.

"Yes, my absolute favorite," Kahara assured him, taking another sip from her glass. Again both males looked at each other in surprise. Rom startled her by rising from his seat and bending down on one knee before her.

"Would you do me the great honor of drinking from my glass?" Rom asked.

Remembering her maid warning her not to refuse any gifts, Kahara moved past the oddity of the request and nodded. Rom held out his glass for her but retained possession of it, bringing it to her lips.

She took a sip.

His expression didn't change, but she could feel powerful waves of emotion rolling off of him. Even Rah abandoned his study of the wall, giving her his undivided attention.

"Would you offer me a drink from *your* cup, Kahara?" Rom requested. Picking up her glass, she started to hand it to Rom, but he encircled her fingers on the stem. "From your own hand – would you offer me to drink of your cup from your own hand?"

After a tension filled pause, she did so. Rom closed his eyes and seemed to savor the wine from her glass even though it was the same as his. He placed his fist over his breast and bowed his head.

"You honor me, lady."

Kahara could swear his eyes misted as he stood and returned to his seat before looking at his brother.

"Go to her, Rah."

"Don't you think that is pressing our luck? She and I have hardly exchanged three words."

"Nothing ventured and all of that. What is the worst she can do? Refuse you or request white."

"I don't want to put her off by asking too much."

"I never thought to see you show cowardice, Rah."

"That was a cheap shot." Rah's mental voice was a low growl.

"All is fair in love – as well as war, brother."

Things had been quiet for a while and Kahara was trying to think of what to say to fill the silence, when Rah took a deep breath and stood to approach her. Dropping down on one knee in front of her as his brother had done, he held out his glass to her in both of his large, battle scarred hands, a challenge in his molten silver eyes. Kahara met his eyes unflinchingly, but made no move toward his glass.

"You would refuse me, then?" he growled.

"What would you have me do?"

"Lady, would you do me the great honor of drinking from my glass?" Rah gritted out between clenched teeth, sure she was playing with him. He braced himself for her cruel rejection. Kahara took a drink without hesitation. Finally understanding what was expected – she lifted her own glass and brought it to his lips.

"You offer me to drink of your cup from your own hand?"

"Yes, is that not what comes next? Am I doing it wrong?"

Closing his eyes in what appeared to be agony, he accepted the drink as tremors ran through his massive frame. He remained before her on one knee, head down, eyes closed, as he seemed to gather himself. Finally, he put his fist over his chest.

"Lady, there are no words," he said with a roughened voice.

Standing, he returned to his seat, looking at her as if he had suddenly discovered a brand new species. He swallowed repeatedly but said nothing more.

The men were stunned. By participating in the ceremony of the red goblet with them both, she had granted them exclusive courting rights. No other house would be allowed to approach her. No other could sire her children. It was now up to the twins to gentle her to their hand and obtain her agreement for final bonding and submission to their mating.

Had she asked for white wine, they would have had to allow others to court her as well, all parties showering her with gifts and great riches. If she had chosen the white or drank the red without sharing it, the right to sire her offspring would remain undecided until she participated in the ceremony of the red goblet with the male of her choice.

True, most women that were predestined mates eventually settled for their soul mate, or in this case, mates, but not until playing the field and a long courtship, basking in gifts and male attention.

In the case of Rom and Rah, as Overlords of their sector, the men had no choice in the matter. Their soul mate was predestined, the only mate in their entire lifetime. They would desire no other. Only ruling lords had destined soul mates. For other males, any Fertile would do.

While there was great competition for the hand of fertile females, the soul mate of the Overlords was doubly desired for political reasons. Only she could successfully bring down the head dynasty by refusing to procreate with them. In the case of the twin lords of

Kari, a full Triad was required for true mating, and in their lifetimes, there would be only one woman.

For Rom and Rah, it was clear that woman was Kahara.

Finally Rom gathered his wits enough to contact the head steward on his lapel com.

"The lady has chosen the red wine and has shared her cup. Please return with the two boxes appropriate for the occasion." Rom had no doubt the steward would know the simple words were cause for great rejoicing and would return in all haste.

"We brought you gifts this evening. Rah, would you like to gift our lady first?"

Never taking his eyes from Kahara, Rah gave a quick negative shake of his head. He did not yet trust himself that close to her.

Kahara didn't know what to make of the man. In spite of Rom's assurances otherwise, she was sure Rah hated her.

Rom took one of the velvet boxes from the table and opened it, revealing a beautiful emerald pendant, set in gold, on a delicate gold chain.

"It's breathtaking, but I…" she paused, remembering her maid telling her not to refuse any gifts. "I don't know what to say."

Rah stood and gathered the other box and opened it for her, displaying striking emerald earrings set in platinum.

"They are absolutely beautiful!" she exclaimed.

The steward arrived with two more small boxes.

Rah produced another pendant, in platinum, on a delicate chain. It was comprised of baguette diamonds set in an oval. Instead of handing it to her, he put it in Rom's hand. It snapped into place over the emerald resting in Rom's palm.

The two men twisted the chains together to form one beautiful emerald necklace, set in gold and platinum, surrounded in sparkling baguettes. The brothers rose together and stood behind her chair. Rom draped the necklace around her throat while Rah fastened the clasps.

"One in all things," the mirror twins said softly. She could feel their hands were shaking.

Rom produced two small circles of baguettes set in gold. Rah held each emerald earring while Rom fitted the circles over them and snapped them into place. Each man put an earring on her earlobe – Rom the left, Rah the right. Once again they murmured, "One in all things."

"I never thought to own such beautiful jewelry. Thank you. I will treasure them always and take good care of them." The men looked at each other, pleased with her obvious appreciation of their gifts, if a bit confused.

"They are our vow to take care of *you,* Lady Kahara," Rom said.

Thinking them a welcome-to-the-dynasty gift, she was overwhelmed.

"I will try to not ever make you sorry you took me in, my lords."

"I don't understand her words," Rah thought to his brother. "How could we ever regret such a great honor she has willingly given us?"

"She is still new to our language and ways. I am sure it is an appropriate phrase from her homeland that loses something in the translation."

Out loud Rom said, "Shall we go dine?"

"That would be lovely. I am quite hungry," Kahara replied.

~ *Chapter 8* ~

Upon their arrival at the great dining hall, Kahara lost her appetite. There were literally hundreds of Karinians in the massive room. At the front of the dining hall, past countless rows of formal tables seating well-dressed members of the oversized race, was the captain's table set for three. The table was attended by a waiter, silver tray tucked under one arm, another man stationed just behind and to the side, and bookended by two massive, fully armed guards standing at attention.

All conversation stopped as every eye turned to them. Kahara froze in place like a rabbit in a snare.

"This may be premature, brother," Rah said on their private channel. *"I can feel her fear. She is about to bolt."* As a precautionary measure, Rom took her by one elbow and Rah grasped the other.

"Be calm, little one, no harm will befall you. Just stay between us and follow our lead."

As Rom gave her time to gather herself, one could have heard a pin drop in the great hall. When he saw her eyes grow determined and her chin come up, he and his brother stepped into the room simultaneously with Kahara proudly displayed between them. Her pendant caught the light and sparkled, clearly stating their exclusive rights. It was missed by no one.

Everyone in the massive room stood as the Triad proceeded to the captain's table located on the dais. The two lords of House Kari glided into the room, the diminutive Kahara floating between them like an emerald draped dream. The Triad was an impressive sight.

"She is doing well. No one can tell she has any trepidation at all," Rah silently praised their mate.

"She is presenting a picture of complete confidence and serenity. We could not have hoped for better," Rom agreed.

Oh, this is so not okay! I am bound to trip over my dress. Shit, the damn table is on a stage where everyone can watch me screw up. I'm so scared I may pee my pants. Maybe puke in my plate. I really don't think I can do this... The litany went on and on in Kahara's head as she let the two formidable warriors lead her to her doom.

Rom and Rah escorted Kahara to the captain's table. Rah held out her chair while Rom helped her sit and arrange her skirts. The two men sat on either side, Rom to her left, Rah on the right, signaling the rest of the room to regain their seats.

Rah turned to the waiter, ordering a bottle of Cabernet and the Ceremonial Goblet of House Kari. The waiter's eyes grew large before he rushed off to do Rah's bidding.

Conversation had just resumed in the room when the waiter returned with the bottle of red wine, a single ornate goblet, and a small glass on the silver tray.

Silence ensued.

"I know you are probably not familiar with this part of the ceremony, little one. Just follow our lead," Rom leaned down, softly whispering into Kahara's ear.

Not familiar with this part? She had not been familiar with any of it, Kahara agonized.

The waiter placed the goblet on the table in front of Kahara. It was gold with platinum around the rim, the stem set with gemstones. The two Crests were on either side, set in braided gold and platinum. Kahara had never seen anything like it. It would fill both of her hands and probably take some effort to lift.

The waiter opened the bottle of wine and poured a small amount into the plain glass on the tray. The man behind him stepped forward and sampled the wine, waited, and nodded his approval. Whether he was approving the wine or checking for poison, Kahara had no clue.

The waiter poured wine into the goblet. Rom and Rah stood and helped Kahara to her feet. Rah lifted the goblet and took a sip before handing it to Kahara.

She was right – it weighed a ton.

Rah watched as she took a sip, and then indicated Rom with his eyes.

Oh, this is like what we did in the parlor, she concluded. She turned to Rom and held the goblet to his lips. He smiled his approval before wrapping his hands over hers on the goblet and taking a sip.

She turned back to Rah. The crowd held its breath as Kahara held the goblet to Rah's lips. Wrapping his scarred hands over hers he took a sip of the wine as well.

Kahara almost jumped out of her skin when the room erupted in applause.

The beautiful, seven course meal was like cardboard on her tongue. The feast passed in a blur. All Kahara could hope was that her table manners were passable, as dish after ornate dish was set before her and later removed, mostly untouched. She nibbled just enough of each to avoid drawing attention to the fact that she was barely eating.

Both men were very attentive, offering her occasional sips from the goblet. Rom carried on light conversation with her while Rah sat, stoic as ever, by her side. She could not help but notice, however, that even Rah's eyes seemed to be shining with emotion throughout the evening.

~

Every day, from that night onward, the brothers would have a beautiful gown delivered to her room. Every evening, they arrived to escort her to the formal dinner. After getting over the initial performance anxiety, Kahara found herself looking forward to the meals with the two Karinian giants. They would arrive at the same time every night and share wine with her, but they never again asked to drink from her cup. Instead, there were numerous vintages in crystal stemware to sample before dinner.

Rom was always warm and attentive, while Rah remained distant and formal. After dinner, the brothers would escort her back to her quarters and share an after dinner beverage with her. Every night, Rom would enquire if there was anything she desired of them. When she said no, they would bid her good rest and leave.

Kahara spent her days furthering her studies. Occasionally, Rom would stop in to visit during the day and take her for a walk. They would visit the greenhouse of the ship or the promenade deck. She never seemed to tire of looking at the stars through the thick transparency.

The past week, she had noticed Rom becoming uncharacteristically edgy. While before, their conversations had been comfortable and spontaneous, now he spoke less frequently. She would catch him observing her with strange intensity when he thought she wasn't looking.

He used to place his hand at the small of her back when escorting her into a room. Now if he touched her at all, his hand would shake before he snatched it away as if burned. His afternoon visits became less frequent, and at dinners he became increasingly distant. When he asked if there was anything she desired from him or Rah, the simple inquiry seemed to have more of a charge. When she said no, the departure was more abrupt.

One afternoon, he surprised her with a visit, inviting her to walk with him to the greenhouse. When they arrived, he further surprised her by taking her to a back portion of the facility where she had not been before. To her absolute delight, it was filled with every flower imaginable. Some, like roses, carnations, and tulips, she recognized as having come from Earth. Others were totally unfamiliar, but nonetheless fragrant and beautiful. Butterflies filled the air, adding a surreal atmosphere.

"Do me the honor of sitting with me, lady," Rom said, indicating an ornate wrought iron bench next to the stone path running through the greenhouse. Kahara sat, arranging her ivory skirts around her as she scooted over, making room for his large frame.

"I have a favor to ask of you, Kahara." He reached under his shirt and pulled out a gold pendant on a heavy gold chain. "Would you wear this for me?" he asked, pulling it over his head and extending it to her in the palm of his hand.

"It's beautiful, Rom." She touched it with one finger in awe. It was a solid disk with a raised, ornate Celtic knot– the same as the insignia he always wore on his uniform.

"It is for your protection. Please honor me by wearing it under your garments always, next to your heart. Should anything happen to me, just wear this on the outside of your gown and you will be safe and cared for by my brother and all of our people." He placed it around her neck.

"I don't understand, Rom. What could happen to you?" The thought of anything happening to this gentle giant filled her heart with grief.

"I have another favor to ask, lady," he said, ignoring her question.

"What is it, Rom?"

"I know it is premature – that you have repeatedly said you want nothing from me. I know that I am asking much, but could you let me taste of your mouth, just once?"

"You mean…kiss me?"

"Yes, Kahara, would you let me kiss you?"

"Yes," she whispered, after searching his tortured eyes. God, how she wanted this man, yet he had never before indicated any interest in her as a woman. Had she been missing the signs? She felt off balance and confused, as if something very important were taking place that was completely over her head.

Rom placed his hands on either side of her face and drew her to him. Ever so slowly, he lowered his face to hers, as if to give her ample time to pull away, before brushing his full, warm lips over hers. She could feel his hands shaking in restraint. He sipped at the side of her lips, covered her mouth with his, and ran his tongue along the seam of her lips. She readily opened for him and received him into her mouth.

Rom was sure his heart would explode. His woman was welcoming him into her mouth with such sweet, open trust and abandon. Her little arms reached up and encircled his neck. He was sure he would die.

He plunged his tongue in and out of her mouth, leaving no corner unexplored. Her taste was ambrosia, he was rapidly losing himself in her. Too easily, he could lose all control left to him and ravage her. The thought of such sacrilege, in the face of her innocent trust, had him backing out of their kiss and pulling away. It was, by far, the hardest thing he had ever done. Kahara looked up at him with dazed, passion glazed eyes, and it was almost his undoing.

His kiss was the most devastating thing Kahara had ever experienced. Just a kiss, and she was about to come totally undone. She wanted it to last forever. Too soon, he pulled away and looked down at her with feverish longing in his molten silver eyes.

He silently stood, wrapped her arm over his, and placed his huge, warm hand over her smaller one where it rested on his forearm. He escorted her back to her chambers in silence. As soon as she stepped through the door, he placed his fist over his crest, bowed, turned on his heel and was gone.

It was the last she saw of him. The next night, Rah arrived alone to escort her to dinner. He was even more surly than usual. After sharing their after dinner drink, he asked if there was anything she desired from him or Rom. When she said no, he looked down at her for the longest time as if he would say more, then turned and slammed out of her chambers without another word.

After three more days of the same, Kahara was fed up. She set out to find Rom and demand what was going on. The moment she stepped out of her chambers, she was surrounded by guards.

"How can we serve you, lady?" one inquired.

"You can take me to Lord Rom."

"He is in the medical facility. I have obtained clearance to escort you there," the guard replied after a short conversation on his com.

When they arrived at the medical unit, she was directed to a large, metal door that swung open at a command from the guard. She stepped through and the door shut with the guard still on the outside. She looked around the large sterile room, noticing a raised metal platform with a man lying on it, covered with a sheet. Hearing her arrival, he turned his face toward her and pinned her with molten silver eyes.

"Lady, you have come to me," Rom rasped.

"Rom! Are you sick?" Kahara rushed over to him in concern.

He did not answer, silently drinking in the sight of her.

At the side of the platform, she put her hand on his forehead to find him burning with fever. He shook under her touch. Looking around in desperation, she noticed a pitcher of water and a glass on a side table.

"Are you thirsty?"

Rom nodded slowly, never taking his eyes from her. "Can you hold your own glass?" A slow shake of his head her only answer. "Can I touch you to help you take a drink?"

Rom's grey eyes turned to molten silver and his nostrils flared with a quick intake of breath. A muscle in his jaw tightened visibly, his entire body becoming rigid, yet he remained still. His steely gaze never left her eyes, as if he could reach inside her soul.

Oh no, now she had done it. She had pissed him off. She tried not to let his rejection hurt, as she stepped back from the platform, giving him space.

"You may touch me any way you like," he surprised her by saying.

His words, softly spoken in his accented, smoke and whisky voice, were so at odds with his body language, Kahara took another step back.

"Kahara, never fear me. You must know I would cut off my own hand rather than harm you in any way."

Uncomfortable with his mixed message and embarrassed by her cowardly retreat, she changed subjects.

"Are you ill?"

"No"

"Then why are you in bed?"

"It is not a bed, it is a restraining platform."

The hair rose on the back of Kahara's neck at his words. She had to know. She approached him slowly.

His nostrils flared as if taking in the scent of her. She carefully reached up, pulling the blanket to his waist, and was greeted with a view of his bare, muscled chest. The unexpected sight of his bronze skin made her weak in the knees. Undressed and lying down, he appeared even more massive.

Seven feet of prone, honed warrior was a formidable sight. His arms were straight down by his sides, biceps bulging, while his wrists and hands were still covered by the now tented blanket.

Careful to not touch him or uncover anything vital, she lifted the side of the blanket to see his wrist and hand. As she had feared, he was restrained to a metal platform. His wrist shackle was thick and wide. On top of the band was an inset area shaped exactly the same as the Celtic knot pendant he had gifted her.

She remembered his words as he had placed it around her neck, his big hands shaking.

"This is for your protection. Please honor me by wearing it always, next to your heart."

At the time, there seemed to be formality and deeper meaning behind his words, but in spite of her repeated questions, he would say no more on the subject.

"Who has done this to you?" she demanded. Forgetting herself in her distress, she reached out and placed her small hand on his massive upper arm. Rom arched his back at the contact. He hissed out a breath between his teeth and started to tremble. Kahara jerked her hand back as if burned.

"I'm sorry," she said in a small voice, wondering how her touch could have brought him such pain.

"No, it is I who am sorry. I thought we had more time."

Kahara waited but he said no more, continuing to devour her with molten eyes. Occasional tremors shuddered across his large frame. She was about to press him for clarification when the door behind her burst open, slamming against the wall with such force, the entire chamber shook. Filling the doorway, looking like death descending, Rom's twin brother stalked into the room and slammed the door shut with equal force.

"What is this I hear about you requesting the Satra?" Rah shouted before stopping dead in his tracks, staring at his brother's exposed chest. "Where is your pendent?" he demanded. Suddenly, Rah's silver eyes fell on Kahara and narrowed dangerously.

In one long stride, he was standing in front of her. Taking her chin in his hand, he forced her to look up at him, nostrils flaring as he took in her scent. Rah reached up with his other hand, grabbed the front of her silk gown and ripped it to her waist, exposing her full pink tipped breasts, between which hung the pendent in question.

"Rah, unhand her!" Rom shouted at his brother, struggling against his restraints.

Rah's eyes drank in the beautiful sight of their destined mate before resting upon the pendent.

"She wears your seal, you have already committed to her, yet I find you locked in Satra!"

His eyes returned to Kahara's face, ice cold, blazing hot. "You! You have brought him to this, you selfish woman-child. Have you come to gloat?" His voice was dangerously low and menacing. "You repeatedly say you want nothing from us, yet I find you standing here, tormenting him. You would watch him writhe in agony, see his heart explode, rather than trust us with your precious body?"

"What do you mean? What's going on here? Who has restrained him?" Kahara hated the tremor in her voice as she confronted the raging giant, placing herself between him and Rom, her arms crossed protectively over her breasts.

"This has gone on long enough, brother. If you will not make the move in fear of offending her delicate sensibilities, then, as second male in this Triad, I will!" Rage, fear for his brother's life, and unrequited lust overcame Rah. He turned on Kahara, whirled her around and forced her to bend over the platform. Kahara's hands shot out onto Rom's bare chest to prevent falling on him.

Rah held her down, threw her gown over her shoulders and ripped off her panties.

"I can smell her heat-scent now. All it will take is one pulse of my mating hormone in her sweet, tight rear and this problem will be solved," Rah growled, as he shoved her down on Rom with a hand in the center of her back, his other hand freeing his massive erection.

"Rah, NO!" Rom shouted, as soon as he had recovered enough air in his lungs from the delicious devastation of Kahara's bare breasts pressed to his chest. "She is innocent. I have not told her."

Rah seemed momentarily frozen by Rom's statement, giving Kahara a chance to push away from Rom's chest and turn in Rah's grasp.

Horror and humiliation had driven Kahara beyond rage. All etiquette forgotten, with no thought of the possible ramifications, she put all her power and training behind a high punch that landed in the center of her assailant's nose. She was delighted by the resulting crunch and gush of blood. By no means mollified, she grabbed the heavy water vessel and smashed it alongside of his head.

"Brother-be-damned! I don't know who you think you are, or what you think you are doing, but you will release Rom immediately," she shrieked like a banshee, while whirling and driving her elbow into his groin and stomping on the instep of his right foot.

The resulting pain drove Rah into action in an attempt to subdue her. With his large, bloodied hands, he turned her back against him and wrapped his arms around her, lifting her off her feet. She tried to head-butt his nose, but he was so large, she only managed hitting the back of her head against his well-muscled chest, tearing her hair from its artfully arranged chignon. Hip length and flaming red, the curling tresses flew around them both, as she kicked and flailed at him, gifting Rom with occasional glimpses of her lush breasts and pebble tight nipples.

Restrained as he was, all Rom could do was watch in amazement as their gentle mate turned into a spitfire in his brother's arms. Rah's blood was dripping on her naked breasts from his bleeding nose, and running down the side of his face onto her shoulder from his head wound. He definitely looked like a male with a tigress by the tail. Had the situation not been so dire, Rom would have laughed.

Kahara proceeded to kick Rah's shins and reach behind her, imbedding her sharp little nails into his abdomen, tearing his shirt and drawing more blood. She punctuated every kick with ear splitting curses from her home planet and demands for Rom's release.

"Brother, do something! I am afraid she is going to hurt herself on me!" Rah roared.

"I am a little tied up at the moment, in case you have forgotten," was the droll reply.

Left with few options, shy of risking damage to her, Rah put her to sleep with his will. Kahara was immediately rendered unconscious, falling limp in his arms. The silence was deafening.

"Now what?" Rah asked after a lengthy pause.

"After that brilliant display in handling our destined mate? I haven't a clue," Rom responded.

Rah stood with a limp, partially disrobed and bloody Kahara draped over his arms, looking dazed and clearly at a loss.

Rom felt another absurd urge to laugh. The mating hormones must be melting both he and his brother's brains.

~ *Chapter 9* ~

Through use of the lords of Kari's private transport chamber, Rah delivered an unconscious Kahara, wrapped in a blanket, to her quarters. Her maid was surprised at the unexpected arrival.

"Your lady is in need of a bath and fresh clothing. I do not wish to awaken her before she has been put back to order, so I will assist you."

"There is so much blood, my lord, has she been injured?"

"No. The blood is mine." Shan dared a quick glance at his face and gasped.

"Can I see to your injuries, my lord, or do you need the medical unit?"

"First we attend your lady. I will go to the unit while she rests."

"Forgive my impertinence, my lord, but she is an unmated female. It is not proper for you to attend her bath."

Knowing it was going to be a fight with the protective maid, Rah gently placed Kahara on her sleeping platform. Careful to not touch her skin, he hooked a finger under the chain around her neck and drew the forth pendant for Shan to see.

"Oh, this is wondrous news, my lord, congratulations to the three of you."

"It is by no means secured – there is yet much danger to us all. I know you to be trustworthy and will hold your silence in all things pertaining to your lady. Her safety may depend on it."

Nodding, the maid proceeded to the bathing chamber and filled the large sunken marble tub with perfumed water. Returning to the sleeping chamber, she began undressing Kahara. As inch after inch of flawless beauty was exposed, Rah's leather pants became uncomfortably tight over his straining erection. It occurred to him that he may not be up to the task after all. Or rather, he was too up to the task, as it were.

Engaging his iron control and turning from the sight of their beautiful mate, he stripped to his undergarments. When Kahara was gloriously naked, he took her in his arms and descended the stairs into the full tub. Walking to the edge so the maid could bathe Kahara, he stood like a statue with her in his arms, looking anywhere but at her beautiful body. Her velvet skin sliding against his arms and chest was torture enough.

As the maid washed Kahara's hair, it feathered down his arm, across his hip and brushed his legs in a sensuous caress. Sainted – he would have to be sainted. Suddenly, Rom's desperate move was beginning to make sense. Much more of this, and he and his brother would end up shackled in Satra together.

After what seemed like a millennium, Kahara's bath was complete and he was able to lay her on the drying sheet her maid had placed on the bed. Girding his loins against rising lust, he helped the maid dress Kahara in a simple silk gown, and lifted her for the maid to remove the drying sheet. Placing her back down, he gently drew her amazing hair from beneath her and allowed it to hang off the bed for the maid to dry while he dressed.

"I will go to the medical unit. Watch over her and do not let anyone else in until I return." Looking down at her sleeping face, he ran his knuckles across her flawless cheek before reluctantly leaving the room.

Rah returned a short time later, healed, bathed and wearing a fresh uniform. Kahara slept peacefully while her maid sat in a chair next to the platform.

"Leave us," Rah ordered, and the maid silently complied.

For a while, he drank in Kahara's beauty. Her scent blended with the perfumed oils and soaps from the bath, creating a heavenly combination. Her long lashes were crescents on peaches and cream cheeks. Her hair, dried and glistening, was once again arranged in the intricate chignon he had become accustomed to seeing.

It would be so easy to leave her sleeping, roll her over and breach her, sending her into the mating frenzy, allowing him and his brother to make her truly theirs before it was too late. Gods knew, he ached to do so, but in the end, she would hate them both rather than just him, as she did now.

He could not do that to her. He understood Rom more and more as the hours passed. She was a treasure, well worth any cost to preserve. He could not bring himself to force her to their mating.

With a sigh of regret, he sat in the chair next to the bed and sent the command to awaken her. Slowly she stretched and opened sleepy emerald eyes. After a while, she focused on him. He braced himself for her anger. Still drowsy, she took on the softest look and smiled at him. His heart leapt in his chest.

"Lord Rom, why are you in my chamber?"

Oh gods, to be his brother for a day and be gifted that soft look, to deserve her smile.

Unable to help himself, he reached out and ran his knuckles down her velvet cheek. He knew he should correct her and inform her of his identity. Wait just a little while longer – just a while.

"What have you been told of your position with us?" he asked, remembering her earlier confusion as he had confronted her.

"I am aware that I owe you everything. You saved my life and that of my friend Rhiannon," she replied, confused at his question.

"Have you been informed of your relationship to the lords of Kari, of the choices you need to make?"

"Only that I am your ward and thrall. I am not to speak until spoken to and am never to touch either of you. I am not aware of any choices."

"You have not been told that you are to spend time coming to know both of us, in order to see if you can find it in your heart to pledge yourself to us?" he asked, incredulous.

"No, I thought I was already your thrall."

"Thrall? What is a thrall?"

"Slave, property."

Rah felt his rage building as a terrible picture was painted. Emerging was the image of betrayal - a betrayal that may well have cost his brother's life or the life of their lady, resulting in the downfall of House Kari.

"Who has been responsible for teaching you these things?" he asked in a soft, dangerous voice.

"I can't lay the blame on Zana for my attack of your brother. She was very clear that I was not to touch either of you. It was entirely my fault."

"Security, pick Zana up and put her in containment," Rah snapped into his com. "Take a regiment as she will not go willingly. No one is to have access to her until I have interrogated her. Is that clear?"

His brisk manner and harsh command prompted Kahara to look at the crest on his shirt. It was silver. This was not Rom. It was Rah and he was clearly furious.

Rah was aware of the moment she discovered he was not his brother. She became silent. Her face blanched and she sat up, edging away from him on the bed.

He had earned her fear, but gods, it hurt.

"Don't back down from me now, spitfire, things were just starting to get interesting," he snarled to cover his pain.

Her chin rose, eyes flashing at the challenge, but she remained silent. Rah silently cursed himself for speaking harshly to her – again. Taking a deep, calming breath, he gathered himself and tried for a fresh start.

"Put your hand in mine, Kahara," he said, reaching his right hand out to her, palm up. Kahara looked first at his hand, then to his molten eyes, but did not comply.

"You will not indulge me?"

"Why do you want me to touch you when you so clearly hate me? Is this a trick?"

"What I feel for you is as far from hate as the furthest reaches of our universe, little spitfire. There is no trick. This is the prelude to a vow I wish to give you."

What was it with these two men and their vows, and what was she feeling from him? He was clearly enraged, but his eyes shone with something else as well. Slowly, she complied.

As soon as her palm rested in his hand, it closed over hers. Enormous, calloused and battle scarred, it was so warm as to almost burn her flesh. She remembered the heat of his brother's forehead that morning and could not miss the similarity. Was that a tremor she felt running through him?

"You have been gravely wronged by me. That we have all been deceived by another is no excuse. I vow never again to raise my hand to you in violence. For my transgression, I will endure any punishment you care to choose, including forfeiting my life. I ask only that you find it in your heart to try to save my brother before it is too late."

"Whoa!" she exclaimed, jerking her hand from his. "Stop – I'm so lost. I have no desire to punish you. I wish you had not humiliated me by man-handling me and tearing my dress, but after that I was clearly in the wrong. I would do anything to save Rom – but from what? Why did you have him shackled?"

"You have not been informed of any of our ways, have you?"

"Not any that makes this understandable."

"Gods, what a mess, I don't even know where to begin."

"If I may make a humble suggestion, my lord, I have found the beginning to be the best."

"I will have to give you the short version. My brother's life hangs in the balance and we have little time. You were not rescued by chance but by design. My brother and I sensed your birth and have waited your entire lifetime to claim you."

"I don't understand."

"House Kari is the dynasty that rules the empire. This dynasty is always ruled by two fertile Overlords – identical brothers – one in all things," Rah continued. "We have not been cloned. Clones are sterile. To each set of twins, there is only one soul mate. She is always from another planet because, outside of the cloning process, we can sire only male children.

"At the birth of a soul mate, her mates become aware she lives and set out to find her. She is not to be taken from her home, nor is she to be interfered with in any way until the time of her death to avoid altering her life's path. At that point, she is rescued, healed, and trained in our ways.

"When she is deemed stable, she is introduced to her intended mates. If she chooses to share the red goblet with them, granting exclusive courtship rights, the courtship begins. During that time, her mates will periodically inquire if there is anything she desires from them. When she is ready to receive them, she will respond that she requires their presence in her bed. If she is not comfortable choosing to give herself to them before her heat cycle is fully upon her, Comasatra is activated in her mates by her advancing season.

"In the Comasatra, the first born is the first to succumb. At this point, he can either choose to force claiming or request Satra. Satra is voluntary submission to restraints in order to prevent the mating lust from driving him to force mating upon his soul mate. If his mate still chooses to deny him, his member will continue to swell until intercourse is either impossible or deadly to the female. Eventually, his heart will give out under the strain. His blood literally begins to boil. It is not a pleasant way to die. It is then left to the surviving brother to convince her to accept him before he is faced with the same choice.

"Once a successful mating has occurred, the lords or remaining lord pledge their lives to their lady, gifting her with the crest of their station. In your case, Rom has made his pledge before mating by gifting you his pendent. This means that if he dies in Satra, I cannot force you. If you choose not to accept me, I will die also, leaving you as undisputed ruler of our dynasty.

"You have, however, granted us exclusive rights to your offspring in the ritual of the red goblet, so you will not bear children to any other house. You will rule, unmated, until your natural death, at which time our line is ended and our dynasty will be dismantled and distributed to the remaining fertile dynasties."

"Holy shit! No wonder you were pissed!" Kahara exclaimed, forgetting all of her recent training in etiquette. "Okay, my head is really spinning now. Do you mean to tell me that I am not your ward or slave, that I am actually your and Rom's mate?"

"Yes, that is what I am telling you. Did you not listen?"

"So, how does this work – I have a husband and a backup husband?"

"Not exactly. This was also to have been included in your training. While I am aware your culture has couples, in the mating format the lords of Kari have Triads. We are both your mates."

"Good god, how is that even possible?" Kahara gasped, looking the giant up and down. Two of the gorgeous monsters? No way!

"Trust me, it is very possible. For now, we have to solve the problem at hand. Do you have any fondness for Rom?"

"Yes, I do."

"Do you find him sexually attractive?"

"Yes, that too," Kahara confessed, blushing.

"Could you ever find it in your heart to tolerate me?" Kahara searched his eyes for a time. Rah held his breath. He did not want to face how devastating her answer could be to him.

"You have to understand, I thought you hated me, Rah."

"Yes, I am regretfully aware of that fact."

"We have not had a chance to get to know each other."

"I know that and regret it as well."

"I hate to admit, I am somewhat afraid of you. Can we help Rom now, and you and I wait until we have had more time?"

"I am sorry, Kahara, there is no time. The mating must be with the full Triad unless one of the twins is dead. I did offer you my life – the offer still stands."

"You would die for your brother, Rah?"

"I would gladly die for both of you, Kahara. You are my heart."

Kahara stood from the bed where she had been seated during their discussion. Rah stood also, bracing himself for her rejection and the request for his execution. Her emerald eyes searched his silver ones. He felt her reach into him with her heart.

"I think you are more volatile than your brother."

"That I cannot deny."

"I also think it makes you a formidable warrior."

"Gentleness has not come easy to me – that is true." His heart sank. He knew what was coming and could not blame her. How could he expect her to trust him after his earlier brutality?

"As a warrior, you have had occasion to kill."

"Yes, many times, as I probably will again." He gave her brutal honesty, feeling he owed her that even though it condemned him in her eyes.

Without another word, Kahara reached up to let down her
magnificent hair. Sinking into a low curtsy, she pooled it at
Rah's feet.

~

Heading down the hall to the Satra chamber, both dressed in
full length white Comasatra robes, Rah tried to debrief Kahara
on what would be needed to save his brother.

"To my deep regret, you have not been prepared for this in any
way, and now there is no time. To complicate things, you once
again became a virgin in the healing chamber. That, combined
with our disparate mating practices, renders any prior
experience useless. Over the course of a year, before your heat
cycle commenced, you were to have been instructed on what to
expect. During that time, we would have courted you."

"A year? But I have always cycled every 28 days."

Rah stopped in his tracks and turned to her in shock.

"Are you an exception among your people?"

"No, most of our women cycle monthly."

Rah's eyes widened as the ramifications of that little fact hit
home. Quickly, he activated his com.

"Connect me with the medical unit," he barked. "Are any
females from Earth out of the healing cylinders yet?" Kahara
could not hear the other side of the conversation as it was fed
directly into an implant in his ear. "Put them all in stasis
immediately until further notice."

Rom took Kahara's arm in a steely grip and headed toward the
Satra chamber at a greatly accelerated pace. Suddenly, the
rapid progression of the Comasatra made sense. He feared to

see his brother's condition after the two hours they had been gone.

"Rah, what is it? What did I say?"

"We have even less time than I thought. It may be too late already."

"No!"

"There is no time for explanations or instructions, little firebrand. You will have to put yourself entirely in my care, doing as I say in all things. I am not a gentle man, Kahara, but I will do my best to minimize the harm to you. There is no way this will be easy, if it is even possible."

"Leave us and secure the chamber. Her ladyship has chosen to release her lord," Rah roared the order, as they hurried into the room. Everyone scrambled to comply, but not before Kahara saw the disbelieving looks from medical staff.

"Prepare the Triad healing chamber and have emergency staff on hand, but do not enter until I bid you do so."

As the doors slammed shut and were secured, Kahara ran to the platform holding Rom. She gasped at the sight of him.

His eyes were glowing, two violet lasers. The irises had become slits, like cat eyes. Blood dripped from restraints not only around his wrists, but now around his neck and ankles as well. His fingers were tipped with vicious claws. A cloth over his privates was his only covering. When he caught sight of her, he struggled anew, roaring his desperation and fury.

"Dear gods, we are too late. Step back from him, Kahara!" Rah shouted in agony.

"No, I won't believe that, I will not accept it. Do you hear me?"

Rah reached out to force her compliance but she jerked free. In desperation, Rah grabbed Kahara by the hair at her nape, forcing her to look as he reached out and pulled the covering from Rom, exposing his enormous, raging erection.

"Do you think you can take that on, lady?" he shouted in her face. "He will rip you asunder and that, he would never survive, nor will I."

"I will not accept failure in this, Rah. I am not the weakling you may think. Our women give birth – it's not *that* big – yet." Close, she thought, nowhere near as sure as she sounded.

"This I cannot allow."

"It is my choice, you cannot prevent me!" Kahara shouted back, shaking Rom's pendent in Rah's face. Rah had told her that the pendant would release Rom's shackles, like a key in a lock, when placed over the indented Celtic knots engraved into the shackles' surface.

By law, it was her choice – he had no right to stop her.

"Oh Rom, what am I to do?" Kahara silently beseeched the writhing warrior.

Rom heard his lady's voice in his mind. He could not believe it. She had spoken to him on a private path. She was telepathic even though they had not yet bonded as a Triad. It was unheard of. Out of his mind, mouth full of fangs, he was unable to answer her – but he had heard.

"Do not release him, Kahara, he has lost all control. There is another way."

"Then, by god, show me, Rah!"

Rah closed his eyes in agony and hung his head, rubbing the back of his neck.

"Okay, little firebrand, it is to life or death for the three of us."

He pulled her to him and removed the robe from her slight frame. As was custom, she was naked beneath. He allowed his own robe to drop, leaving him naked as well. Fully engorged and aching, he realized he was not far behind his brother.

"Lady, if we survive this, you will surely hate me more than you already do."

Before Kahara could respond, Rah pulled her to his chest and covered her mouth in a ravaging kiss. Plunging his tongue into her warm depths and his thigh between her legs, he ground her sex against his leg and her abdomen against his erection, while Rom roared and writhed upon the platform. Shocked to her core, Kahara tried to pull away.

"DO NOT fight me Kahara – it is too late for regrets. To fight me will only hasten my own demon. Submit, damn you, submit!" Each word was punctuated with a shake as he held her nape in a crushing grip.

She had given him her trust when she had pooled her hair at his feet. She realized there was no choice but to follow through. Kahara immediately softened into him, allowing him his way.

"That's it, little firebrand, now give me your passion, lady – want me."

He released her hair, holding her in place with an arm around the small of her back. With the other hand, he reached behind her and sank one large, callused finger into her tight, wet folds from behind, continuing to grind her clitoris against his hair-roughened thigh. Lifting her entirely off her feet as if she weighed nothing, he ravished her mouth. His finger stretched her with a burning sensation, just before passion engulfed her.

His breathing doubled, body temperature soaring. Rah had to use all his control to avoid crushing her. He felt the moment she ignited for him, bathing his hand with her sweet nectar. Gods, he wanted this woman. He had no idea it would be like this. His entire body began to shake as he added a second finger to the first, and felt her inner muscles convulse against the additional invasion. She whimpered.

Rom was burning up. The sight of his beloved brother preparing their bride for the mating was the most beautiful thing he had ever seen. Though his demon writhed and roared, his heart rejoiced. He knew it was too late for him, but this made it all worthwhile. With Rah successfully mating Kahara, Rom's portion of the genetic seed could be taken from his dying body to inseminate her as well. The dynasty would go on – Rah would love and take care of Kahara for them both.

Rah added a third finger and thrust into Kahara's depths with savage force. There was no time for the gentleness he wished he could show her. She seemed to understand and softened further into his invasion, her maidenhead suddenly giving way in his hand.

His nostrils flared at the scent of blood added to her sweet nectar. She shuddered against him but made no sound to indicate the pain he must be causing her. Instead, her little arms tightened around his thick neck and she participated more fully in their kiss.

Rah could feel his erection swelling further, and realized he had to take it to the next level while he still could. He carried her to the platform where his brother was restrained, and pulled his fingers out of her delicious depths. He turned her in his arms, laying her across Rom's chest. Rom became more agitated, arching on the platform, shaking his head back and forth. If Rah was not sure his brother was fully out of his mind, he would swear he was protesting.

Rom threw his head back, black hair loose and flying, fangs erupting through his gums, as he roared. The feel of Kahara's full breasts and beaded nipples crushed against his torrid chest was sensual beyond belief. He longed to grab her and sink into her with claw, fang, and rod.

Kahara's nipples ached where they pressed against the scorching heat of Rom's muscled chest. She was out of her mind with desire and terror as Rah held her down from behind. He moistened her untouched rosette with her juices while Rom's massive, burning erection pressed against her ribs.

"Push out against me, spitfire," Rah growled, as he started to sink his forefinger into her rear.

Kahara complied, the burning and stretching somehow as erotic as it was painful.

"That's it, lady, relax," he rumbled, as he moved his finger in and out of her tight hole in shallow thrusts while stimulating her clitoris with his other hand. A second finger joined in, followed by more stretching and burning.

Rom was bucking and writhing beneath her, further stimulating her breasts and impaling Rah's fingers – his searing erection a brand in her side.

"Gods, I am sorry, lady, we are out of time," Rah groaned into her ear, as he removed his fingers and replaced them with his enormous member. She could feel the massive, hot head pressed against the tiny untried entrance and was sure he would rip her apart.

"Push out for me, lady, push out and relax. Oh gods, you are so hot and tight."

She could feel his massive form blanketing her back, shaking at the restraint required not to drive forward and fully sink into her. In spite of her compliance, the pressure increased and the burning reached an almost unbearable level.

"Take it in, lady, to the hilt, take all of me," he gritted.

Just when she was sure she would scream from the pain, his cock bathed her over-stretched muscles with pre-cum laced with his mating hormone. Relief was immediate, followed by such intense desire, she thrashed under him and thrust her hips back, trying to impale herself further.

"God, Rah, I want you! I want all of you now," she screamed, not recognizing herself.

Rah lunged forward so violently, Kahara felt his heavy sack slam against her womanhood from behind. With great effort, Rah froze in place. He could feel her untried muscles convulsing around his shaft as she whimpered in passion and thrust back at him, trying to take more of him in.

"It is alright, lady, just give me a minute."

More pre-cum, less pain, more passion, Kahara was beyond herself as Rah lifted her by the waist, still impaled in her rear.

He climbed onto the platform between his brother's shackled legs.

"Spread your legs and straddle Rom, lady, that's it – now take his cock and guide it inside."

Kahara managed to follow his instructions. But as the scalding head of Rom's massive shaft seated itself at her entrance, she was sure there was no way she could take him.

"Relax, firebrand, you can do this, just move up and down a little until he releases his hormone to ease you."

Easier said than done. Rom was a thrashing beast, growling, arching his back and snapping his fangs. Sandwiched between the two massive men, Kahara began to panic.

"I am with you, Kahara, we are in this together – give over to me," Rah whispered into her ear as he took her by the waist, helping her move on his brother.

With a roar, Rom released his scalding pre-cum. Her pain became passion. Rah pushed down on her hips, sinking his brother's agonized flesh into their mate before her muscles could tighten up. Delicate tissues tearing, Kahara screamed in agony/ecstasy as she exploded into the orgasm of her life.

Both men released more pre-cum in response and she went wild between them, propelling them into action. Rom drove into her convulsing sheath as Rah retreated. Rom drew back, preparing for another mindless thrust, as Rah drove deep into her tight rear.

It was up to Rah to time his thrusts in order to protect their mate's vulnerable body. Rom set the pace, as he was completely lost in the throes of the Comasatra.

Harder, faster, deeper they drove, pounding unmercifully, while Kahara screamed until all three exploded into orgasm. Hearts, minds and spirits melded as both men swelled further, locking into Kahara's body. Three became one and Kahara lost consciousness.

~

Rah was devastated. She had pooled her hair at his feet, and in return, he had hurt her – damaged her lovely body. She now lay, petite and childlike, mercifully unconscious in his arms.

He put his fingers to her throat. To his relief, he found a steady pulse. His eyes met his brother's now lucid gaze.

"She lives," was all he could manage. Rom closed his eyes and wept.

"Gods, what have we done, brother, what have we done?"

The link-up would not release for several hours, but Rah was unwilling to wait to ascertain the damage they had inflicted on their courageous little mate. Activating his throat com, he ordered the staff to put all three of them in the healing chamber before she regained consciousness and suffered further.

His brother needed healing from the rigors of the Satra. Where Rah was damaged, however, could not be healed. He had failed to protect their mate – she would surely loathe him. His heart was devastated beyond repair.

~ *Chapter 10* ~

"The outing will be good for her. She is fully recovered," Rom insisted to his brother.

"Security is too difficult to maintain. I will not risk her," Rah repeated for the third time.

"We have a no-technology treaty with the indigenous race of Planet Taron. It could not be safer. Besides, Kahara is unused to space travel and she is showing signs of claustrophobia."

"Why did you not tell me? When did this begin?" Rah's immediate concern delighted his brother.

Rah had been like a Taronion ice bear with a wounded paw ever since the mating, walking large circles around Kahara. He avoided contact at every opportunity while observing her at a distance with hungry eyes when he thought no one was watching.

"You never stay around long enough for me to tell you anything, brother. Did you think I would not notice? You have to give her a chance, Rah. We are a Triad now. There is no changing that."

"Three weeks!" Rah suddenly erupted, roaring at his twin. "She was in the healing chamber for three full weeks. I am sure she is not anxious to be in my presence."

"You were not to blame."

"Easy for you to say. It was at *my* feet she pooled her hair. She must despise me."

"She has never given indication that is so, yet you block your mind from her. How do you expect her to get to know you, when all you do is glower, growl or avoid her altogether?"

"I am sure she knows all of me she will ever care to."

Rah could hardly restrain himself from ravaging her again every time he caught her sweet scent. It was the last thing he wanted her to know. He blocked her from his mind to assure she did not see what an animal he really was. Problem being, the block went both ways. He could not read her if he blocked her from reading him. Rah could only guess what went through her beautiful head, and he had a grim imagination.

"I insist we take her on an outing to Ice Planet Taron after first bell tomorrow. I also insist you be on your best behavior. This has gone on long enough, Rah, and well you know it."

Yes, Rah knew it had to change, that the courtship of their lady had to move forward. He just did not know how to change it. He decided to bow to his brother's superior diplomatic skills. With a curt nod, he turned on his heel and headed to the bridge to arrange their outing.

~

Shan helped her dress for dinner in one of the beautiful gowns the twins sent to her every evening. Kahara, letting her mind wander, could not help but wonder at their strange mating practices. Once out of the medical unit, their lives continued as if nothing had happened. She had expected them to share quarters now, but had been escorted back to the one she occupied - alone.

Rah was cold and distant, and Rom, while attentive and kind, treated her as if they had never been intimate. Meanwhile, she could not look at either male and not want him.

Yes, the mating had been wild and fraught with discomfort – but it was also beyond wonderful. She had been looking forward to further intimacy when the situation was not so dire. Had she been that much of a disappointment? She knew she had not conceived and was now receiving shots to prevent ovulation. Had they had changed their minds about wanting her?

Rom and Rah arrived on time, as usual, and as usual, were devastatingly handsome in their formal uniforms. The brothers took her breath away as they stood to greet her when she joined them in the sitting room.

"Lady, you are a vision," Rom complimented.

She was wearing a gown of dusty lavender silk. Cut low in front, it lovingly hugged her form to the dropped waist where it flared out in graceful folds grazing the floor.

"Thank you both for the lovely dress."

"Sit and talk to us, little one, we have a surprise for you," Rom said, taking her hand and leading her to one of the chairs.

"A surprise?"

"Yes, we are approaching Ice Planet Taron, one of the allied planets in the Daguronian Sector. Rah and I thought you might enjoy an outing in one of our transports to see it up close. It has three moons, is covered with snow and glistens like a diamond in the night. I think you will find it to be a very impressive sight."

"I would love that!" Kahara exclaimed, pleasing the brothers with her enthusiasm.

"Wonderful. We will depart just after first meal tomorrow morning."

~

The following day, Kahara found travel garments had been sent from her lords. A form fitting, long sleeved, white bodysuit and full, white floor length wraparound skirt, rested on her bed. A white, fur lined, hooded cape and knee high mukluks completed the ensemble.

When the time came for the brothers to pick her up, only Rah appeared at the door.

"Good morning, Lord Rah," she greeted him, unsure if she should address the absence of his brother.

"Good morning, lady. I regret Rom was called to an emergency meeting of the council and will be unable to leave the ship today. We can reschedule if you do not wish to go alone with me."

His voice was flat and controlled, stance military straight. He did not meet her eyes. She reached out with her gift, feeling his trepidation. Tired of playing cat and mouse with this man – her mate – she took the bull by the horns.

"I guess I have to ask if *you* have a problem going alone with *me*. Am I an unpleasant obligation to you? If so, I will forgo the outing. If not, I would be delighted to have you take me to see the ice planet."

Rah was floored – unpleasant obligation? How could she not know she was his life? She wanted to go alone with him? Would be delighted to have him take her? Where was her well-deserved, fear and loathing of him????

As Rah stood, staring at her, his face unreadable, she took it as rejection and turned to leave the room rather than let him see her pain. Seeing her turn to leave him, he reached out, grasped her upper arm and spun her to face him.

"It is my pride and privilege to escort you anywhere you would care to go. You are not an obligation to me, lady."

"What *am* I to you, Rah?"

"My mate. You are my mate and therefore my life, Lady Kahara."

Realizing he still held her captive by the arm, he hastily released her.

"I apologize. I have no right to handle you so. Have I caused you harm?" Gods, if he had so much as bruised her delicate skin, he would cut off his own hand.

"No, Rah, you didn't hurt me. I welcome the touch of both my mates," she said honestly.

"If you welcome our touch, why do you repeatedly tell us you have no need of us?"

"When did I ever say I did not need you?"

"Every night lady. You tell us every night."

Was that pain she was feeling from him? Totally lost, Kahara decided to let the matter drop for now and take it up with Rom later. She and Rah communicated poorly at best, and she did not want to spoil their day.

She stepped closer, shocking him by lacing her arm through his.

"About that outing, shall we go? I am really looking forward to some time off this ship, and to spending the day with you."

Rah's heart filled with pride as he escorted his lady on his arm. She walked calm and serene by his side, as if she felt she belonged there, as if she viewed him as her mate and protector, rather than the animal that had ravaged her.

~

Once they were secured in the cockpit of the shuttle, Kahara watched Rah from under her lashes as he prepared for departure. He spoke softly into his throat com implant, his long tapered fingers flying over the control screen. His black flight suit was impeccable, encasing his magnificent body like a second skin. He sat, somehow relaxed, and at the same time military straight. His thick black hair, secured at the base of his neck, hung down to the middle of his back between massive shoulders. There was no doubt he was fully in charge. He seemed not to know she was there.

Taking off with Kahara, alone, in a small shuttle transport, was not the most brilliant idea, Rah decided. Her proximity, seated next to him as he did his preflight check, was raising havoc with his concentration. Thank the gods, he was the fleet's best pilot, or he would have doubted his ability to fly the damn thing.

At another of Rah's soft spoken commands, the hanger doors raised, revealing black space filled with brilliant stars. Kahara caught her breath at the sight. In space – it never ceased to awe her that she was actually in outer space.

"Do you fear for your safety, Kahara?" Rah asked, observing her closely. After all, she was not born to space travel and had not yet been confronted with open space. She was undoubtedly terrified.

"No, I fully trust your abilities, Rah."

As her eyes met his, he saw excitement, rather than fear, sparkling in the emerald depths. How many other ways had he misjudged her?

With practiced hands, Rah reached over to check Kahara's seat restraints and neck support, careful not to touch her more than necessary. She calmly watched as he leaned near her, surprising him when she did not flinch or look away.

"Rest your head on the neck support," he instructed. Kahara complied as he lowered a built-in helmet over her head and secured it to the cowl neck of her jumpsuit. She heard a rush of air as it equalized pressure. Her head was firmly held in place. She felt somewhat trapped.

"This is only for takeoff, to protect your smaller neck. We will be pulling quite a few positive G-forces until we leave the gravitational pull of the transport ship."

His voice was intimate in her ear and she realized his throat com implant was broadcast through speakers in her helmet. The sound of his voice helped immeasurably.

"Are you alright?"

Kahara gave him a smile and thumbs up.

"We will also experience some negative G's during our decent, at which time you will feel panels in your flight suit tighten on your legs to prevent the blood from rushing from your head," Rah explained, as he secured his own helmet and restraints.

Good thing to know. She was not sure she would have taken kindly to her clothing coming alive without his forewarning. When Rah had given her the flight suit and instructed her to put it on over her clothing, the bodysuit design of the travel garments suddenly made sense. Now, after his explanation, she understood the design of the flight suit.

Rah's fingers flew over the touch panel, and she could hear, as well as feel, the ship building power. Suddenly, the thrusters fired and they shot into open space.

Yup, that was a whiplash waiting for a place to happen. Thank god for the helmet restraints protecting her neck. It was so breathtaking! Kahara began to laugh.

At the unfamiliar sound in his ear com, Rah quickly looked to Kahara, expecting an emotional breakdown. Preparing to use his will to sedate her, he instead observed wonder and joy shining in her beautiful face.

I underestimate her at every turn, he thought.

"How is our little mate doing, brother?" Rom asked over their private mental channel.

"She is beyond belief, taking to it as if she were born in space," Rah replied. *"How is your emergency meeting going?"*

"Boring. You enjoy yourselves and I will see you at third meal."

Rom had made the right choice, he was sure of that now. It was not easy for him to feel justified misleading the other two members of his Triad, but sometimes results must prevail over means. Besides, he had managed to avoid outright lying. That he could not bring himself to do. Arranging the last minute meeting taking himself out of the picture – to give his beloved brother and mate some much needed personal time – was a brilliant strategy. He congratulated himself.

As the small ship approached the beautiful white planet, Kahara felt a building sense of excitement. Rah had told her they would not land, as they had a no-technology treaty with the native species. It was also extremely cold, but they could view it from low level flight. Taron's three moons were a spectacular sight as they rose from above the planet. Kahara abruptly noticed one of the moons seemed to have three smaller objects appearing from behind it.

"What is that next to the third moon?" she asked Rah just before alarms blared and all hell broke loose.

"Command, we are under siege – initiating evasive format," Rah calmly announced into the com as he banked the craft. He reached over and secured Kahara's helm, looking into her eyes. "Slight change of plans, lady."

"So I gathered," she coolly responded. Unexpectedly, the craft rocked as an explosion of light appeared between them and the transport ship, forcing Rah to bank again.

Kahara felt her flight suit tightening around her legs, and spots appeared in front of her eyes as her body tripled in weight.

"We have been fired upon – loading weapons and engaging shields."

A second control screen dropped down in front of Kahara.

"I take it I am in Rom's seat?"

"Gunners station, but don't worry, I can manage from here," Rah assured her, as another silent blast forced a rapid change in direction.

"Not to doubt your obvious prowess, but it looks to me like you are up to your ass in alligators, Rah. Now would be a really good time to give me access to our mental link."

Rah could not believe what he was hearing. She should be hysterical, yet she was calm and logical.

Another blast – another shudder, but this time they listed heavily to the right.

"We've taken a hit to the starboard thruster, shields one quarter down," Rah pragmatically reported to command. "Switching to manual flight." Rah's control screen rose up out of the way and a flight stick took its place. The craft was clearly unstable, requiring both of his hands to keep it on course.

"Alright, little scrapper, you are on."

Rah dropped his mental block, giving Kahara direct access to weapons operation as he turned the shuttle, heading straight at one of the three attacking crafts.

Kahara was suddenly seeing double – his view as well as her own – but his knowledge was accessible. Closing her eyes, she let her fingers do the walking, using Rah's sight rather than hers.

"Laser loaded – locked – firing," she steadily narrated her movements to Rah who banked the craft at the perfect moment. It was a direct hit, the fighter's shields giving way at such close range. The craft disintegrated in eerie silence as debris bounced off the remaining shields of the crippled shuttle.

Rah banked again, hoping to retreat to the transport ship, but it was not to be. A second fighter pulled up, forcing a change in direction with a weapons blast that had the small craft shuddering.

"Pull a 360, I've had it with this bastard," Kahara demanded.

Rah complied, amazed at her daring. He allowed the craft to continue its spin from the blast until they were once again facing the fighter.

"Loaded, locked and firing," she conveyed.

"Remind me to never anger you," Rah exclaimed in wonder as he struggled with the controls. "We are down to one thruster, all other engines offline and shields down – caught in gravitational pull – will have to take her down. Heading for coordinates..." Rah rattled off headings to command.

Kahara saw they were indeed rapidly descending at an alarming rate.

"Rah, turn over entry calculations to me," Kahara demanded. She had drawn from his knowledge, combined it with her space shuttle flight simulation training and come to a realization. He could not pilot the damaged craft and manually discern the proper angle to enter the atmosphere. Rah complied, turning over the calculations to her, leaving his mind open for her to draw on.

"At my mark, bank left and lift the nose 20°. Three, two, one, turn, stop turn – and lift."

The craft shuddered and shook. Kahara hit the appropriate sequence on her terminal to redirect their failing power to the heat shields, and saw them flare as the shuttle entered the atmosphere.

Soon, the snow covered ground was rushing up to meet them as Rah wrestled with the controls, calmly searching for the best place to set them down. They were skimming the tree tops before an opening finally presented itself.

The landing was not pretty as they roared across the tundra, slamming into the wall of a rock cliff. At the last moment, Rah managed to turn the craft so the impact was on his side, rather than Kahara's. As the skin of the craft buckled against his left leg, he was glad he had managed to do so. Closing down their mental link and blocking his pain, Rah turned to check on Kahara.

She was sitting, composed, with her hands folded on her lap. He reached over and released her helm. Slowly she turned her head to look at him.

"Damn! What a rush! You are really good."

He couldn't believe the female.

"Are you unharmed?"

"I think all parts are still functional. How about you?"

"The remaining fighter will no doubt send a landing crew to capture us," Rah avoided her question.

"What makes you think they want to capture us?"

"They could have taken us with a direct hit when our shields went down. They are trying to obtain you."

"Me? Why me?"

"You still have no idea of your value, little scrapper. Trust me, it is you they are after. Can you get out of your seat?"

"I think so."

After some struggling, Kahara managed to release her restraints.

"Now I need you to climb in back and open the emergency supply locker."

Kahara followed his instructions. Soon she was outfitted with a pack, snow shoes, extra garments and a guidance device. Rah took the device, set it to particular coordinates and demonstrated its use.

"This will take you to a fully supplied shelter. Use it only as much as you have to, turning it off between times so it cannot be detected by the enemy. Go there and wait until Rom comes for you. They were preparing a rescue team as we entered the atmosphere."

"Wait, Rah, I am *not* going without you."

"It is you they seek. You need to hide until help arrives."

"So, we hide together."

Suddenly she noticed Rah's pallor and the lines of strain around his mouth.

"You've been hurt and are hiding it from me. Let me see."

"I am fine. Go now, Kahara."

"In a pig's ass. You are *not* fine and I am *not* going anywhere."

"What does this have to do with an even-toed ungulate's gluteus maximus?" Rah puzzled aloud.

"Let. Me. See." she ordered, running her hands over Rah's body, looking for damage. Brushing his left leg, she encountered warm moisture. Pulling her hand back she found it covered with blood.

"Dear god! Is it broken?"

"Yes, little scrapper, in two places. I cannot accompany you and you must leave the site of the crash."

"How bad is the bleeding?" she demanded, ignoring his instructions.

"I have lost some blood but my body repairs quickly. The bleeding will stop before it becomes life threatening. The leg, however, is useless until I visit a healing chamber. Now go."

He failed to mention that the ones after her would not let him live to see a healing chamber. He planned to hold them off as long as he could with the weapons he had on hand, buying time for Rom to reach their precious mate.

"How about *no*, not going to happen, so forget it."

"Kahara, I am the commanding officer. I demand you obey me!" he shouted in desperation.

"Rah, you are my mate, I will *not* leave you!" she shouted back at him.

A long, shocked silence followed.

"Why?" Rah finally asked in a quiet voice.

"I love you," Kahara whispered, grabbing his face with both hands, tears running down her cheeks. She had whispered, but with his superior hearing he had heard – heard and rejoiced – as she covered his mouth in a searing kiss.

"Open your mind to me, Rah," Kahara demanded in the next breath – as if her confession and the kiss had not taken place – as if she had not just rocked his entire world. "I need to know the emergency operations of this beast."

~

Much time and jury-rigging later, Kahara managed to convert a stretcher into a travois with a harness made of wide, stout strap. She covered the stretcher with her fur lined, wool cape, trading it for a white tundra jumpsuit, pack boots and hooded parka she found in the emergency supplies.

She was wearing a fully loaded weapons belt as if born to it. Kahara used a small manual crane to lift Rah out of the pilot's seat after releasing the canopy. Helping him ease into the makeshift travois, she handed him a hooded parka and fur lined mittens, along with his weapons belt. After checking the inflated air splint on his broken leg, she covered his legs with her cape.

"Kahara, lady, you can't hope to pull this. Even without all the extra gear, I weigh in at over 300 pounds in full uniform."

"Rah, baby, stop being so negative. I have hidden talents."

After checking the travois, strapping and supplies one more time, Kahara sat down in the snow, cross legged, and closed her eyes.

Was she was finally seeing reason? Rah wondered. Though she was very impressive and resourceful, this was exhausting her and wasting time. There was no hope of getting them both to safety.

Kahara opened all of her senses, reaching out to the natural world around her, seeking, searching… There!

As she had prayed, there was abundant wildlife on the frozen tundra, similar in signature to her helpers on Earth. With intense focus, she sent out her call, stating her intention and her desperate need. She started to sing an ancient song - beseeching all of her relations, on this distant planet, to come to her aid. When she was sure she had been heard, she came back into her body and opened her eyes.

Rah was watching her intently, a concerned look on his face. It was clear he was afraid she was losing it altogether.

"You sing beautifully, Kahara," Rah said in awe. "It is as if the entire planet responds to your song."

More to the man than meets the eye. Kahara had always known this but his words confirmed it. Well, no time like the present to edify him and probably lose any ground she had gained with him.

"Rah, there is something you need to know about me. I am not like others. Not even the other people from Earth."

"No, Kahara, you are not. You are exceptional in every way."

Oh, you have no idea, she thought.

"You know I can't get us to safety without help," she forged ahead.

"Yes, this I have been telling you," he agreed. She decided to let that slide.

"You also know, at best, Rom and his troops are still days out from being able to find us."

"Yes, Kahara, you have assessed the situation most accurately. I am sorry to have failed you."

"You have done no such thing, Rah. You evaded the fighters and put that craft down safely against all odds. I need you to know I have called in some new friends to help. You are not to shoot them when they show up, okay?"

"Called how? What friends? There is no one here but us."

"Well, no humans."

"What are you saying, Kahara?"

"I am more of the natural worlds than of man, Rah. I commune with nature in all of its forms."

Shaman! Ancient One! Oracle! Rah had heard of these. They were the most revered of beings, and had not been born into his race for generations.

"Why have you not told us of this, Kahara? We would have been more sensitive to your needs."

"I have never been accepted. All my life, people have feared me or tried to exploit me. I've learned it is best to keep my own counsel."

"Not from your mates, never from your mates! We need to be informed in order to care for and protect you. Who else knows this thing?"

"I think Zana suspected. She walked in on me when I was trying to find comfort in the ship's greenhouse and saw the plants leaning into me. They tend to seek me out at the most inopportune times. After that, she acted increasingly strange toward me."

Abruptly Kahara's eyes became glazed and distant. "They have come."

Rah looked up and saw huge forms materializing out of the mist as Kahara stood and walked to them.

"Kahara, Stand back! They are dangerous!"

"Be at ease, Rah, I am safe with them. Good god! Is everything of giant proportions in your worlds?"

Kahara gaped at a beautiful pack of wolves approximating the size of small horses. "I'm going to have to adjust those harnesses. Wow! With these puppies we can pull a supply sled as well."

Rah was speechless as she fearlessly approached the black alpha female. Putting her small hand on the beast's shoulder, she closed her eyes and communed.

Less than an hour later, after disabling all detectable instrumentation and power sources on the wrecked craft, they were under way. Kahara rode the beautiful grey and black wolf that pulled Rah's travois effortlessly.

Other members of the pack had carried the alpha pair's small litter of pups by the nape to the crash site. The pups were now in the travois, tucked in close to Rah. He and the pups were secured under Kahara's cape and laced in with waterproof, heat reflecting tarps. Another wolf, a gray, was pulling a supply sled rigged from some of the wreckage. The silver alpha male and black alpha female were in the lead, the rest of the pack surrounding them. They were moving at an amazing pace.

The streak of a craft entering the atmosphere sliced through the sky. The entire pack howled at the intrusion. Kahara called out to the alpha male who turned to her. The pack halted and Kahara jumped off her mount, sinking into the snow. Not bothering to get up, she rolled over to the supply sleigh where she reached in, pulling out snow shoes. Once she had them on, she stood, shook herself off, faced the direction of the wrecked shuttle, raised her arms to the heavens and began to sing.

The wolves howled in perfect harmony as an aurora borealis lit up the sky. The wind kicked up and Rah could see a storm approaching from where they had come. Kahara checked on him, removing her mitten and placing her cool hand on his forehead, searching his eyes. Then she returned to the grey and black wolf, removed her snow shoes, looped them together by their bindings and hung them over furry shoulders. The massive lupine lay down so she could remount and they were again under way.

They traversed the barren tundra for hours under the light of the three moons as Rah slipped in and out of consciousness. He was weak from blood loss and pain, feverish from the breaks in his leg, and he could tell infection that was setting in. The large pack moved silently as the storm followed behind, never overtaking them, but obliterating all signs of their passage.

~

"I cannot help but notice this is not the shelter I directed you to, Kahara," Rah whispered during one of his increasingly fewer lucid moments. He was gazing up at the ceiling of the cave. It was lovely, with colorful stalactites that sparkled in the light of the fire. Kahara had been careful to keep the fire small, and located directly under a geothermal vent so as not to be detected by the ones pursuing them. The underground hot springs kept them warm, but she hesitated to use the artificial lights in their emergency kits, not knowing if the power source could be tracked.

The storm she had conjured had finally hit, sealing them in the wolf pack's den while eliminating all signs of their presence. The wolves could easily dig out if necessary, but seemed content after procuring oversized rabbit-like creatures for food. She had skinned and gutted one of the creatures, securing it on a spit over the fire.

She melted snow and was heating the water in a metal container from the survival kit on a horseshoe of stones set in the flames. Small chunks of game floated in the water, making a broth in the event Rah couldn't eat solid food.

"The enemy craft entered the atmosphere not long after we were under way, so I didn't feel I could risk using the directional device. The wolves brought us to their den instead. How are you feeling?"

"You seem very capable in the wilderness. Where did you learn these skills?"

"I taught wilderness survival and I was part of a search and rescue team," she said, managing not to lie to him while avoiding mention of her special ops training. "Don't think I didn't notice you circumvented my question, Rah."

"Well, let's just say, I would not be opposed to a healing chamber."

"What is your pain level?" she asked, supporting his neck and holding a container of water from their supplies for him to drink. She had been making every effort to keep him hydrated.

"Oh, it's there."

"I take that to mean high."

Rah didn't comment. Instead, he silently ran his eyes over Kahara in a fever laced caress before closing them again, seeming to go back to sleep.

"Rom, where are you? Are you in range yet? I am pretty much useless and am having to leave the care of our woman in the paws of a wolf pack."

No answer. He must still be out of telepathic range. Rah was beginning to worry he was running out of time. It was becoming harder and harder to maintain consciousness. Dying in front of their beloved was not high on his list of how best to care for her.

Rah had been sleeping for some time when the scout wolf came in from the small bolt hole at the back of the cave. The scout approached the alpha, whining and licking him on the side of the mouth, showing acceptance of his dominance while exchanging information.

"The vile ones are heading this way. Their course is too direct for them not to have some way of detecting our presence," the alpha male shared with Kahara.

"All of our equipment is off, as you requested, so they must be using some sort of scan that detects life forms."

"We know they have such capabilities, but can only discern life form, not species," the alpha informed her. *"Your pack has not yet pierced the sky, though we can detect the disturbance of their craft in orbit. The vile ones will be upon us before your pack can reach us. They are violating the no-technological weapons treaty. We will try to protect you, but claw and fang is no defense against their weapons, little sister."*

"I will not put your family at risk. They want to take me alive, but would kill my mate. I'll go out and lead them away from him and your pack. Can we move my mate into the nursery den with your pups to make him more difficult to detect, and send members of your pack out to make wolf sign around your den?"

"Yes, your plan is a good one."

"After I am a safe distance from your den and the storm covers my tracks, I will turn on my navigation device to draw them to me."

"You are a formidable warrior, little sister. We will do as you say. I will send some scouts from the pack to keep track of you, and two others to guide your pack to the den when they arrive on planet."

"I am mated to identical twins. We are a Triad. When my people land, they will be led by my other mate. I will be able to communicate with him as I do with you. I'll tell him you are allies and to expect you. I don't think he can communicate with you as I do, so I'll make sure he understands. Thank you so much for all you have done for us. I will not forget my promises to you."

After getting Rah settled into the nursery, Kahara looked down at him, tears filling her eyes. He had not awakened, even during the move.

"Don't you dare die on me Rah. I wouldn't want to go on if I lost either of you," she whispered, leaning down to brush a kiss across his lips.

Though Rah's body was deep in trance trying to maintain life – rendering him unable to respond – his awareness was present. What was she up to? When she kissed him, he could feel her tears splash onto his burning face. Then she was gone. The wolf pups were nestling around him in the small den, comforting his body, yet there was a yawning vacancy in his heart in the wake of her departure. Dear gods, he loved their little mate and had not the strength to link with her in order to tell her. He had never felt more helpless.

Kahara was dressed and packed, her snow shoes and weapons belt on. It was still dark. How long were the nights here? she idly wondered. The Alpha pair approached her and rubbed noses. *"Please care for my mate until our pack comes,"* Kahara beseeched them.

"We will be honored to do so," the alpha male assured her.

"I will treat him as one of my pups and nape him if he gives me trouble," the alpha female teased.

"Our scout will give you a ride from here to save time. We will trust you to cover his tracks when he leaves you."

"Once again, thank you."

Kahara turned to leave before she broke down in front of the pair. She had no illusions about the likelihood of her returning. At least the pack and Rah would be protected until Rom could get to them.

"Be well, little sister."

"Be well, my friends."

~ *Chapter 11* ~

The night was clear. It was bitter cold and barren where she and the scout parted. She conjured the wind to cover his tracks as he loped away. Kahara set out in the opposite direction, turning on her navigation device.

"Okay, you bastards, take the bait. Come and get me," she muttered under her breath.

She had been under way for a good hour when she saw the flash of Rom's craft entering the atmosphere.

"It's about time you got here, good lookin'," she called on their mental path, not expecting to reach him.

"Kahara! Where are you? I have been unable to contact Rah on his com or our mental link."

"The answer to the first question is – I haven't got a clue. The second – Rah is unconscious. His leg was broken in the crash. He has an infection with a high fever."

"Are you harmed? Is he with you? Are you at the site of the crash?"

"No, to all three questions. I changed our location and turned off all nav equipment to avoid being found by the enemy. Even so, they seem to have located where we were hidden. It was clear they would reach us before you could provide backup. We were outnumbered and Rah was out of commission. I am out trying to draw them away from his position with my nav unit."

"And he agreed to this?" Rom was incredulous.

"No, he has been unconscious for hours."

"We have located your beacon. Turn off the unit, make a 90° turn to your right and head straight for the mountain range you will see there. I will intercept you as soon as I am able."

"WILCO, but don't bother trying to track me. I will leave no tracks to be followed. And Rom, I have allies here – large wolves will meet you and guide you to Rah. He needs medical attention as soon as possible. See to him first. I am fine for now."

"You are not fine, Kahara! You are one small woman, alone, on an alien planet, in the arctic, at subzero temperatures, with the enemy on your tail."

Kahara noticed that, even though his voice was even and commanding, Rom did not seem to be his usual cool, calm self. It brought a small smile to her frozen mouth.

"I have the advantage. They want me alive and I am no stranger to the wilderness, no matter how it presents itself. Take care of Rah and watch your back. I have no doubt they want you both dead."

Not long after Rom's shuttle set down and his landing crew disembarked, they were approached by a pack of huge arctic wolves. How his lady had managed to communicate with wolves– much less befriend them – was beyond him, but he was not about to look a gift wolf in the muzzle. Rom sent his search and rescue team with the wolves to retrieve his brother, and then set out with his highly trained, special ops team to find Kahara.

~

Kahara saw the enemy before they detected her. They were fanned out, searching the area. Easily as large and powerfully built as Rom's race, she knew it wouldn't take long for them to find her. Dropping down behind a small drift, the only cover for miles, she made sure the white fur of her hood concealed her face, and became very still. She knew that every second she could buy Rom could make the difference.

"Kahara, where are you, lady?" Rom's mental voice was emotionless and direct.

"Can you detect the enemy near where I turned off my nav unit?"

"Yes, we have them."

"They are about to step on me."

Kahara heard what could only be swearing in his native language before Rom cut their connection.

"Rom, was that a foul explicative?"

Out alone, in the arctic night, on an alien planet, the enemy upon her and she was teasing him? He could not believe her calm courage.

One of the enemy ground team spotted her and shouted to the others over his com.

"Ah, man! Shit is about to go down," Kahara warned Rom, as she jumped up and headed out as fast as her snowshoes would allow - not making it three steps when one of them fired. She was struck with a brilliant, agonizing light, and hit the ground convulsing.

"Kahara, report, are you hit?" Rom's mental voice remained calm and commanding, but his heart was in his throat.

"Must have been some kind of stun set for someone twice my size. I am conscious but paralyzed—except for the convulsions."

"Do not move."

"Not like I have many other options, Rom," Kahara bristled at his clipped order.

"Control, do a sweep and disable all power units. They have violated the no-technological weapons treaty. Kahara is down, we're going in hand to hand," Rom addressed the mother ship via his implanted throat com.

Kahara was lying on the frozen tundra, completely helpless, when one of the aliens reached her.

"I have the female," he bellowed into his com as he roughly lifted her by one arm. Kahara could only guess what he said as it was in his native language, coarse and guttural, interspersed with clicks and growls. Just her luck, it was not among the hundreds of dialects she had mastered during her studies.

The enemy landing party converged upon them as she dangled by one arm. She could feel her body coming around. She braced herself against the pain and tried to act as if she were unconscious, still paralyzed, in hopes of gaining an advantage. Catching a glimpse behind her captor, she saw shadows on the horizon.

"Rom, is that you coming in?"

"Yes, hold steady, lady, we will get to you."

"I'll give you some cover."

"What?"

Kahara closed her eyes and summoned the wind. Suddenly, the enemy forces were encased in a ground blizzard. Rom was amazed. While he and his men were still unobstructed, standing under the light of the moons, the enemy was in a cloud of snow. Though he could see their forms, he would lay bets they could not see their hands in front of their faces.

"If that is your storm, you can let it go now. We have you surrounded," Rom communicated to her as his team fell into position. Kahara immediately complied, knowing she needed all of her strength to stay conscious.

Tall, muscular, with hood pushed back and long black hair flying in the wind, Rom emerged like a wraith from the flying snow. He tore his way through the enemy wielding, of all things, a giant broadsword. He blazed a path toward her, pausing only briefly to take out anything and everything standing between. His eyes glowed liquid silver, his expression stone cold.

Two of her captors rushed him from either side, equally large swords swinging. Rom spun, crushing one windpipe with an elbow – while beheading the other with his sword – not breaking stride. There was no hesitation in him, just cold, determined fury that left a path of bodies in his wake. Kahara had never seen a more formidable warrior. His team was definitely taking care of business, yet Rom downed three men to their every one without even breathing hard.

The man holding Kahara ripped her hood off, grabbed her by the hair and put a knife to her throat. He held her between himself and the rapidly approaching Rom. The attack was so sudden that Kahara let out a startled cry, giving away her conscious state.

"Don't move, Kahara." His mental voice was calm and expressionless.

He spoke to her captor in the enemy's guttural language.

"Rom, I have a knife. I am going to create a distraction on the count of three... one, two, three."

Kahara convulsed, seeming to pass out, slumping forward over her captor's knife. He pulled away to prevent cutting her throat and leaving him with a dead, and therefore useless, shield.

The man suddenly stiffened, lifting slightly away from Kahara, a shocked look in his eyes. Rom did not hesitate. Lunging forward, he swung his sword over Kahara, taking the top of the man's head off. He pulled the headless man off his mate and threw him a good fifteen feet. As the body landed, Rom saw the hilt of a standard issue, emergency blade sticking out of the dead man's gut.

His men took position to cover them, dispatching the rest of the enemy, while Rom examined Kahara for injury. Though covered in her captor's blood, the only place she appeared to be bleeding was where the sharp blade had come into contact with her throat. Thankfully, it was just a shallow flesh wound and not life threatening. However, her right shoulder was dislocated where she had been jerked up from the ground. As he looked into her enormous, pain filled green eyes he could hardly contain his fury.

At the wild, enraged look on his blood splattered face, Kahara started to scuttle away from him on the snow.

"Kahara, do not fear me," Rom demanded.

How could he expect her to see him as anything but a vicious animal? He had just butchered over twenty men in front of her. Unable to help himself, he pulled her into his arms even though he was sure she could not welcome his touch.

"I am sorry, it was all just so…much," she whimpered in a small voice against his neck. As he pulled her to his chest, she could feel the thundering of his heart and the tremors that ran through his muscular frame. "Did you get to Rah in time? Is he okay?"

"He is on the med ship in a healing chamber as we speak."

"Thank you, Rom, you're wonderful."

"Hardly. If I were even adequate, you would not be harmed, nor would you fear me, Kahara."

"Oh, but what fun would that have been? I rather enjoyed my little outing. I suppose you are going to take me back up to that overrated tin can and never let me out again."

"The thought has merit, and that happens to be the revered flagship of the exalted Daguronian Fleet you are so maligning, lady."

All Rom could do was hold her to his chest. He couldn't bring himself to let her go long enough for his team to bind her shoulder and put her on a sled.

"By the way, Rom, I thought you were the diplomat," Kahara teased, looking around them at the gory carnage.

"When someone is trying to harm my mate, that is as diplomatic as I get," Rom grimly informed her in a quiet voice.

Kahara took that moment to look down at her white, insulated jumpsuit. It was covered in blood and other gore, but it was the brain matter that did it. Without warning, and to her abject humiliation, she promptly passed out in earnest.

~ *Chapter 12* ~

Having his ship disable the power units on the planet's surface worked both ways. Rom's team was now on foot, several days from the shuttles that sat on the only suitable landing site in the entire area. The shuttles themselves were grounded until another arrived from the main fleet with more power units.

Thank the gods, Rah was back on the medical unit and the rest of the enemy had been taken out by the Daguronian fighters. Everyone else was safely off planet. He only had Kahara and his special ops team with him. The six men were the absolute best he had, well capable of seeing to his mate's safety – with or without the power units and jet sleighs.

Taking advantage of Kahara's unconscious state, Rom kept her under with his will and had the medic of his team, Saul, reset and bind her shoulder for travel. Rom was down on one knee, cradling Kahara so Saul could attend her.

She was so petite and childlike in his arms, her skeins of flaming hair flowed over his arm and pooled on the snow. It was hard to believe she had been able to communicate with the local race of wolves, outsmart an entire squadron of the enemy, transport and protect his critically injured brother, travel the frozen tundra alone *and* call in the wind to assist his team. She had kept her head, helping orchestrate her own release.

He was still amazed by her knife in the gut of her abductor. He was relatively sure she was in shock by the time he managed to pull the body off of her, but she responded with wit and humor rather than the hysteria one would expect from any female in her position. The only concession to her gender had been passing out at the end, but that, no doubt, was as much from pain as emotional trauma.

"Would you like me to have one of the manual supply sleds prepared for her, my lord?" Marc, the head of the special ops team, inquired.

"No, I will carry her. Her weight is not significant and I don't want her jostled more than necessary."

The medic approached with a thick, white fur to wrap around Kahara.

"With your permission, I would pull up your lady's hood."

"Yes, thank you, Saul." All three looked down at Kahara where she slept in Rom's arms.

"She is a fitting bride for the Lords of Kari, my lord. Our lady is an unbelievable warrior." It was the highest praise from the head of special ops. In spite of her gender, diminutive size and gentle demeanor, after this day, none of them doubted her ability, skills or courage.

"It was she that summoned the wind! Our lady is a gifted Wield as well. Without her help, we would surely have lost men, approaching without cover as we were," Kev, the teams tactician added. His ability to read people and situations made him the best in his field.

"She will give you and Lord Rah fine sons, my lord," another of his men complimented.

If I can regain her trust, Rom thought grimly as he stood with his precious package.

After deploying Zeb to scout ahead and prepare a camp, Rom instructed Marc to send coordinates back to the mother ship for a clean-up team to collect all technology from the planet. As far as he was concerned, the arctic bears were welcome to the bodies. Such treachery did not deserve retrieval or burials.

Soon, the team was under way. The night was clear, the stars looking like diamonds as the three moons began to set.

Kahara woke and snuggled deeper into Rom's powerful arms about an hour into their march. She looked up into his perfect, masculine face, highlighted in gold by the last setting moon. His ebony hair flowed about his shoulders, lifting and falling with his long strides. How could anyone be so graceful in snow shoes?

"Where are we?"

"The middle of nowhere, as I believe you would call it."

"How long have I been out?"

"Not long."

"With a little help from my mate?"

"Yes. I did not want you to suffer and you clearly need the rest."

"Have you been carrying me all this time?"

"You weigh nothing at all, little one."

"Put me down, Rom, I can walk."

"Indulge me, we will stop and camp soon. Let me carry you until then." His heart was breaking at her apparent reluctance to be near him.

Kahara could see they were about to reach the foothills of the mountain range Rom had directed her to before the enemy found her. She hated to admit it, but she was still tired from her ordeal, and he felt so good. Resting her head against his chest, she enjoyed the warmth and comfort of his arms.

At least she tolerated his touch enough to allow him to continue carrying her. It must speak of her exhaustion, Rom concluded. He savored the feel of her in his arms.

Zeb had set up Rom's tent by the time they arrived at a stand of trees beside a river. Kahara could hear the river gurgling under a thick layer of ice, and assumed there must be geothermal activity nearby keeping the water running so close to the surface. She could detect sulfur on the night air.

As Rom set her down in the vestibule of the arctic tent, she saw that Zeb had brought them several large containers of warm water, fragrant soap, and drying cloths. Other containers of the hot spring water sat around the interior of the tent, providing much needed warmth. Two boxes of provisions, and drinking water were also provided. A large sleeping pallet of high tech blankets covered with a large white fur sat to one side.

While quite roomy due to the size of Rom's race, the vestibule and tent interior were too low for the massive warrior to stand. Kahara realized the design was to preserve heat. The advanced material of the tent floor provided insulation from the snow beneath. Glowing clusters of crystals, that had been slipped into clear pockets in the ceiling, provided surprisingly adequate lighting.

"Oh, tent, sweet tent!" she exclaimed. "I'm in heaven!"

"The females I have encountered would not be so delighted," Rom said, looking at her strangely. "Though we are still unfamiliar with the customs and peculiarities of your home planet, while I was there, I could not help notice – most never left their artificial structures. It is doubtful to me any of them would have appreciation for a tent in the arctic night."

"Yes, well, I am considered a bit of a freak by my people." Rom could hear defiance laced with pain in her simple comment.

"*My* people consider you a gift, lady."

Rom longed to stroke her delicate face, but held back. He was relatively sure she would not welcome his touch.

~

Rom had gone to consult with his men, giving Kahara privacy to wash up. After doing so, she could not bring herself to redress in her gore spattered gear. Having no fresh clothes, she wrapped herself using one of the blankets like a sari with the end thrown back over her shoulder, leaving the other bare. It was the thinnest of gossamer, silver silk, yet amazingly warm, and hung to her ankles.

She was sitting on the pallet, both legs to one side, brushing out her hair with a brush she had found in the bathing kit, when Rom returned. He carried a bottle of wine and a warm meal in a small insulated package.

The sight of her sitting there like an angel in silver, with her flaming hair flowing past her hips, shining crimson in the soft lighting, would have brought him to his knees – if he had not already been kneeling in the low vestibule. Gods, she was a beauty. Not even in her heat cycle, she had him constantly hard and aching. He had never heard of this happening to a male before, and was sure she would not be pleased.

The few fertile women he knew begrudgingly tolerated their mate or mates once a year during their heat cycle, and only until they conceived. How was he going to survive until then? How was he going to survive if he could not win back her trust, after the way they had ravaged her?

"Something smells delicious." Kahara turned and smiled at him. "The food's not bad, either."

There was something about the man that brought out the devil in her. Maybe it was because he was always so contained and unerringly proper or, more likely, because he was just so damned gorgeous.

He was as still as any predator, regarding her with unreadable silver eyes. She could tell he'd taken time to clean up as well. He wore fresh clothing and his long hair was still damp, hanging around his broad shoulders in a straight, thick fall of midnight. Freshly shaven, all signs of the earlier battle were gone except for a bruise on his prominent cheekbone.

His features struck her as very Native American, with his black hair, bronze skin and high cheekbones. His eyes were the only exception, a startling, steely blue-grey, glowing from his dark face and lashes. The contrast was arresting.

"I am sorry, lady, we did not expect to be out overnight so we only have emergency gear. I have no clean garments for you. Neither did we bring you a tent of your own. I will sleep in the vestibule if my proximity there does not make you too uncomfortable. I would have you well guarded, but cannot bring myself to let another of my team do the guarding."

What was this about, she wondered. Didn't he want to share the tent with her?

"Is that wine I see?" she asked, deciding to jump in with both feet.

"Yes, red, as I know to be your preference." A flush rose on his bronze cheeks in remembrance.

"Well, come in and sit down," she invited, patting the pallet next to her. "Let's share some."

Rom set down the packages and removed his pack boots and white outer gear. Dressed in a form fitting, black flight suit, he was careful not to crowd her, as he slowly moved into the tent proper and closed the flap to the vestibule.

"You wish to share wine with me, lady?" Rom was shocked to his core. He had brought the wine for her enjoyment alone.

"Is it okay to share wine when Rah is not able to be with us?"

"Yes, he would be overjoyed you wish to share wine with us through me. We are one in all things."

Rom reached into the one of the packages he had brought and pulled out a single goblet.

"I have only one goblet." His silver eyes searched hers.

"Well – then pour and we will share."

"You would share the red goblet with me, Kahara?" his voice was a husky whisper.

"It's not like we haven't done so before." She was becoming confused.

"To do so again now would reconfirm your commitment to us, in spite of what we have done and put you through, lady. Are you sure that is your wish?"

"What have you done to me and why would I need to reconfirm my commitment?"

Rom hung his head in shame. So she was playing with him. Gods knew he deserved no better. What they had done was unforgivable.

"Rom?"

Kahara reached out and put her hand under his strong, square chin, forcing his head up to look into her eyes. She was taken aback by the torment there.

"Please answer me. I don't understand."

"We ravaged you, lady. You were in the healing chamber for three weeks. Please do not pretend you do not remember. We are well aware of our crime against you and that there can be no forgiveness. Is that torture not punishment enough?"

So that's what this was all about. It wasn't that they didn't want her or had changed their minds. Perversely, Kahara was overjoyed.

"Does the reconfirmation require a witness?"

"Yes."

"Then I will wait while you go get one."

Now she wished to shame him by denying him in front of one of his men? So be it. He would not begrudge her any form of revenge she desired. He reached to the sleeping pallet and drew another silver blanket around her shoulders. He could not stand to have another male gazing at her flawless skin.

"I will return shortly."

When Rom reentered with Marc, his face was unreadable while Marc's was glowing with pride. Both men sat cross legged, Rom on the pallet next to Kahara and Marc on the tent floor in front of the couple.

Marc poured the wine into the goblet and took a sip, waiting a moment before handing it to Kahara. She sipped, her eyes meeting Rom's over the rim of the goblet, before holding it out to him. He covered her hands with his, fully expecting her to jerk back and throw the wine in his face. Instead, she gently put it to his lips and offered him to drink. He cautiously did so, savoring the moment.

"In order to complete the ceremony, I must share the goblet by proxy for Rah." He was sure this would earn him the wine in the face. She paused, her eyes saddening.

"I wish he could be here in person. Are you sure he is healing well?"

"Yes, he will be out of the cylinder upon our return." What was she up to?

"Okay, by proxy, for now, but we'll have to do it in person when we return." She took another sip before bringing the goblet to Rom's lips again.

"For Rah."

"For Rah," he whispered, before taking the wine.

"It has been witnessed, it is done," Marc solemnly pronounced, as he placed his fist over his heart. "I will share the news with the others. This is cause for great rejoicing." Then he was gone, silently closing them in the tent together. Moments later, men's voices raised in a cheer that rent the silent arctic night.

"I do not understand you, lady."

Rom was staring at Kahara as if he had never seen her before.

"I think there must be much misunderstanding between all three of us, Rom. I had come to think you and Rah did not want me."

"Not want you? How could you ever think such a thing?"

"I thought we were mated, but you both left me living alone, in my own quarters, never touching me again."

"The female of your people are not honored their own quarters?"

"As a rule, we live and sleep with our mates."

"How do your men stand it?"

"Excuse me? You find me so disgusting then?" Kahara was getting pissed, but she couldn't help herself.

"Gods no, lady. I do not think we could sleep with you and keep our hands off of you until your next heat cycle."

"Who said anything about keeping your hands off of me?"

"You would let us touch you?"

"This is madness! Rom, in my world, men and women committed to each other enjoy sharing their bodies all the time, not just to procreate. I can't look at you without wanting you. I want you to touch me – I want to touch you. You just have to be patient with me while I figure out what to do with two men, rather than one."

"Lady, you unman me," Rom groaned. His cock was growing so hard at her words, he feared he would explode.

"Okay, look, it's clear we don't understand each other's ways, so let's start over and find our own way. Pour some more wine. We will share it and make our rules as we go."

"Whatever is your pleasure, lady."

His head was spinning with what he had learned. This woman was absolutely out of the experience of all of his people in every way. Their woman – their mate – had recommitted to them. He would do whatever it took to keep her.

They shared another large goblet, without Rom making one single advance. Kahara, emboldened by the strong wine on an empty stomach, decided it would be up to her. She took another sip and held it in her mouth. Reaching up to where he sat towering beside her, she pulled Rom's head down to hers and placed her lips to his. As his silver eyes met hers questioningly, she fed him the wine from her mouth.

Rom's massive frame shook as he took the warmed wine directly from his mate. Never had he experienced anything as erotic as the red wine, directly from his lady's lips. Unable to stop himself, he thrust his tongue into the sweet depths and ravaged her with a hungry kiss. Kahara's small arms encircled his thick neck as she pulled herself flush against his chest, deepening the kiss further.

"You, sir, are completely overdressed," she whispered to him, when they finally came up for air.

She reached to unfasten the high collar of his flight suit and continued down the front, exposing his massive, bronze chest. She ran her tiny hands over the firm slab of pectoral muscles exposed by her actions. Rom gasped, grabbing her small wrist, holding her hand still against his chest.

"You don't want me to touch you?" she asked, trying not to sound as hurt as she felt.

"I am yours to do with as you will, lady. Touch me any way you like." His voice was a deep, needy rumble.

"What do you want, Rom?"

"You, lady. I want you till I fear I will die with the wanting."

Rom could not lie to her, not even to avoid frightening her. It was the raw, shameful truth.

Kahara rose to her knees, letting the blanket pool onto the pallet. Unable to help himself, Rom reached up, reverently and gently, to caress one pink nipple. It pearled at his touch. He ran his fingertips over her belly and across a hip, coming to rest at the very top of the red curls shrouding her womanhood.

"Ah, lady, I have never seen anything so beautiful," he whispered, overwhelmed by her actions in the face of his confession.

"May I see you as well?"

Rom undressed for his lady. Every efficient move exposing lean, powerful muscle encased in bronze. Kahara drank him in with her eyes. His massive chest rose and fell with every rapid breath. Long fingered hands made short work of removing clothing until he knelt on the pallet before her in his naked, fully aroused glory.

And, my god, was he glorious! His thick rod stood proud and full, reaching well above his navel. Ebony hair flowed over massive shoulders, framing a powerful face and molten silver eyes that scorched her body as they caressed every quivering inch of her.

"Oh, Rom, you take my breath away."

Kahara reached out, running her forefinger from his throat to his navel, following the path of soft black hair growing there, to his groin.

Rom let out a low moan, shuddering at her feather touch. She boldly encircled his throbbing member with one tiny hand. Her fingers could not begin to reach around his girth. Rom shuddered again, but held steady, not wanting to frighten her. As long as it took for her to familiarize herself with his body, he would endure, in order to have her trust them during her next heat cycle.

When she slowly bent over, taking his mushroom head into her hot mouth, Rom nearly exploded.

"Mmm, you are delicious, Rom," she cooed around her mouthful.

Oh, gods, he was not going to live through this. She took one of his hands and placed it over her full, lush breast. The erect nipple pressed against his callused palm. She ran her tongue around the throbbing head of his erection while stroking up and down the shaft with her fist.

Rom shook from head to foot, hips helplessly thrusting him deeper into the warm cavern of her mouth. Grabbing her by the hair, he gently but firmly pulled her away from his uncontrollable groin and back to his hungry mouth. She lunged at him, pushing him backwards to lie on the pallet.

"Got ya!" she laughed, as she climbed on top of his scorching body, her wild hair falling against his skin.

Rom lay perfectly still, letting her have her way. He feared moving so much as a single muscle. Any movement might not only frighten her, but drive him into action. While he was renowned for his control in all things, she was just about to break him.

Kahara straddled him, crushing her bare breasts into his chest, as she bent to indulge herself in another, mind blowing kiss. He responded, sinking his tongue into her mouth, but did not otherwise touch her. Instead, his hands were fisted in the bedding until his muscled arms shook.

"Would you please hold me, Rom?"

"Oh, lady, I cannot trust myself."

"I trust you, Rom."

Slowly and ever so carefully, he brought his huge arms around her small frame.

"I won't break," she encouraged.

"I will, lady. I am afraid I will."

She rubbed herself against him, kissing his throat. He shuddered, shaking uncontrollably now, as they shared another drugging kiss – then another – yet he made no move to take her.

Yup, looks like this was going to be entirely up to her. She pulled back from his embrace. Reluctantly, he let her go. Sitting up on her knees to straddle him, she took hold of his blistering rod and directed the full, pulsing head against her wet core.

"Lady, you are not in your cycle, I will have no mating hormone to ease you," Rom moaned, gently grabbing her hips to prevent her taking him into her body.

"The men of my species never have any. I want you, Rom, it will be okay."

"I am yours, Kahara, take of me as you will."

He released her hips and grabbed fistfuls of the pallet on either side of him. His molten silver eyes met her emerald green ones and held. Slowly, she sank onto him, impaling herself on his massive erection, inch by incredible inch. He could feel her inner muscles quivering in protest at his size. Every so often, she would stop and give herself time to adjust.

God, he was unbelievable! So huge she had to work to accommodate him, even when he was not in the mating madness. She backed off slightly – Rom groaned. He still did not touch her or restrict her in any way. Carefully, her emerald eyes never leaving his, Kahara moved herself up and down on the huge head, gradually taking more of him each time she sank down. The stimulation had her drenching him with her cream.

Rom was in agony – he was in ecstasy. Her sheath was a tight, wet, quivering fist around the head of his member. Her emerald eyes were full of passion. Her full breasts swung with the motion, as her long hair flowed down her back, pooling on his scalding sack.

"Rom, would you put your hands on my breasts?" Gladly, he complied.

"Pinch my nipples," she panted.

"I don't want to hurt you," he moaned.

"You won't. I need you to pinch them, rub them back and forth between your fingers. Oh God, yes, now pull on them."

As Rom followed her instructions, she drew up again until he was almost free of her tight sheath, before sinking back down on him in one fluid stroke, taking him deeply. Her inner muscles convulsed around the invasion.

Rom lost himself, thrusting up, forcing further into her hot depths, and roared. Kahara's orgasm was immediate and unending. She screamed his name, over and over, as she flew apart on top of him. He felt his balls pulling up under the fall of her hair, electricity running up his spine.

Helplessly, he thrust up again – once, twice, and then losing all control, he grabbed her slender hips and savagely pounded into her, again and again, until he exploded, his scalding seed jetting into her in powerful surges. She whimpered and collapsed onto his chest.

"Damn, what a rush!" she breathed.

~

As Rom returned from the madness of his passion, he was devastated. Gods, what had he done to her? What had he done? His brother had been right. They did not deserve Kahara and could not be trusted to care for her. Gently he lifted her limp body from his chest and placed her on the pallet. Getting up, he put on his flight suit.

"Rom? What is it?"

"Ah, lady, I know there can be no forgiveness this time."

He was on his knees in the low tent, his back to her, head hanging, black hair veiling his face, arms helplessly at his sides as his big hands fisted in anguish.

"I will send in our medic. My team will surround and guard you. They will see you to safety. I will not impose myself on you further."

He fully intended to walk into the arctic night and never return. Kahara could feel it.

He heard her rise from the bed upon which he had just ravaged her – again. Standing in front of him, wearing only her glorious hair, she reached to push his hair from his face, tucking it behind his ears. Holding his strong jaw, she searched his eyes. Her cheeks were flushed, lips swollen from his brutal kisses. Kahara was amazed to see tears filling his silver eyes. Then she sank before him naked and vulnerable, pooling her hair at his knees.

"Don't leave me, Rom. That was the most beautiful moment of my life. If you reject me now, I don't think I could stand it," she whispered, tears in her voice.

"Gods, lady, what would you have me do?"

"Get undressed – let's go back to bed. I want to have you hold me for a while and then we can do it again. This time though, you get to be on top." She smiled up at him, her eyes misty, tears on her face.

"You put yourself back in my hands? Pool your hair in front of me, when I have just broken your trust and ravaged you again?" Rom shouted as he pulled her from the floor to stand in front of him. "What madness is this, Kahara? What madness?"

"That was not ravagement. That was making love. Did you not enjoy it?"

"Lady, you gave me ecstasy such as I have never known."

"As you did me."

"How can this be? I made you scream! You screamed my name for mercy. I gave you none."

"You didn't hurt me and that was not screaming for mercy. I love you, Rom. I want to make love to you again. Make me scream again."

The last was a mere whisper as she wrapped her arms around his neck, brushing her lips back and forth across his. She could feel his erection, full and throbbing, through his flight suit where it pressed against her soft belly. Leaning down, he covered her lush mouth with his and was lost.

~

Rom was unerringly gentle with her. At her request, he was on top and spent a long time kissing and suckling her to a fevered pitch. His warm tongue teased her nipples to hard peaks, then he would nip her with his sharp, white teeth, only to lick and suckle again. He nuzzled the tender cords of her neck, then drew hard, leaving his mark.

Working his way down her body, he paid special attention to her navel and the insides of her thighs. The backs of her knees

140

seemed to fascinate him, so he left his mark there as well. On his way back up, he spread her legs wide and gently parted the lips of her throbbing womanhood. She was drenched for him, shiny and swollen, mindless with desire.

"You are so beautiful. I want to taste you. I want to drink your nectar."

"Oh, God, Rom," she gasped.

"Please, Kahara, I will not hurt you. I must know you like this. I need your taste on my tongue."

"Yes, oh god, yes, lick me, suck on me, please," she whimpered, arching toward his mouth.

Rom could not believe his good fortune. Though his wild desires for her concerned him greatly, their lady eagerly met him at every turn. His pleasure seemed to be hers as well. Though she whimpered and writhed, he held a mental link with her to be sure he caused no harm. He was learning to understand it was not in pain that she writhed.

He lowered his head to her, his long hair brushing her thighs as he covered her with his hot mouth. She was absolute ambrosia. He could not get enough. When he sank his lapping tongue deep into her cleft, he had to hold her hips to still her as she bucked, quivered and shook. He captured her sensitive button between his teeth, flicking it with the tip of his tongue as he simultaneously sank one long finger into her depths. Her wet sheath caressed his finger.

She was so small! However had she accommodated him? Yet he could detect no tearing or signs of damage from their earlier encounter. She was rearing up to meet him now, in spite of his restraining hands.

"Another finger, please, Rom, put another in me," she panted.

As he did so, he was amazed to feel her tissues stretch to accommodate while still caressing his fingers on all sides.

His objective observations ended abruptly as she came apart for him. He could feel her orgasm ripping through their mental link, taking him with her, as he spilled his seed without warning. His cock pumped out spurt after spurt of pearly white onto her legs and the blanket beneath, but did not soften. He sucked hard on her clitoris, marking her there as well, and sank a third finger deeply as she screamed his name. He decided he could learn to like her screaming.

Suddenly, he had to be inside her. His cock, still spewing and rock hard – throbbed for her depths.

"I want in, oh gods, lady, I want inside you now!"

She pulled him up her body and wrapped her long slender legs around his waist.

"I can't be gentle. I fear hurting you," he warned in a guttural growl, his swollen mushroom head pressing against her hot entrance, still ejaculating endlessly. "Tell me no, and I will find a way to leave you."

"You won't hurt me, Rom. Take me now," she panted, her own orgasm not having abated.

They were caught in a feedback loop of their mental link. The results were mind blowing.

He thrust down as she rose to meet him. She was wet, scalding and wild, the fit perfect, as she took every throbbing inch of him into her thrashing body.

He held her to him, buried deep, shuddering with his continuing ejaculation, until he could control himself no longer. Pulling out, he slammed home again, so hard he felt his scalding sack pressed against that sweet rosette that should be filled with his brother. He reached between them, and lubricated his fingers in their combined juices.

Still driving into her in long, deep thrusts, he sank the moistened fingers into her rear on his next wild plunge. Kahara screamed, peaking again. He pounded into her even deeper, rotating his hips and adding a third finger. Kahara came apart. Rom threw his head back and bellowed in final release. They both lost consciousness, waking much later, wet and chilled, with Rom still swollen and locked in Kahara's body.

She wiggled enticingly. He thrust in and out in a slow, sensual stroke, and they were lost to each other again. Thus went the rest of the night.

The man was tireless – she woke with him moving within her again. His stamina was a thing of legends, not that she was complaining. It seemed she couldn't get enough of him.

Rom was amazed at the welcome he found in his lady. She met him, thrust for thrust, time and time again until he lost count of his releases. He would doze for a short period only to wake again, finding his desire for her insatiable. As he filled her with his seed, she filled every corner of his big alien heart to overflowing.

He felt his love for her to the depths of his soul. Never had he known such ecstasy as he found in the arms of his tiny mate. When sleep finally claimed him, it was the deep sleep of the sated, his heart having finally found its home.

~ *Chapter 13* ~

After six hours of sleep, it was time to get under way. Zeb was planning to set out ahead of the group to find the best route to the landing area, where they would rendezvous with the shuttles sent from the fleet. Ever mindful of their precious cargo – the lords' beautiful, petite mate, Zeb intended to make the trip as short and smooth as possible. The thought of the lady having to traverse the harsh frozen tundra, without technological support, did not sit well with him. She should be in a heated jet sled, not on snow shoes. Hell, she should not be on this harsh planet at all.

As he stepped out of his tent, Kev, who had been on guard, silently stopped him with a hand on his arm, indicating the tree line. Zeb looked up to see the camp converged upon by giant wolves. Soundless and stealthy, the wolves surrounded the camp and sat on their haunches, in seeming formation, regarding the two men from about twenty-five feet away.

Armed only with swords and short knives, they regarded the pack in alarm. There were at least fifty of the beasts, sitting in silence on the moonlit snow, each the size of a small horse. They sat quietly as if awaiting something when, to the men's amazement, Lady Kahara emerged from Lord Rom's tent – alone.

Ethereal in the golden light of the three moons, she was barefoot in the snow. Her only covering was a draped, silver, heat generating blanket that sparkled in the moonlight. Long red curls fell wild and untamed around her tiny body.

As a large, black wolf stood and approached her, both men drew their swords. They were fully prepared to take on the entire pack, sacrificing their lives to protect their lady.

"Do not," she whispered to the men. "They are allies."

The wolf approached the lady and lay at her feet in the snow. To their utter disbelief, Kahara got on its back and arranged the blanket to cover her bare legs. The wolf stood and returned to the pack, the tiny woman sitting its back as if born to it.

Several of the pack stood and joined the black wolf bearing their lady. They frolicked around her in joy, some putting their massive muzzles close to her face. She reached to each in turn, hugging them to her, scuffing their fur and rubbing noses.

The men's attention was drawn back to the Lord's tent as it began to shake and shudder. For a while, it looked as if it would walk off on its own before a distraught Lord Rom Andor emerged, shirtless, hopping on one foot as he pulled on a pack boot, looking around desperately. His wild silver eyes came to rest on the two men. Kev pointed, drawing the lord's attention to his mate and the pack of wolves.

Rom froze in place, fear for his mate paralyzing him.

When he woke to find her gone, he had died a thousand deaths. There was nowhere safe outside the tent for her to be. The last thing he expected was to find her sitting a giant wolf in the middle of a huge pack of the beasts. He held steady, fearing movement could trigger an attack. Opening all of his formidable senses, he attempted to ascertain the mood of the pack. Kahara met his eyes.

"I am well, Rom. They are allies," she sent to him.

"Kahara, lady, you will be the death of me," Rom responded on their private path.

"They have come to provide protection and escort to the landing site. They also have brought an ambassador. He wishes to speak with you, Lord Rom," Kahara shared aloud so all the men could be informed.

"They are the pack that helped Rah and I. I took the liberty of offering to set up a meeting with you. They want to have their race represented in the federation. I hope I didn't overstep my authority," she added, on their telepathic link.

"You have done well, little one. We have been trying to reestablish relations with them for years but have been unable to do so. They tend to be a very reclusive and independent race." Rom marveled at his mate's communication and diplomatic skills.

The formation of the pack parted, and a black and silver wolf with green flecked yellow eyes came forward. He was slightly smaller in stature than the rest of the pack, but still formidable in size and structure.

"Greetings, Lord Rom Andor. May I have permission to communicate with you?" the wolf addressed him on a common mental channel.

"It would be an honor," Rom formally replied in kind, surprised by the clear, telepathic communication.

"I am Lord Jarl Lyall, commander of the Taronian forces. Your lady-shaman is greatly revered by my people and has convinced the alpha pair it would be in our best interest to become allies with your race. She informed us, it is with you we must negotiate for the privilege. I have been chosen to serve as ambassador for my race, due to my cross-species communication skills."

"Your skills are indeed impressive. We have been unable to communicate well with your people in the past. It has been several hundred years since Ambassador Santi, our last skilled cross-species communicator, set up the no-technological weapons treaty with your race. Once he was lost to us, we have been unable to contact your people."

"Yes, I have heard of the good ambassador. He and the shaman of our people, my great-great grandsire, Lord Belinu Lyall,

negotiated the treaty. I am sorry to hear of your loss," Jarl respectfully offered his condolences.

"Thank you, he was a great ambassador and is sorely missed."

"As your lady-shaman said, we have come to offer protection and transport to your landing site. Might I respectfully suggest, in consideration of your easily chilled bodies, we get your people loaded up and under way? We can discuss details en route," Jarl said. Rom detected humor lacing the wolf's mental communication.

"Thank you for your consideration. Hairless wonders that we are, we are not so well suited to your arctic conditions. I would offer to hold council in one of our tents, but I don't think you would fit," Rom responded with a smile, deciding he liked the lupine commander: turned ambassador.

Kahara returned to Rom's tent, put on her soiled clothing from the day before, and braided her hair. Camp was quickly broken – the loaded sleds to be pulled behind several wolves of the Taronian pack. A giant wolf lay down in front of each of the Karinians.

"What do they want?" Marc questioned, still leery of the oversized lupines in their midst and particularly of the monster before him.

"He is offering you a ride. I suggest you take him up on it or you will be left in the dust – or snow as it were. They are really fast cross country," Kahara advised, as she comfortably remounted the black alpha female. Kahara saw the silver alpha male offer himself to Rom.

"I thank you for offering to carry my mate, dear friend," she sent to the wolf.

"It is only fitting. We are both alpha and the largest of our respective packs," was the pragmatic response.

As they headed out, Rom and Kahara, mounted on the alpha pair, took up the lead – Lord Jarl slightly out in front of them. They were followed by the other members of the landing party, each mounted on a wolf. Behind them, the wolves pulling sleds fell into line. The rest of the pack surrounded them in tight formation, with the exception of the twelve scout wolves. Three patrolled ahead, three behind and three off to each side, with noses to the ground, circling back as they went.

"Can you hear any communication between the wolves?" Rom asked Kahara privately, impressed by the military precision of the pack.

"Yes, Lord Jarl is directing them. The four scout teams each have a leader that is in constant contact with Jarl. The alpha pair seems content to leave the operation to him," she replied, clearly understanding Rom's query and the reasons behind it.

"Are you familiar with Lord Jarl?"

"No. Like you, I just met him. He was not with the ones that answered my call for assist after the crash."

"What is your take on him?" Rom asked, respecting his mate's intuitive abilities.

"He is clearly very gifted and a respected leader. If he is the great-great grandson of the shaman, I suspect he has inherited shamanic gifts and has been well trained. This would explain his communication skills."

"Like yours."

"Yes, like mine," Kahara confessed, not comfortable with the topic.

"Do you think we can trust him?" Sensing her discomfort, Rom changed the subject.

"He doesn't block me when I scan him and I pick up no deception. This race may be reclusive but they are honest and pragmatic, just as their counter parts on Earth. I fear this sets them up to be taken advantage of by unscrupulous deceptive

races. That's why I suggested the allegiance with you. They need protection and at the same time will prove to be valuable allies."

"You are precognizant as well?" Rom did not miss her accurate reading of possible future events.

"Yes," she answered honestly. Again Rom could feel her discomfort.

"You see my race as honest?"

"No, there is much deception and betrayal operating among your people. I see you and Rah as honest with great integrity. I know I can trust you both to treat my new friends fairly."

She had communicated with him as clearly and accurately as any of his military leaders. Rom did not miss the professionalism or her ability to use her gifts in a combat setting. There was much more to their lady than met the eye. Not for the first time, he wondered about her life before they had acquired her.

"You speak to me not as your mate, but as your commander."

"Yes."

"Why?"

"We are in a precarious situation and military format. I can best serve you as a subordinate. I will be glad to resume my station as mate tonight," she said, looking over at him with a secretive smile, causing his heart to take up double time and his cock to rear its head. Gods, but she was a provocative enigma.

~ Chapter 14 ~

Lord Jarl and Belinu Lyall had discussed in length, the prophesized appearance of Kahara on their planet. Both shaman had recognized deep purpose between themselves and the powerful, female shadow walker. There was much positive change that would be brought by this one petite human and it was their duty to assist her any way they could.

Jarl had agreed to turn over his position as commander of the Taronian forces to his trusted second. He would willingly sacrifice his chances of finding a mate in order to travel with the Karinians and serve the lady shaman as ambassador for his people. He just hoped he could earn their trust enough for them to be willing to accept him. Time was short and the stakes were high.

"We have picked up the scent of more vile ones," his lead scout informed him.

"How many?" Jarl inquired.

"The stench is strong, probably an entire unit."

Not good, he thought as he asked, *"How far?"*

"No more than five miles due north and we smell the presence of technological transport and weaponry."

"Lady and Lord Andor, we have encountered a problem. There is a unit of vile ones, five miles north of our location. They appear to be armed with technological weaponry and heading our way."

"All of our technology is down. I have no way to contact my fleet in order to disarm them," Rom informed the Taronion commander.

"We will need to find cover in order to defend ourselves," Jarl advised. *"It is likely they will reach us before we can do so. I will stay here with my troops and hold them off in order to buy time for the alpha pair to carry you and your lady to safety."*

"That is a suicide mission," Rom stated.

"Your lady must live – at all cost."

"Lord Jarl," Kahara addressed the commander. *"Am I correct in assuming you are gifted and trained in the shamanic way?"*

"Yes, lady, but I am no match for their weaponry."

"How are you on illusion?"

"Fair, for short periods of time."

"Can you unite powers with another?"

"I have done so with my great-great grandsire, but he is my teacher."

"Rom, I think we can buy us all some time without sacrificing Lord Jarl and his troops. However there is no time for explanations and I will have to go with Lord Jarl while you go with the Alphas."

"You are my lady mate. It is mine to protect you, or die trying," Rom protested.

"This is the best way to protect all of us. I have trusted you with my love and my life – can you not trust me as well?"

"What do you have in mind?"

"Lord Jarl, are you willing to carry me? The physical contact will better unite our power and traveling as one there will be less to shield from view."

"With your mate's permission, it will be my honor."

Rom looked from his lady to the Taronion commander and back again.

"It is the rest of my life and my twin's life you carry, Lord Jarl," he said by way of permission.

"She is the key to the rest of all our lives. Lord Rom, I will not fail your trust or our lady shaman."

The alpha female lay, allowing Kahara to dismount and Jarl lay as well, offering her his back. Kahara spun an illusion of herself on the back of the female, who rejoined her mate and Rom.

"Your lady and I will provide distraction without endangering her. I leave you in command of my troops to set up an ambush from the cover of the forest one mile west of this location. Because you cannot communicate with them, I will direct my troops as you direct me. Are you able to read pictures and concepts as well as words on our channel?"

Jarl sent Rom an image of the location he had indicated and a common battle formation of his troops as he spoke.

"Yes, that is very clear," Rom marveled.

"Your lady can as well. In this way we will all three command the entire operation as a psychic Triad. Send me a picture of where you want whom and I will make it so."

Satisfied that the two formidable leaders were in full cooperation, Kahara stayed in the background as she set up the bonding of her power to that of Lord Jarl. He had left himself entirely open to her, hiding nothing, enabling her to accurately and synergistically align their gifts.

Jarl, in turn, used his superior communication skills to allow Rom to experience everything he and Kahara were doing, thus keeping him appraised of their capabilities as well as their actions.

While his every instinct was to shelter and protect her, Rom could not help but consider what a powerful tactical Triad he and his brother could form with their lady. It was becoming clear she could participate and excel in their operations, ultimately providing more safety for them all. He was not so macho he could not bend to the superior arrangement. His brother, on the other hand, may take some convincing.

Rom set off with the Taronion troops at a westerly heading while Kahara, mounted on Jarl, appeared to waver out of existence. Though he knew it to be an illusion, he took comfort in the sight of his lady's image on the back of the alpha female running next to him.

"Lord Rom, if you will lean forward and hang on, I will have the alpha pair increase the pace," Jarl directed him. Rom had no sooner complied when the alpha lunged with an impressive bunching of muscles and show of strength.

Looking back over his shoulder, he saw a ground blizzard forming between his group and the north – courtesy of his lady, he thought with a smile. She had been kind enough to leave the distance between him and the forest clear and calm while the winds of hell obliterated all sign of his passage and shielded the Taronion troops from view. Her precision amazed him.

Soon, Rom received a remote picture of the enemy unit on the newly formed Triad channel. They were seventy-five strong and well-armed, traversing the tundra riding open jet sleds. Or at least they had been, until the blizzard ground them to a halt.

Rom saw an image of wolf forces coming at them out of the blowing snow, eyes glowing and fangs dripping. They appeared twice their actual size, numbering several hundred. He could hear the sound of lasers going off in the distance as he watched the panicked unit fire upon illusionary wolves who seemed to disappear back into the blizzard and circle around them yapping and howling in challenge.

"What is your location, Lord Rom?" Jarl asked.

Rom responded by sending a picture of his view of the tundra with the tree line becoming visible in the distance.

"When you are in position, we can drive the enemy your direction. How would you like to set up the troops?"

"What would you suggest? You are more familiar with their capabilities than I," Rom respectfully deferred to the Taronion leader.

"They will need to remain unseen until the unit is close enough for the pack to attack and pull them off of their jet sleds. The enemy has little chance of winning a ground fight if they are separated from their sleds and weapons for even a short time."

"Let us split your warriors into three groups as we approach the tree line and position them behind the trees. Instruct Kahara to cover our tracks and movements with her blizzard. We will use your troop's superior vision and sense of smell to ambush the enemy when you drive them into the gauntlet formed by two of our groups. The third group can cut the alien forces off and get any that the two sides miss," Rom suggested, as he sent a visual diagram of the operation.

"Nice tactics for a diplomat," Jarl complimented.

"I'm not feeling overly diplomatic," Rom assured him.

The Taronion pack divided into three groups and took up position in the exact format Rom had sent Jarl. They were swift and sure as they silently disappeared into the trees. As soon as they were in position, Rom sent Jarl and Kahara a picture formation. The wind immediately picked up and covered their tracks before dying down, replaced with a dense fog hanging low in the trees.

Rom received a picture of the totally panicked men on jet sleds. Jarl and Kahara had managed to cause members of the enemy units to appear as attacking wolves, causing the men to fire on each other.

The enemy leader, realizing they were being taken out by friendly fire, yelled for a cease fire and retreat. The illusionary wolf pack rushed the panicked men from behind, driving them forward. The ground blizzard let up, exposing the tree line where the real wolves waited under the cover of ground fog. The fleeing troops took the bait. Karinian warriors and Taronian wolves fell upon the enemy and it was over in a matter of minutes.

The fog cleared, exposing the dead and dying in gruesome detail, just as Jarl and Kahara shimmered into visibility at the tree line.

"Casualties?" Jarl asked Rom.

"None on our side," he responded, looking in disgust at the carnage left of the enemy unit. *"Your people don't believe in taking prisoners for questioning, do they?"*

"They have no way to question them," Jarl reminded him.

"Yes, well I suppose there is that."

"We managed to read the leader and know their intent before we attacked," Kahara told Rom.

"What was their intent?"

"Kill you and take me."

"Why?"

"He didn't know that."

"Who sent them?"

"Other than his superior officer, he didn't know that either."

Suddenly, Rom was aware of the carnage in clear view of his gentle mate.

"Lady, let me take you from this place," he offered in a concerned voice.

"It's not the first time I have seen death, Rom."

"I deeply regret that," Rom stated, hanging his head in shame for having killed in front of her – yet again.

"You are a powerful warrior, Rom. Do not feel shame for your ability and willingness to protect me. It brings me great pride to have you as mate. I saw much unjust killing before leaving earth. This is not the same," she hastened to assure him on their private channel.

"Your mate and his warriors do an impressive dance with the silver fang. We are honored to have fought by their side," the alpha male told Kahara, who in turn shared his words with Rom.

"Silver fang?" Rom asked.

"I think he means your sword, Rom," she enlightened him with a smile.

"Tell him we are honored to have him and his powerful pack as allies. They risked their lives for us today. It will not be forgotten."

"You and your men could have picked up and put to use the technological weapons of the fallen enemy but did not. It would have evened the odds considerably," Jarl observed.

"It would have been in violation of our treaty. Only as a last resort to protect my lady would I have done such," Rom answered in all honesty.

"In order to protect our lady shaman, you would have been welcome to do so," Jarl assured him.

"For one without claw or fang you do quite well. I hope someday to witness you dance the silver fang again," the Alpha informed Rom after Jarl translated their conversation.

"It will always be my honor to fight by your side," Rom responded and Jarl translated.

Thus the alliance was formed between the two races. By the time they reached the landing site, plans had been made for Jarl to accompany Rom and Kahara back to their fleet.

Jarl and Belinu were capable of communicating over great distances, even galaxies away. Staying in touch with his people in order to represent them would be possible without technological support. It was clear why Jarl had been chosen as ambassador, though it took him from his position as commander of the Taronian forces where he would be sorely missed.

~

As Rah came out of stasis, his first awareness was a soft, warm hand, caressing the side of his whisker roughened jaw. It was not something he had ever experienced in his long lifetime. His eyes snapped open to meet the worried, emerald green gaze of his mate.

She lived! His hand flew up to hers, trapping it against his face. He shuddered in relief. She lived. He squeezed his eyes shut, holding her hand to him reverently.

"Lady, do not ever leave me again," Kahara heard him whisper in a rough, unused voice.

When he opened his eyes, he noticed Rom standing beside their mate.

"Hello brother," Rom greeted him. "As you can see, I managed to recover our wayward little mate." To Rah's amazement, Kahara responded by punching Rom soundly in the shoulder.

"It is still undecided as to who recovered whom," she countered in feigned ferocity. "How are you feeling, Rah?" she said in a much gentler voice.

"She punches me, then coos at you. I was the one that rescued the two of you. I should be the hero here. Where is the justice in life?" Rom teased.

Rom never teased! For that matter, no one ever punched him and remained standing! What world did he just wake up in, Rah wondered.

He had cause to wonder that again, the very next day, when Kahara arrived in his recovery room. She was accompanied by a black and silver Taronion wolf whose shoulder was on a level with hers.

"Rah, I would like you to meet Ambassador Lord Jarl Lyall. Lord Jarl, this is Commander and Chief Lord Rah Andor, my mate."

Was that pride Rah heard in her voice when she introduced him to the wolf? Could she actually be proud he was her mate? He also noticed she did not say *other* mate.

"It is my honor to make your acquaintance, Lord Rah." Jarl amazed him by addressing him on a telepathic channel.

Rom, and recently their lady mate, had been the only ones Rah had ever communicated with telepathically. At Rah's mental flinch, Jarl went on, *"I am well versed in nonverbal communication and therefore able to honor your privacy. I will only detect what you choose to say to me directly. If you prefer, I can speak with your lady mate and she will translate for us."*

"Can you understand me if I speak?" Rah asked out loud.

"Yes."

"Then I will speak and you can send. Is that acceptable to you?"

"Whatever makes you the most comfortable. I regret I have not the palate for speech," Jarl replied with a smile in his mental voice.

"How are you feeling today, Rah?" Kahara asked. She amazed him by voluntarily reaching out and touching his cheek. "Medical Officer Saul gave me permission to move you to your chambers, provided I take care of you and not let you up and about until tomorrow."

"You would choose to care for me when we have a perfectly good medical center to do so?"

"Yes."

"Why?"

"I thought you would be more comfortable in your own quarters and I would much rather have you there." Her tone of voice clearly indicated she did not understand what *he* did not understand.

"Why?"

"So I can fuss over you and otherwise make your life miserable," she answered in exasperation. "Would you rather stay here?"

"No, I would not rather stay here. I think I would like to experience some of this fussing of which you speak."

"Good, I will go make arrangements," she tossed over her shoulder as she left the room, the giant wolf in tow.

~

He could get used to the fussing, Rah decided, as his beautiful mate tucked the covers around his huge shoulders and gently brushed his long hair out of his face. He watched her closely, not saying a word. The monstrous Taronion wolf lay curled up in front of the bedroom door.

When Kahara asked if Jarl would like her to find him more comfortable quarters, the wolf considerately answered on a common channel so both she and Rah could hear.

"I will take guard duty until Lord Rah is strong enough to do so, or Lord Rom relieves me," Jarl had calmly stated.

"Why do you think we need guarding?" Rah asked, somewhat put off by the wolf's proprietary attitude.

"There were several attempts on our lady shaman while she was on Taron. Someone is clearly invested in acquiring her."

"Several? Why was I not informed another attempt was made?" Rah demanded, looking at Kahara.

"Do not get your balls in an uproar," Rom sent him on their private channel, as he walked into the room. *"I have come to debrief you."*

"Oh, good, you're here, Rom," Kahara greeted him. "I will leave you two to catch up while Lord Jarl and I go see to setting up quarters to accommodate his lupine nature."

Once again she amazed Rah by leaning down and kissing him on the cheek. Standing on tiptoe to do the same to Rom, she left in a fragrant swirl of peach silk and red curls. As usual, the wolf fell in behind her.

~ *Chapter 15* ~

It had been several days since Rah had been strong enough to return to duty. Kahara hadn't seen much of the Commander and Chief since. She knew there was much demanding the attention of both brothers who were trying to catch up after their time on the ice planet and Rah's convalescence.

Both of her mates had been grabbing meals on the run rather than participating in the formal dinners on board the ship. Kahara's former quarters had been modified to accommodate Lord Jarl. This was to be her first night with her mates in their newly remodeled quarters.

The brothers had not yet arrived when Jarl escorted her to her new residence, so he settled with a thump and a lupine sigh to take up watch at the front door. She had already eaten, so she decided to enjoy a bath before bed. She located a lovely dressing room containing her belongings, which connected to the large bathing chamber.

When Kahara emerged from her dressing room after her bath, she was wearing a soft, flowing, mauve satin dressing gown. It crossed at the tailored bodice, gathering into a full skirt that attached to a wide wraparound sash accentuating her tiny waist. Brushing the floor, the skirt opened with each step, showing a flash of shapely leg. Matching high heeled slippers encased her dainty feet. Her flaming hair was banded by a wide ribbon and left free to flow down her back to her hips.

The sensual combination of dusty mauve satin, flaming red tresses and velvet ivory skin took Rah's breath away. Having just bathed, using the exotically perfumed soaps he and his brother had given her, she smelled of amber spice and sin, mixed with her own unique scent. At the sight and smell of her, his already raging desire increased tenfold.

He could tell the moment she sensed she was not alone in the living room of their quarters. She froze, flowing skirts swirling around her legs, before coming to rest. She looked over at the fireplace where he stood. Her emerald eyes widened, pink lips opened slightly and her beautiful full breasts rose with her sudden inhalation.

Kahara was rarely taken by surprise. She was usually aware when someone was near. That Rah was in the room without her knowledge was a bit shocking. But there he was, muscular arms crossed over his massive chest, leaning into the mantel of the large fireplace. Bare feet crossed at the ankles, he looked deceptively relaxed. For a man usually so military straight and contained, he appeared uncharacteristically casual.

His black, silk uniform shirt was partially unbuttoned, exposing the pendent resting against bronzed skin. He was not wearing his ever present weapons belt. Her eyes met his, emerald fused with molten silver. Her heart rate increased and she had to fight for her next breath. His nostrils flared, as if taking in her scent but he said nothing. Kahara noticed the Taronion wolf was no longer in residence.

"Rah! Hello, what a surprise." Could she sound any more asinine?

"What is so surprising? These are my quarters, after all."

Oh god – that voice, smoke and whisky, a challenging caress. Was that a slight lift of his full lips? Kahara was left speechless.

Gods, how he loved seeing her in his and his brothers quarters, fresh from her bath. Nothing could be more provocative, their woman – his woman, sharing their space. It would be the death of him.

"Come, sit. We need to talk." Rah left the fireplace and approached her. Taking her hand, he led her to the couch in front of the fire and sat her down. "Would you care for some wine?"

The glass table in front of them held a bottle of red wine and the ornate ceremonial goblet. "Rom shared his memories of your time on Taron. I would be most honored to share the red goblet in person, if that is still your desire."

"I would love to share the red goblet with you, Rah."

He poured the wine and sipped before handing Kahara the goblet. She took a sip and held it to his full, sensual lips, her eyes never leaving his. Covering her hands with his much larger ones, Rah drank from the goblet.

His heart turned over, his cock became granite. Firelight danced in her hair and in her eyes. His hands shook with desire where he held them over hers. Would she also offer her body as she had to Rom? Could she also trust and desire him in such a way? He took the goblet from her and put it back on the table.

"Kahara?"

"Yes?"

"He shared *all* of his memories – we are one in all things."

Kahara's cheeks flamed but she did not look away from him.

"Did you find that upsetting?" She was not sure of his meaning or his intent.

"There is much upsetting me at this time, little one. But watching my brother pleasure you – making you ours in all ways was the most beautiful thing I have ever had the privilege of sharing." His voice was a soft, deep rumble that had her womb churning and her nipples beading under the satin of her gown. His molten eyes searched hers.

"I am not the diplomat that Rom is. Kahara, all I know is plain speaking. I have no soft words or gentle ways to ease things for you." Taking a deep breath, he forged ahead. "The males of our world know that we are considered beasts by our females. Karinians do not impose themselves upon a mate, should we be lucky enough to find one, until her season is upon her. Nor do we go into the mating frenzy until that time. It is unheard of.

"We offer our protection and provide for our mate's every want and need for her lifetime in exchange for the privilege of fertilizing the one or two viable eggs she possesses. Once that is done, we never impose ourselves upon her again.

"She is treasured above all things. We would give our lives to protect her. This is the way it has been as long as we have record."

"I didn't know, Rah, have I done something wrong?"

"Ah, no, little one, never that, never fear that. You are beyond all we could ever have hoped or imagined. The problem is with me."

"You don't want me?"

"Believe me, *that* is not the problem, I desire you with every breath. It is wrong, shameful, and disrespectful, but I am hard for you day and night though you are not in season. My every thought is of ravaging you, of sinking into you and taking you, even though it is not for the purpose of procreation. So great is my desire, I do not trust myself with you. When I sank into your beautiful tight flesh, I could not stop.

"My brother was lost to the Comasatra. That is understandable. But I am second born. It was up to me to control the mating and protect you. Yet I lost myself as well, and we ravaged you until your beautiful flesh tore – still I want more. Even my shame cannot dull my lust.

"I should be put down as the rabid animal that I have become. You have every right to demand it, but instead, once again you share the red goblet with us. Though not in season, you shared your body with my brother. I have repeatedly failed to protect you, allowing you to be taken on Taron, yet you willingly move into our quarters.

"You are out of my experience. I am lost."

"So this is why you have been cold to me and push me away at every turn?"

"Yes." His shame was complete.

"Rah, I want you to want me. I want you. For my race, this is natural between mates."

"So Rom assures me, yet I fear for your safety with me. I am not as controlled or refined as my brother. I do not think I could stop or control myself as he was able to do. I am but a coarse warrior, I have no gentleness in me and my passions run high. I can become the berserker in battle and, I fear, in lust as well."

Kahara stood. Rah was sure she would leave in disgust after his shameful confession.

"Do you think you could ever come to love me, Rah?"

"Ah, little scrapper, how could you not know I love you. Though brute I may be, I love you with all that I am," he whispered in his smoky voice, looking at her with intense predator eyes.

Instead of turning away, Kahara untied her sash, her gown pooled on the floor at her feet. She was left standing before him wearing only high heeled slippers and mauve hair ribbon.

"Oh gods of all that is holy, have mercy." His voice quaked, fists clenched to keep from grabbing her. His member raged against his leather pants, demanding freedom.

She sat in his lap, reaching behind his neck and the leather that held his thick, ebony hair. Running her fingers through its satiny length, she freed it to fall on his wide shoulders and leaned to nibble at his full lower lip.

"I trust our love to gentle you," she whispered.

167

"Kahara, oh please, lady, at least have Rom present to stop me if I cannot stop myself. I beg of you, for your safety, let me call my brother to be with us."

Rah's mental call had already reached Rom who quietly flowed into the dimly lit room. His beloved brother and mate sat before the fire, Kahara's beautiful naked body draped over his brother's lap. Rah shredded the leather seat in an attempt to keep his hands off of her.

"I am here."

"Hi Rom. Rah seems to have some misgivings," Kahara blushed. She was still unaccustomed to the unity of the brothers and the novelty of having two mates rather than one.

"I was trying to soften him to my wiles but he is proving rather resistant."

"I know you are trying to get used to us one at a time, but Rah feels it best that we are all here for this. Can you bring yourself to embrace us as a Triad?" Rom wanted nothing more than to witness and support the bonding of the two most beloved people in his life.

"I trust your judgment and I trust both of you." Truth be told, she still felt a bit awkward. Yet the way Rom's eyes drank in the sight of them together, the silver depths full of passion and love, was one heck of a turn on.

"Rom, I am not sure what to do," Kahara confessed on her private link with him.

"Looks like you are doing fine. You have his full attention."

"Rom, if I start to harm her in any way, put me down," Rah pleaded on the private link with his brother.

Rom settled himself in the chair across from the couple, stretching out and crossing his booted feet at the ankles. He looked deceptively relaxed. Both regarded him with worried eyes.

"You might try undressing him, Kahara. As I recall, that was my undoing."

"You're actually enjoying this, Rom!" she admonished.

"You have no idea, lady. You have no idea," he winked at her.

Taking the challenge, Kahara returned her full attention to Rah. His eyes were blazing, his body shaking and he was looking at her as if she were a viper about to lay down the fang.

She unbuttoned his shirt, leaned over and nuzzled his neck while one delicate hand slipped under the garment and fondled a pectoral slab and male nipple. He shuddered beneath her touch. Emboldened, she pushed the shirt off of his muscular shoulders and ran her hands over their corded strength.

"You are so beautiful to me, Rah, I love touching you," she whispered into his ear, as she took the lobe into her mouth and bit down gently.

Rah finally released the tortured seat cushion, reached up and grabbed her by the hair at her nape, forcing her mouth to his and ravaging it. His other arm pulled her tightly into him, crushing her bare breasts against his chest. His tongue mimicked what his cock wanted to do, thrusting in and out of her warm depths. Said member was pressing against her bare rear through his supple leather pants as one searing kiss lead to another, leaving them both panting.

Kahara extracted herself from Rah's arms and stood in front of him, her legs braced apart, still wearing her high heeled slippers and nothing else. He looked up at her, eyes blazing.

From where Rom sat, he could see his brother's impassioned face through his mate's long shapely legs and beautiful bare behind peeking from under her flaming fall of hair. Kahara took Rah by the hand and pulled him up to stand in front of her. She looked up at him, holding his eyes while she reached down to unfasten the fly of his leather pants, freeing his raging erection. Rah moaned as his aching member sprang free.

Kahara slid his pants down and, kneeling, helped him step out of them. She looked up at him, standing naked before her. He was long legged, dense muscled and lean. Wide shoulders tapered to narrow hips, his cock rose proud, thick and full. She could see it throb with his heartbeat. His large, heavy sack was pulled tight, as if in anticipation. His hands were fisted at his sides while his deep chest rose and fell with rapid breaths. He looked down at her with an unreadable expression, eyes deep pools of molten silver.

Placing the palms of both hands on his inner thighs just below his groin, she ran them down his legs and back up again. She could not resist running her nails close to his groin, causing him to buck and shudder. She looked up, emerald melding with molten silver. Taking him into one hand, while the other rested behind his knee, she covered him with her hot mouth, never letting her eyes leave his. He was so huge her jaw ached, but she took him deep into her throat.

Rom had freed his own raging cock and was slowly stroking himself as he watched his lady drive his brother out of his mind. He felt her mind in his, drawing from his knowledge in order to pleasure Rah.

"Take your clothes off, too. It's only fair. I want to see you." Kahara's voice was a siren's call in Rom's mind. He complied, stripping for his mate, while she watched him, her mouth full of his brother's raging cock.

Losing himself, Rah fisted his massive, scarred hands in her hair, hips thrusting forward. Throwing his head back, he moaned with the intensity of his passion. It was the most provocative thing Rom had ever witnessed.

Rah was out of his mind. Nothing in his life had prepared him for this. He was shaking from head to foot. His lady was kneeling before him, her tongue swirling around the engorged head of his cock, her sharp little teeth raking his shaft. He could feel her throat spasm around him as he thrust into her hot mouth.

Through their connection as twins, Rah could sense Rom's passion rising where he sat across from the couple, watching as he stroked his own engorged member. Rah could see Kahara and himself through Rom's eyes, his cock plunging into her pink, swollen mouth, her beautiful full breasts swinging back and forth with the power of each thrust.

Kahara was so hot, she was drenching wet. Sucking Rah's huge cock while watching Rom beat off was the most erotic thing she had ever experienced. When she reached up and dragged her sharp little nails over Rah's heavy sack, he came unhinged.

He roared, jerked her up by the hair, grabbed her by the waist and slammed her down to the plush rug. He fell on her. Eyes molten and wild, he shoved her legs over his shoulders, ramming into her in one savage thrust. Kahara reached over her head to find something to hold on to, and latched on to Rom's thick ankles. Looking up, she met his hot eyes past his massive, engorged erection, as Rah slammed home again.

"Lady, are you well? Should I stop him?" Rom sounded concerned at his brother's sudden brutality.

"I'm good." (Another driving thrust, this time to the hilt.) *"Oh god, I'm good. Don't you dare make him stop."*

"Brother, Rom, I am beyond myself, out of control. I must be ripping her apart. Stop me!"

"Our lady informs me she is well. Should that change, you can trust me to intervene."

Kahara was stretched and filled with Rah's sudden invasion. Her legs over his muscled shoulders spread wide, opened her fully to him, and he was relentless. Pounding into her again and again, she could feel him against her womb. As she gripped Rom's ankles to hold steady, she looked into Rah's beautiful, passion ravaged face and saw the anguish there.

"Rah, oh god Rah, you are so good, fill me – I want all of you, I want you buried in me – deeper," she cried. Damned if she would let him think she was not with him all the way.

"I can't stop. I am unable to spare you!" he roared.

"I don't want you to stop. Give me all you've got, Rah."

He pounded into her endlessly. His heavy sack slammed against her tight ass as her clitoris was crushed against his pelvis with each driving thrust. His cock was so huge, her hips had to spread further to accommodate his girth. The agony/pleasure pushed her over the edge as she screamed her endless orgasm.

He reared up on his massive arms – with a circular motion of his hips, churned into her and bellowed, pumping his scalding seed deep into her ravaged depths. Rah shuddered, Kahara came again, her convulsing sheath driving him into another orgasm as he slammed home.

"Oh gods, brother, I can't stand it. Roll her over, I need in." Rom's mental voice was desperate and feverish.

Rah complied, rolling over and settling Kahara astride him, still seated in her to the hilt.

"Rom needs to be inside you with me, Kahara, can you give my brother that?"

Kahara looked over her shoulder at Rom as he approached her, his raging cock in hand, pleading in his beautiful, molten eyes. She became hot all over again.

"I want you, Rom, come into me please."

"I will go easy, lady, I just have to be inside you."

Good to his word, he moistened his fingers on their combined juices and gently thrust one in to the first knuckle to prepare her. He was shaking – she could feel what it cost him to be gentle. It was so erotic to be astride Rah, full of his still erect, pulsing cock, while Rom laved her neck with his tongue. He pulled on a nipple with one hand and penetrated her rear with the forefinger of the other.

Rah leaned up and took her other nipple into his hot mouth and sucked hard. Grabbing both of her bottom cheeks, he spread her wide for his brother.

"I want you in me there, Rom. Do it now. I want you inside me too," she moaned. His huge engorged head replaced his fingers and he pressed in, slowly, relentlessly.

"Push out against me, lady, I don't want to hurt you. Gods, you are so tight."

The pressure built, burning and stretching until she thought she would scream. Finally, the swollen head of Rom's cock pierced the tight ring of her sphincter muscles, granting him entrance. He held still, giving her time to adjust. Slowly and carefully, he started to move in gentle thrusts, each penetrating deeper than the last, while Rah held steady, his still erect and throbbing cock buried in her hot tight, sheath.

"Oh gods, lady, I'm coming in," Rom roared. With a last powerful thrust, he buried himself in her tight rear.

Both brothers were in her now, only the thin membrane of her body separating them. The men could feel each other's cocks filling her and throbbing. It was painful and wonderful at the same time. She was stretched beyond imagining.

"It is up to you, little scrapper," Rah said between clenched teeth. "Take us as you will."

Kahara started slowly rocking back and forth. As she thrust backward, Rom filled her ass and as she rocked forward, Rah filled her sheath. Rah's hands were spreading her cheeks until she burned where Rom's massive cock stretched and filled her.

Rom pinched and pulled on her nipples. Rah reached up and kissed her, thrusting his tongue into her mouth as Rom sank his teeth into the cords of her neck.

Kahara came undone, going wild between them, as they thrust in tandem. Their timing was exquisite, their care for her obvious.

Rom reached around and rolled her clitoris between his thumb and forefinger, pulling, pinching and circling the erect little bud, until Kahara lost her mind and both brothers blew up inside her. Jet after jet of scalding seed filled her, sending her over the edge again and again until she finally collapsed between them, exhausted and spent.

Rom met Rah's eyes over their trembling mate. *"She is now truly ours – we have both spilled our seed into her womb completing the bonding. She is our Chalice, we are a Triad."*

Each brother placed his mouth over her neck on opposite sides, their fangs extended. They bit down, as both men buried their cocks in her with one last savage thrust. They simultaneously filled her body with more scalding cum and their mouths with her blood, mixing DNA and marking her as their mate. All three minds, bodies, hearts and spirits melded. Kahara helplessly convulsed between them in yet another screaming orgasm.

~ *Chapter 16* ~

"You bit me! Both of you! Why did you bite me?" she exclaimed, incredulous.

"All races of the Daguronian Sector have blood rights, some more extensive than others. Karinian blood rights are only performed during mating. If you do not like it, we will not have to do it again," Rom explained.

Rom kissed her shoulder and carefully pulled out of her well used rear. At her flinch, Rah held her face between his hands and searched her eyes.

"Are you harmed? Have we hurt you little one?"

"Just a little sore, you didn't hurt me."

Rah carefully pulled his semi erect cock from her body. Rom lifted her from his brother's chest into his muscular arms and carried her to the bathing room. Rah followed, holding the door open and pulling the ribbon from her hair as they passed. He lit incense and candles.

The cascading waterfall that tumbled into the warm bathing pool was most welcome to her sore, tired muscles. Soon she was submerged in fragrant water with both brothers. The air was full of heady incense. Thick, drugging and cloying, the smoke filled her lungs.

Rom held her afloat on her back, his muscular forearms under her shoulders. He met her gaze with half lidded molten eyes, while his big hands massaged her breasts. Rah stood between her legs, his long fingers administering to the soft tissues at her core with healing salve.

It was so sensual she grew instantly hot. Reaching up behind her, she pulled Rom down to her by his long hair, opening her mouth to the possession of his kiss. Rah pulled her legs over his shoulders and put his hands under her hips. Closing his eyes, long dark lashes fanning over his cheeks, he brought her molten core out of the water and to his mouth.

Both brothers surged their tongues in and out of her in deep penetrating thrusts, while the chest deep water supported and soothed her. Rom pinched and pulled on her hardening nipples. Rah bit down on her erect clitoris and flicked it with his tongue while he sank three, then four fingers into her sheath, massaging and easing her inner muscles. His other hand tended her tight nether hole, inserting one, then two fingers covered with the salve.

"Come for us lady, nice and gentle," Rom encouraged, kissing her neck, while rolling and pulling her nipples between his fingers.

Rah held her entire lower body up by his deeply thrusting fingers, her legs over his shoulders. He alternated nibbling on her clitoris with lapping it with his tongue. Kahara helplessly gave way into a rolling endless climax.

The brothers turned her over in the water. Rom wrapped her arms around his neck, freeing his hands to palm her clitoris and penetrate her with his salve coated fingers, while kissing her senseless. Rah came up behind her and took her by the hips. He gently inserted a fat syringe, filling her rear with cool healing salve, followed by his thick cock. He penetrated her slowly until he was in to the hilt, and then made love to her in deep, leisurely, rotating thrusts. Another mind blowing orgasm crested over her.

Rom replaced his fingers in her sheath with another syringe of cool salve, followed by his torrid member. The brother's massive erections did a meet and greet in her quivering body in slow, deep, circling thrusts. Their cocks danced together inside her while they kissed each other over her shoulder, tongues deep and dueling.

When they broke the kiss, Rah bit the cords of her neck while Rom delved deep into her mouth, tasting of both he and his brother.

"Come with us, Kahara," Rah begged. The brothers never increased their lazy, surging, rolling pace but passion built exponentially.

"Gods, lady, how we love you. Give us your orgasm. Take us to heaven, come with us now."

The three way orgasm was shared on all levels. Slow, controlled, rotating thrusts never accelerated but deepened, while all three exploded into wave after wave of seemingly endless ecstasy.

~

The brothers washed, dried and buffed Kahara's glowing skin. They gently brushed the tangles out her hair. Rah carried her, wrapped in a plush oversized towel, to the bedroom of their suite.

Rom and Rah's rooms had been combined to create a huge, circular master. It had a fireplace of black granite with blue pearlescent flakes, flames dancing out of white sand. In the center of the high silver ceiling was a domed skylight to the stars. Under the skylight a massive bed sat in the center of the room on a raised dais. That and the floor area circling the large round bed was covered in plush black carpet. The rest of the floor was highly polished, black/blue pearlescent granite tile. The bed was dressed in silver satin comforter and pillows.

One entire portion of wall was a floor to ceiling fish tank, full of colorful exotic fish. The rest of the walls were papered in dove grey, topped by an ebony crown molding with recessed lighting. Beautiful plants with fragrant white blossoms surrounded a standing bird cage full of song birds, now roosted for the night cycle – automatically provided by the ship's programmed lighting. Soft music filled the room from an unseen source.

"Oh, this is beautiful!" Kahara exclaimed, "I've never seen anything like it."

"We hope you find it to your liking," Rah said.

"The environment was carefully chosen to include the four elements, in order to help you feel more grounded, Kahara. We consulted with Lord Jarl to help us better understand your shamanic nature, we will do what we can to accommodate your needs," Rom stated, as he drew out a silver satin dressing gown from the hidden closet behind a huge mirrored portion of the wall.

After helping her into her robe, both men donned black robes and led her to the sitting area in front of the fireplace. There was a black leather, circular love seat and a glass and chrome coffee table arranged on a round silver and black area rug. Seating Kahara in the middle, the males sat on either side.

Just looking at the identical brothers took her breath away. She still couldn't believe she was mated to them.

"We don't want to pressure you, little one," Rom ventured. "Because you said the mated couples of your people slept together in the same bed, we took the liberty of designing the bed to hold all three of us. This is entirely up to you. Rah and I will be glad to find other quarters if you need the space to yourself. We had this built for you. It is yours however you choose to enjoy it."

"Thank you for your thoughtfulness. It really means a lot to me. If you are both comfortable with it, I would enjoy having you sleep with me."

Still a little shy with the gorgeous men at her side, and acutely aware of her deliciously sore body, she looked down at her hands folded neatly in her lap.

Rah reached over, placed his fingers under her chin, forcing her to meet his eyes. They were deep pewter, full of emotion, though his face, as always, was unreadable.

"You honor us, lady. Never had either of us thought to enjoy the luxury of sleeping with you in our arms."

He stood, taking her by the hand, and led her to the bed. Rom pulled down the covers while Rah helped her out of her robe and into the center of the bed. Both men stripped and joined her. Rom lay on his back and pulled her to his side, resting her head on his muscular shoulder. Rah curled up behind her, wrapping his massive arm around her waist. Rom leaned down and kissed her on the forehead. Rah kissed the back of her neck.

"Sleep well, lady, know you are safe in our arms."

Kahara felt safe. While sharing a bed with anyone was going to take some getting used to – much less two massive warriors – she felt safe, treasured and loved. It was her last thought as the lights dimmed to darkness and the music faded into silence. She drifted into an exhausted, sated, dreamless sleep under foreign stars, in the beautiful room her mates had built for her.

~

Kahara couldn't help but be excited. After months in space, they were in orbit around planet Amon. Her mates had promised to take her there after first meal. They were to stay docked at the space station for over a week, shuttling back and forth to the planet in order to tend to various affairs.

Amon was inhabited by a race symbiotic to that of her mates. What that involved, Kahara was not sure, but she was attempting to study up on the relationship between the two races. Apparently, it was another vital area of her education Zana failed to provide.

So far, it appeared the Amonian race were born male and served as body guards for the fertile females of the Daguronian Sector. When the females became impregnated by their mate or mates, the Amonians became Surrogates, and actually switched sex. Kahara had no idea what a Surrogate was, but apparently they were deeply involved in the rearing of the children.

When a fertile female was found, she was housed and educated on Amon, or one of many other Surrogate planets like it, until a male contracted for the right to her eggs and the nuptial agreement was agreed upon and signed.

Amon was where the other females, gathered during the trip to earth, would be brought out of stasis and set up residence. Only the ruling lineages had a predestined mate. All other males petitioned for a mate. The genetic line as well as social ranking and relative wealth of the petitioners played a large part in who was considered for the privilege.

Fertile females were often paired with their Surrogates before being paired with their mates. After mating, the Fertiles usually chose to return to one of the Surrogate planets to live out their lives in pampered luxury with their mates footing the bill.

The males of the species were not allowed onto any of the Surrogate planets. Even Ambassador Jarl, the Taronion wolf, had been denied access. Rom and Rah as rulers of the entire Daguronian Sector were the only exceptions. They had diplomatic and policy obligations requiring their presence planet side from time to time. Even so, they were only permitted entrance to the landing zone and selected conference and banquet areas. At no time were they granted free reign of the planet.

Fertiles ready to be matched were transported to various Surrogate planets where they participated in Presentation Balls. At these balls, available fertile females were introduced and offered for. It was at these week-long galas, mates were chosen and prenuptial negotiations were completed.

Kahara was to be received into the center and evaluated in order to pair her with her Surrogate. Because she had not been formally claimed and the nuptial contract had yet to be agreed upon, documented and signed, she would be treated as a promised but un-contracted fertile female.

There was much formal ceremony involved so she was focusing on learning the customs and mores. She didn't want to risk disgracing her mates in her interactions with the natives during the formal events they were required to attend.

While Rom and Rah were as attentive to her as always, much was demanding their time. Rah was deeply involved in bringing the fleet into orbit and coordinating the docking of the transport shuttles at the space port. He was also arranging security for the duration of their visit.

Rom was arranging the multiple diplomatic meetings and events in which he and his brother would be involved. There were also policy setting summits requiring his attendance.

The twins were left with so little spare time, Kahara hesitated to fill it with her many questions.

In addition to her studies, she was attending fittings for yet another wardrobe suitable to the many formal affairs and activities. Apparently, she was required to change dress numerous times a day for different events. She would be expected to attend formal brunches, teas, dinners and balls. Kahara wasn't sure which would be harder to keep track of, the multitude of silverware to use when or what to wear to what.

It was probably a good thing that the transport shuttle of the lords of Kari was approximately the size of the Titanic or they would have needed a freighter to haul all of her clothes.

Kahara was immersed in her data screen when Rom entered the study of their quarters. He glided up behind her, lifted her hair and kissed her on the back of her neck.

"How fares our beautiful mate this morn?"

"Lost in protocol, if you must know," she laughed. "I despair figuring everything out before I am called upon to use it."

"How can I help?"

"Forgive me when I make an ass of myself?"

"That you will never do," Rom assured her while running red curls through the fingers of one hand, the other on her shoulder rubbing out the tension he found there. "The main thing you will need to focus on is choosing your Surrogate. As future Lady of Kari, you will be presented with the best planet Amon has to offer. It is an important decision, so take your time. Interview as many as you like."

"Whoa, wait, my what?"

"Surrogate. This is the major reason for our visit. You must have obtained your Surrogate before you become with child. It is a legal requirement that must be fulfilled before our bonding ceremony. He is the one who will guard you and attend you when Rah and I are absent. Should you choose to travel without us, it is he that will accompany you. He will also midwife and steward our children. It is a very intimate relationship, so you must be sure he pleases you on every level.

"The counselors on Amon will be running compatibility tests in order to properly pair you with your Surrogate. Also, Rah and I agree you need to be educated as to your rights so you can come from an informed and empowered position when negotiating our nuptial agreement. Zana was to have provided you with the information but, regretfully, did not. We feel it would be unfair to expect you to make the decisions necessary without full disclosure."

"I don't feel prepared to make such a decision on my own, Rom. After all, if it involves our children, it involves all three of us. Can't we interview the Surrogates together? As far as the agreement, I totally trust you both. Why can't we just come to the agreement on our own?"

"It has never been done that way." Rom was puzzled. "As a rule, the Fertiles' mates are not even allowed on the planet. Rah and I are an exception due to our diplomatic and ruling roles, or we would not be able to be here with you at all. It is you that must be comfortable with your Surrogate, and find him pleasing. Mates are never consulted in the selection.

"Most females take pride in their Surrogates as a reflection of their refined personal tastes. As to the nuptial agreement, it would be a conflict of interest for either of us to provide the information. It is also very complex and we do not feel qualified to educate you in this. We both want to be entirely fair with you, little one."

"Well, I won't be comfortable unless I can consult with you and Rah."

"Then we will make ourselves available for consultation, Kahara. Your comfort is of paramount importance to us both. All is in readiness. We will leave within the hour. I must go attend things on the transport. Rah will come and get you when it is time for you to board. I will see you then." He brushed her forehead with a kiss and left.

Rah met him in the hall on the way to the loading dock.

"How did she take it?" Rah inquired.

"Too well. I don't think she knows what a Surrogate involves."

"You did not enlighten her?"

"Just to the importance of her selection. I thought it wise to cross one bridge at a time. With her unexpectedly frequent and multiple heat cycles we cannot rely on the shots to postpone them for long without risking her health. It is paramount we have a Surrogate available as soon as possible," Rom replied.

"I bow to your superior diplomatic nature. Damn Zana and her treachery. Kahara should not have to be going through this unprepared and uninformed."

"On that, we are in full agreement, brother."

"I hate the idea of her having a Surrogate. I know it is the only way, that her very life depends on it. But the thought of another male with her, even an Amonian, makes me want to castrate him," Rah growled.

"I feel the same. Just try not to kill any Amonians. It makes it hard on relations," Rom smiled, trying to lighten the mood that both brothers shared.

"She insisted consulting both of us on her choice of Surrogate, saying if it involved our children, it should involve all three of us. She also wanted to come to the nuptial agreement without the benefit of counsel or coaching, saying she trusted us and did not see the need."

"The female never ceases to amaze," Rah stated in awe. "What did we do to deserve her?"

"I do not know, brother, but I do not think I can bring myself to let her go after she conceives. I know it is her right, but I just do not think I can honor it. I cannot imagine our life without her. I fear I would not find it worth living if she chooses to live away from us."

"Nor can I."

Both brothers fell silent. What more could be said?

~ *Chapter 17* ~

Rah was quiet and formal when he came to get Kahara. She could tell that something was weighing heavily on him, but assumed it was his many responsibilities and chose not to further burden him with questions.

He watched their beautiful mate out of the side of his eye as she gracefully walked at his side. She was impeccably groomed and dressed, her lovely flaming hair done up in a formal style. Wearing a lovely, floor length, travel gown of dark indigo velvet, she was the epitome of beauty and grace.

No, he could not – would not let her go. Customs, agreements and rights be damned, he would never let her leave them. If he had to chain her to their Triad bed, he would keep her by their side.

He reached to take her by the elbow, more for the reassurance she would allow the contact, than any real need to help her over the bulkhead as they entered the transport. His heart stopped before taking up double time when she not only welcomed his touch, but smiled up at him.

Kahara could not help but admire Rah in his formal uniform. He was so clearly in charge, having many responsibilities, yet solicitous of her as if nothing were more important than seeing her onto the ship.

"It pleases me greatly you have chosen to wear the mated tanzanite pendant and earrings Rom and I gave you. We are proud to have you display our Triad status, Kahara."

"I am proud to have you as mates, Rah. I love wearing your gifts."

Oh gods, he may just have to kill himself an Amonian before the trip was over. This female was theirs. No other would have her! How were they to stand a Surrogate in their lives and her bed?

"Rah? Is something wrong?" Kahara worried at his sudden fierce expression and bruising grip on her arm.

"I am sorry, little scrapper, I forget my strength." Damn, now he had hurt and frightened her. "I will be more careful of you, I promise." Before she could respond, Rom met them, taking his position on her other side.

"You are a vision of beauty, Kahara. Are you looking forward to spending time on a planet rather than deep space?" Rom asked.

"I'm excited about being in the air and sunshine but, to be honest, a bit uneasy about all that is expected of me. I hope I don't embarrass you both."

"You can never embarrass us, little one, you are our deepest pride," Rom assured her.

"Would you like to join us on the bridge?" Rah inquired. "We have installed a seat for you as our mate. The bridge area is lined with observation windows. You can see the entire trip and docking operation from there."

"I would love that, Rah!"

When they entered the control center of the ship, there was a raised dais facing a floor to ceiling observation window with three black captain's swivel chairs. The entire crew stood at attention until Rah sat Kahara between his brother and him and helped her strap in. When Rah and Rom took their seats, control panels dropped before them.

Though she could sense the officers' curiosity and desire to watch their lord's new mate, some of them never having seen her before, the large crew on the bridge returned to their seats. Each returned to his task in a semicircle behind the dais clearly attuned to Rah who began quietly giving commands on his throat com.

After brief preflight procedures, the hanger doors of the mother ship opened and they were under way. The entire crew worked together like well-oiled machinery. It was clear to Kahara that Rah ran a tight ship and commanded the respect of his people.

Rom was speaking softly into his com and consulting the screen before him. He was communicating with ground, calculating the trajectory, filing their flight plan and coordinating their docking sequence.

Watching the two handsome, competent men as they worked so naturally together was such a turn on, Kahara was sure she would never tire of it. She wanted to be part of that team, not just one of the frivolous pampered creatures that their fertile women appeared to be.

~

"Lords Andor, Lady Kahara, it is a privilege to meet you. I am Maxl-Marissa, the head of Surrogate pairing for the planet Amon Facility. Lords, please allow Drone Nate to show you to our lounge and settle you in with a glass of our famous Amonian wine while I take Lady Kahara to freshen in her quarters."

 Maxl-Marissa was the most androgynous individual Kahara had ever seen. There was also something about him/her that did not sit right, but she supposed it was the strangeness of the race that disturbed her. Drone Nate, on the other hand, was clearly an oversized warrior. From her studies, she realized Nate must be a pre-pairing Surrogate while Maxl-Marissa was a post-midwife one. She was unfamiliar with the Drone classification.

"Are you comfortable with the arrangements, Lady Kahara?" Rom asked her solicitously, his silver eyes searching hers with concern.

"Yes, it would be nice to wash up and change for dinner," she replied, not wanting him to worry. She knew it was a political dinner and he had plenty on his mind.

"Until dinner then, Lady Kahara," Rah said, lifting her hand to his mouth to brush it with his lips as he nodded to the eight massive warriors in his guard. Six of them broke off and surrounded Kahara.

"Your guards will not be necessary in our facility, Lord Andor. We have the security and the safety of your lady well in hand," Maxl-Marissa insisted in a haughty tone.

"I appreciate your most competent security team as I have been interfacing with them most of the day. But when it comes to Lady Kahara, this is nonnegotiable," Rah said in a polite but clipped tone that left no room for argument.

With one more searching look at their mate, Rom and Rah departed with Drone Nate.

Kahara, flanked by her personal Karinian guard, followed Maxl-Marissa down a marbled corridor into the residential portion of the facility. The synchronized clip of the guards' boot heels on the marble tile echoed off the stone walls.

"I'm unfamiliar with the classification of Drone," she queried.

"Yes, I have been informed of the unfortunate circumstance depriving you of the training you will need," Maxl-Marissa replied in her annoying nasal tone. "A Drone is a member of our species that is entirely too coarse and primitive to serve as a Surrogate. They function as guards and laborers in our society."

"Oh." What else could be said to such a callous statement, Kahara wondered?

"Here we are – this will be your quarters during your stay with us. Your luggage has already been delivered and your wardrobe pressed and hung by your assigned maid."

Another seemingly sexless individual stood at attention next to a massive male just inside the entrance. "This is Saul-Sandrah, she will serve you. Drone Kane will see to your protection and escort. Please let them know if there is anything you need for your comfort. Dinner will be in a quarter turn. You will dine with your lords before they return to the docking station."

Three of the six guards entered the quarters and looked into every room, securing the premises before allowing their lady to enter, while the other three closed in around Kahara.

"I was unaware I would be expected to stay here. I prefer to return to the docking station with my lords."

"That would not be expedient. They have much to attend to and you will be very busy with the pairing and educational portion of your stay," Maxl-Marissa replied in a no nonsense tone. "They cannot be expected to take time from their many duties to transport you back and forth, now can they?" With that she swept out of the room, leaving Kahara to Saul-Sandrah and Drone Kane.

Saul-Sandrah was more clearly female than Maxl-Marissa but she still had the unisex look, as Kahara had begun to think of it. She was a tall, lithe brunette with a bobbed haircut and kind gray eyes. Drone Kane, on the other hand, was all muscled male. He stood nearly as tall as her mates with an even stockier build. His long, sandy hair was pulled back and tied at his nape, displaying a raw boned face and high cheek bones. With his piercing, intelligent, electric-blue eyes and tanned skin, he reminded her of a Viking of old earth.

Kahara's guards had nodded to him. They seemed to be familiar with him and his position as her escort. Naturally, Rah would have overseen Kane's appointment and probably knew everything about him down to his shoe size. At the thought, she relaxed somewhat.

"Your quarters are secured, Lady Kahara. Unless you have further need of us, we will stand guard at your door and post at your windows," the head of the special ops informed her.

"Thank you, Marc, I think I am set."

"Sandrah, how long is a quarter turn and what am I expected to wear tonight?" Kahara asked in a resigned tone, once the guards had departed.

"Just long enough to bathe and groom. It will be a formal dinner. I have chosen the hunter green taffeta gown and slippers paired with the emerald Triad pendent and earrings for you tonight. Kane will escort you to the dining room. We are honored to be chosen to serve you, Lady Kahara. We will do our best to make your stay as pleasant as possible."

"Thank you both. I was not expecting to stay on planet when my mates returned to the shuttle so I was caught a bit off guard. I hope I did not appear ungrateful for your presence."

"No, not at all, you are most gracious. Will you require a Surrogate tonight, lady?"

Sandrah indicated a screen displaying pictures and profiles on the table in the sitting area of the plush quarters. "They all have your security's clearance and have been handpicked for you by Maxl-Marissa herself. You can make a selection and Kane will see to the arrangements."

"Tonight? What for?"

Kane and Sandrah exchanged confused looks at the question.

"For your pleasure," Sandra stated.

"I don't understand."

"Maybe our lady is tired after her trip and would prefer to retire alone," Kane graciously suggested.

"Yes, I am quite tired."

This was going to be worse than she thought. In spite of her extensive studies, she didn't understand half of what they were saying. She was also very unsettled by the idea she would be expected to stay here alone among all these foreign people rather than returning with Rom and Rah to the orbiting docking station and their transport.

Her unusual cowardice surprised her. It was not as if she hadn't been dealing with dangerous, challenging situations most of her adult life. Her time served in special ops should have prepared her for anything.

She would not whine about it to her mates, she decided. Maxl-Marissa was right. Rom and Rah had more important things to do than escort her from appointment to appointment. If she wanted to build a team with them, she was going to have to prove she was up to it and stand on her own, no matter how challenging the alien environment.

~

Rom and Rah had been seated in the gathering hall only a short time when Kahara and her escorts entered. At first, she was totally hidden by the massive guards surrounding her. Once safely in the hall, the guards parted, exposing her to the brothers' hungry eyes.

She was a vision in emerald. The strapless gown was form fitting at the bodice embracing her full breasts like a lover, gathered at her petite waist and flowing in crisp folds of taffeta to the floor. Her emerald pendant and earrings sparkled in the soft light, displaying their Triad status. Flaming red hair was drawn up at the crown of her head, held with an emerald and diamond barrette before flowing free in a cascade of curls, well beyond her hips.

Her dainty hand rested on the arm of Drone Kane who escorted her toward their table and the empty seat between the twin lords. At her entrance, every male Surrogate rose from their seats and the entire room seemed to hold its breath, except for Rah – who growled under his breath at the sight of her hand on the Drone's arm.

"Down brother, it is protocol. She is displaying prefect etiquette," Rom cautioned, only to be rewarded with another low feral snarl from Rah.

This was going to be a long stay, Rom decided, no more pleased than his brother at the sight of their mate's hand on another male, drone Surrogate or not.

Just then, she found them in the crowd. Her emerald eyes sparkled with love, her lovely face lighting into a brilliant smile for her mates. Her joy in seeing them was there for all to witness, in harsh contrast to the haughty, self-absorbed fertile females in the room.

Kahara had eyes only for her mates. They were in their formal uniforms at the head of the Lord's Table in the crowded banquet room, standing head and shoulders above the rest in both stature and pure male potency.

At first, Rah looked to be furious. But when their eyes met, his instantly softened and warmed. Rom's eyes caressed her from head to foot with open pride before fusing with hers, his smile enigmatic.

"You favor your mates," Kane softly exclaimed in clear amazement.

"Yes, why would I not?" Kahara looked up at him, confused.

"What has he said to upset her?" Rah demanded of Rom.

"Does something trouble you, little one?" Rom asked on their private channel.

"No, I just don't always understand these people."

"I think she is still trying to get used to communicating with the Amonian race, brother. Remember she has not been exposed to races other than those of her home planet."

"He is looking at her strangely. I like it not."

"I think he is finding her equally confusing. I, for one, can totally empathize," Rom replied with wry humor – Rah snorted.

When Kane and Kahara arrived at the Lord's Table, the brothers reached out and took her hands while Kane pulled out her chair. Once she and her mates were seated, the rest of the male diners returned to their seats and conversation resumed.

Kane took up position standing at the back of Kahara's chair. Her guards circled behind the table, standing with legs splayed, hands held behind their backs, at military rest, eyes surveying the room.

Kahara turned to Rah. "I know after what happened on Taron, caution is advised. But don't you think this is a bit overkill? I can hardly breathe."

"No, lady, I had to fight to get this much of our security on the planet or I would have doubled it," Rah replied.

"Naturally, I will comply with whatever you feel is necessary. I trust your judgment. I just want to be sure you know I don't require all of this to feel safe."

"You have no idea of your value to us, little one," Rom added to the conversation. "We will always require this much and more to feel comfortable with your safety away from the security of our home planet. It is our intention to protect you, not to stifle you. Let us know what adjustments you require for your comfort and we will do our best to comply."

"Well, does Kane really need to stand behind me breathing down my neck when I have one of you on either side?"

"Actually, it is the protocol of the planet. He is here to protect you from our offensive presence, lady."

"Protect me from my mates? That is outrageous!"

Rom and Rah were secretly delighted at Kahara's heated response. Rom observed that Kane had heard her and was pleasantly surprised as well. From the interview he and Rah had with the Drone, Rom could tell he was clearly from the old breed of Surrogates and secretly held to the old ways. Originally, mates were mates and Surrogates protectors, not effeminate sex toys to self-indulgent spoiled brats.

As Kahara settled in to her glass of delicious Amonian wine, she started observing the other occupants of the room. There were many elaborately dressed women, accompanied by extremely effeminate males who hung on their every word. In fact, the fawning and catering was rather nauseating.

The only males that appeared to be men were her mates, the Karinian guards and an occasional Drone. The rest reminded her of overdressed transvestites. The Surrogates wore as much makeup as the women and were, quite frankly, girlish. With carefully styled, longish hair, brightly colored ruffled shirts and leotard-like pants, clearly designed to display their package, they definitely qualified as fops.

As she continued to watch the other diners, she noticed how the women would occasionally fondle the Surrogates' backsides and even said "packages" as if to show off their possessions to the other women.

While the Surrogates kissed, cooed and fawned over the women with much fluttering of their outlandishly long eyelashes, their eyes were cold and calculating. A foreboding shudder ran down Kahara's spine.

"Are you well, little one?" Rom, never missing anything, asked.

"I'm really trying not to be judgmental, Rom, but are those normal Surrogates?" Kahara asked.

"Yes, these are considered to be the cream of the crop, to quote earth idiom."

"Well, I sure hope they have more going on than they appear, because they don't look like they could protect anything more than their long nails. I can't see where they would be the influence I would want on our children. Are you sure it is necessary to get one? Surely one of your guards and a female nanny would better serve our purposes."

Rom choked on his wine. Rah sat back and regarded his brother, one eyebrow raised, his look saying he was very interested in seeing how he got out of this one.

"Let's say they have hidden talents," Rom evaded.

"Darn well hidden if you ask me," Kahara muttered under her breath, but all three males heard her. It was Rah's turn to choke on his wine and a distinctive, muffled snort came from the Drone behind her chair.

A waiter came to replenish their drinks and an orchestra appeared on stage at one side of the room and began to play. Several of the women got up to dance with their Surrogates.

"Would you do me the honor of dancing with me, little one?" Rom asked, taking her hand and helping her from her seat.

"I don't know your steps, but if you don't mind dragging me around the floor, I'm willing to try," she responded with a smile.

"We were made to dance together, Kahara," Rom stated as he escorted her to the floor with one large warm hand resting at the small of her back.

When they reached the polished wooden surface, he took her into his arms and swept her onto the floor in steps similar to the ballroom dancing she had so enjoyed on earth. Her wide taffeta skirts whirled around them as they flowed across the dance floor, moving as one.

Rah watched his brother dancing with their mate with pride. They were poetry in motion, every step in perfect accord, making a mockery of the other couples' flamboyant attempts at drawing attention to themselves.

Soon, he could see the focus of the entire room settling on the gorgeous couple in their midst. The women either glared at

Kahara in her simple elegant gown, or curled their lips in disdain at the massive warrior in his formal uniform. The Surrogates looked on speculatively and the Drones in admiration. Soon, Rom could catch snippets of conversation from the crowd:

"Who does she think she is, dancing with that brute?"

"Any self-respecting female would have a Surrogate by now."

"Would you look at her plain gown, you would think the lords of Kari could provide something better."

"Someone should tell her to cut that garish hair."

"I can't believe she is letting him touch her."

"She is sure not much to look at."

On and on it went until Rah was growling under his breath.

"Looks like Lady Kahara's grace and beauty has hit some nerves, my lord," Kane said to Rah, seeing his outrage. "Fertile females are notoriously jealous and petty."

"They had best not do anything to hurt her," Rah snarled.

"I will do my upmost to shelter her from their venom during her stay my lord," Kane assured him.

Oblivious to the stir they were causing in the room, Rom was glorying in the feel of his mate in his arms. She followed him effortlessly, seeming not to object to his holding her in public. Her warm little hand on his arm was relaxed and her soft smile, genuine. She was clearly enjoying their dance.

Tilting her head back, she smiled up into his face – hair and gown fanning out behind her, as he guided her in a graceful, flowing turn.

"I love you Rom."

It was whispered but he heard it. Overcome, he pressed her into his chest, as if to absorb her confession into the deepest stratum of his being.

"You humble me, little one. I only pray I can do you justice. You are the center of my heart, forever engraved into my soul. I will live and die for you, this I can promise."

As the music ended and they returned to their table, Kahara saw Rah watching them, his expression fierce.

"Do you think Rah feels left out?" she asked Rom, concerned.

"No, we are one in all things. There is clearly something bothering him, but it is not us or our dance, of that you can be sure," Rom replied, wondering at his brother's worry.

"What troubles you, brother?" Rom sent the query to Rah.

"There is much hostility toward our lady. Drone Kane indicates the other fertile females are jealous and may try to hurt her."

"Do you dance, Rah?" Kahara asked him as they returned to the table, hoping to dance with him as well.

"Nothing like my brother, but watching you was deeply satisfying," he replied, as he stood to help her to her seat. "I do have hidden talents though," he said with a wink.

"Yes, you do, and some not so hidden," Kahara responded, running a teasing look up and down his impressive frame. On impulse, she stood on tiptoe and kissed him on the cheek before taking her seat.

Rah thought his heart would explode out of his chest. Right there, in front of the most haughty and venomous members of his society, she openly displayed her affection for him. Gods, it was humbling how much he loved their lady. He would do anything to protect her from the harsh world into which she was being thrust.

All too soon, the night was over and Kahara was saying goodnight to her mates.

"Are you sure you will be comfortable here, little one?" Rom inquired, for the fiftieth time.

"Yes, Rom, everyone is quite attentive and my quarters very comfortable. I have half the population of Kari as guard. I'll be fine. I will miss you both though."

"You can always return to the transport with us tonight and we will bring you back for your appointments in the morning," Rah ventured.

"You have better things to do than haul me around between appointments, but thanks for the offer. Hopefully this will be a very temporary situation and we can conclude our tasks here in short order."

Her answer seemed to mollify the brothers, though Rah still looked less than pleased. Kahara decided that being head of security made for an understandable tendency toward paranoia.

"Until tomorrow at first meal then, lady."

Both brothers kissed her hands before releasing her to her drone and guards for escort to her quarters. They would have preferred to see her there themselves but were not allowed in the residential portion of the structure.

"I do not like having her away from our side. Something is not sitting right about the arrangements or her ready compliance with them," Rah grumbled.

"Remember, she is not accustomed to space travel. She is probably enjoying her time on planet and reluctant to return to the ship before she has to," Rom assured his brooding brother. He was not happy with the arrangements himself. He had not realized how difficult it would be to have her away from them or how wrong it felt to let her go, leaving her to the care of others.

~ *Chapter 18* ~

"This is totally unacceptable," Maxl-Marissa snarled as she paced back and forth in front of her superior's desk. "She is making a spectacle of herself, fawning over those two brutes, in front of the entire room of Fertiles."

"I agree. We will need to take action right away to avoid compromising the other Fertiles' programming. We will start her training first thing in the morning and either break or destroy her," Frank-Felecia, the head of operations dictated.

"How can we do that without having her running to those two animals for shelter? This is turning out to be a disaster!" Maxl-Marissa complained.

"We knew it would be difficult to deal with her lack of programming when we heard the twins had found their mate in that remote sector. What we had not planned on was for her to be in love with them. Who would have thought such a thing was even possible? I had counted heavily on the wiles of our Surrogates – yet her maid informs us she has refused to have one brought to her bed."

"This could destroy everything we have built," Maxl-Marissa warned.

Unbeknownst to the entire system, the Surrogate planets had formed a monopoly on the mating practices and therefore the economy. Fertile females were brought to the planet under the guise of protection and education where they were carefully programmed, through sexual and emotional abuse, to hate and fear their mates and crave Surrogates.

Control the procreation, control the universe, was the motto and the Surrogate planets had held to it tenaciously for generations. Kahara's arrival on the scene was definitely a threat that Frank-Felecia intended to deal with posthaste.

"Inform the Andorian twins the lady has requested sanctuary, and have her guards apprehended and escorted off planet," she commanded.

"Brilliant!" Maxl-Marissa praised. "It is simple, clean, believable and expedient."

"Arrange to have her moved as soon as the guards are in custody. We will house her in the programming facility. No time like the present to whip the little bitch into shape," Frank-Felecia ordered. "I will enjoy breaking her myself. We wouldn't want me to get out of practice, now would we?"

"We recorded the lord's voices for synthesis during the meal. We have all we need from them so we can easily ban them from the planet," Maxl-Marissa responded on her way out to see to the arrangements for Kahara's transfer.

~

"Sanctuary! Our lady has requested sanctuary?" Rah roared. "I knew it was too good to be true, the way she seemed to accept us. Now it becomes clear why she was so glad to stay behind last night. I expected her reluctance, even her rejection, but not this treachery."

"Use your head, brother, what would she have to gain by pretending to accept us? She could have been well rid of us both easily enough. No one expected her to give herself to me when her unexpected heat threw me into Comasatra. She barely knew us. It was generally expected she would let me die in Satra. She could have left you in the wreckage of the shuttle on Taron, when you requested she do so and no one would have blamed her for your death."

"Don't ask me, I have never understood the illogic of females," Rah ranted.

"You speak of the spoiled Fertiles we have been exposed to over the years. When has our mate ever displayed anything but perfect logic? You think with your fear of losing her, not the level head I have always known you to have," Rom admonished his raging brother.

"Yet, you say she has requested sanctuary?"

"So they tell me, but I believe it not," Rom replied. "They have escorted our guard off planet. To a male, they required healing chambers from fighting to stay at her side. She is now alone and at their mercy. Gods only know what they are doing to her as we speak."

"Not entirely alone, I have an ally in her drone, Kane. I handpicked him for his integrity, intelligence, prowess in battle and belief in the old ways. I also secretly set him up with a com. Hopefully we will hear from him shortly," Rah informed his distraught brother. "We will get her back if I have to tear the entire planet apart. She had better be innocent or I will not be responsible for my actions."

"Brother, you must trust me when I say our lady is innocent, I know her heart is true. What do they hope to gain by earning our wrath? It was obvious at dinner that she was well pleased with us as mates. She did not act like a frightened, traumatized damsel in need of sanctuary," Rom mused aloud.

"You are right, Rom. Well I remember her sweet yielding, the passion of her body between us. That had to have been real, and you are in her mind. You have seen her love of us. Forgive me, I am not myself."

"There is nothing to forgive, Rah – we are both crazed by her loss."

"First Zana's betrayal, then the attempted abduction on Taron, and now this. Something big is afoot. I fear we will not be pleased with what we find. I knew we should not have left her no matter how she craved ground time.

"Damn my pride, I should have established and maintained our telepathic link no matter how I feared her rejection," Rah admonished himself.

"It would have not done you any good. We are too far away for telepathic contact. Believe me, I have tried to reach her. It is to our advantage that the Amonians have no way of knowing we have telepathic abilities with her. It is so uncommon as to have been forgotten over the ages. If we can get back in range, we can contact her without them knowing we are on the ground."

~

"Lady, forgive me, but I thought you were pleased with your mates," Kane quietly inquired, as he escorted her to her first appointment at the training center.

"I am. What would make you question it?"

"Then why have you requested sanctuary?"

"Sanctuary? What is that?"

"Sanctuary is provided by our planet upon request. It is protection and seclusion from an unwanted mate. It is every Fertile's right not to be forced into mating."

"I requested no such thing, Kane. I am already mated and I love my mates!"

"It is as I feared then, a conspiracy is afoot. Your guard has been apprehended and escorted off planet and your mates banned from returning. Lord Rah warned me to trust no one where your safety was concerned and now I begin to see why. We may have little time. It is likely they will force me from your side. You must trust me no matter what I am forced say or do. I will do all I can to see to your safe return to your mates, lady. Upon my life, I will serve you above all others in the old way of our people," Kane fervently vowed, as he saw Maxl-Marissa bearing down upon them.

"There has been a change of plan, Drone. Escort the female to the programming facility, the head of operations will meet you there," Maxl-Marissa ordered.

"The programming facility? Is something amiss?" Kane inquired.

"Do you question my authority?" Maxl-Marissa snapped.

"No, director," he hastily replied, "I will see her there at once."

Taking Kahara by the elbow, he changed directions, leading her toward the new destination. Once they were well out of Maxl-Marissa's hearing he whispered to Kahara, "Lady, it is worse than I feared. You must be strong and not lose faith in your mates. I have heard whispers of this place that do not bode well. Gladly I would stand and fight for you, but they would kill me before I was able to win your release. I will comply for now, freeing me to get word to your mates. Together we will have a much better chance of foiling their plans."

The programming facility was a maximum security unit with double lock down doors and barred windows. It was clear to Kahara that they were not even trying to pretend to have her best interest at heart. It occurred to her to act as if Kane had not kept her informed.

"Why have you brought me here? Take me back to my quarters at once. I insist to speak to my mates," she demanded in a loud voice.

Kane pretended to tighten his grip on her arm and drag her along, his respect for her increasing. She was intelligent as well as loyal and beautiful.

"Let me go, Drone, you are hurting my arm," she continued to berate him as they entered the building. "Get this animal off me," she demanded as the head of operations approached them in the hall. "He is manhandling me! Don't you realize who I am? I am the intended of your rulers and I will report this to my mates. I will see to it you are all very sorry."

Frank-Felecia brutally backhanded her. "I am your ruler now, bitch, best not to forget in the future." Turning to Kane she ordered, "Take her into the interrogation chamber and restrain her on the table."

"No!" Kahara screamed and sobbed hysterically and quite convincingly.

"Gag her while you are at it. I have heard all the whining I care to hear," Frank-Felecia called at Kane's back as he appeared to drag a struggling Kahara down the hall.

The room was barren and foreboding with a metal exam table anchored to the floor in the center. Restraints for wrists were at the top of the table and movable stirrups, sporting ankle restraints, at the bottom. Hooks on the wall held various threatening items, among which were gags with straps and metal buckles.

There was a massive Drone guard on either side of the table and two at the door. Kahara's frightened eyes met Kane's anguished ones. Neither of them spoke. It was clear there was nothing Kane could do to help her here and she prayed he didn't try. Better he have a shot at getting to Rom and Rah than to die in this room, as she was sure he would, should he indicate in any way he was not in full compliance.

"Strip her," one of the Drones by the table ordered. The other took a large knife from its sheath at his hip and cut her gown down the front. Kahara felt Kane's hand tighten then tremble on her arm. Her eyes met his, her look meaningful, just before she kicked him in the shin.

"You bastard, you are supposed to protect me," she shrieked. "Let me go, you filthy monsters, you have no right to lay your paws on me."

Kane knew she had just warned him off interfering as he was about to attempt. It was agony watching her mistreated and humiliated. It took all he had to pretend anger at her. Lifting her off her feet, he pinned her down on the table, while the drone with the knife made quick work of the rest of her clothes. Better his hands on her than theirs.

Leaning in close to her ear under the guise of securing one of the wrist shackles he whispered, "Hold true, lady, I will return for you."

As he leaned back, he snarled loudly "That is the last kick you will get at me, you haughty little bitch."

He secured her other wrist while the two other Drones strapped her ankles to the stirrups. Reaching up, he grabbed a gag. Leaning close to attach it behind her head he whispered. "Forgive me, lady, if there were another way…"

"We will have no further need of you here, Drone Kane," Frank-Felecia announced as she entered the room. "You may return to the resort and your duties there."

"As you wish," he replied, trying to look disappointed at having his "revenge" cut short. It cost him more than he could say to turn on his heel and leave her there naked and at their mercy.

~ *Chapter 19* ~

"We have had contact from Drone Kane," Rah announced, as he blasted into the war room of the ship. "They are holding and torturing her in a maximum security facility. We have to make our move at once."

"By all that is sacred, they dare torture our lady?" Rom roared, his chair crashing behind him as he surged to his feet – no easy deed as it had been secured to the deck. "I will see them all dead!"

"Trust me brother, they have touched what is mine. They are dead Amonians walking."

Rah was ice cold and contained, more formidable in his rage than if he had been bellowing at the top of his lungs. The berserker shown from his blazing silver eyes, fangs appeared at the sides of his mouth, claws tipped his powerful fingers. All that knew him were well aware they were in the presence of a lethal killer. He was a feral predator on the hunt, cold and calculating. None would get between him and his foe and live.

"The stealth pods are prepared. My special ops team is already under way. They will disable planetary security. We will leave now and the fighters will follow as soon as the planet's shields are down."

The stealth pods could penetrate the planetary shields undetected, but had no weaponry and little maneuverability. Rom and Rah would meet Drone Kane on the surface at the coordinates he had provided. Rah had the foresight to leave a weapons stash on the surface that Kane had already procured. Kane had gathered other

Drones, faithful followers of the old ways, who were now armed and ready to assist their lords.

~

Kahara was naked, cold and shivering. They had put an IV in her arm and were administering what had to be a cross between a hallucinogen and an aphrodisiac. Her arms were shackled above her head and her legs splayed, bent at the knees, exposing her innermost core. The gag stretched her mouth wide and her jaws ached.

"Let's see if we can soften you up to one of our lovely Surrogates now, shall we?" Frank-Felecia gloated from the foot of the table as she tapped her own leg with a leather crop. "Rupert should do nicely – he is such a pretty boy with an amazing tongue."

The indicated blond, fair-skinned Surrogate approached her, naked and erect with cold lust in his eyes. Kahara violently shook her head no and struggled with her bonds.

"Wrong attitude bitch," Frank-Felecia snarled bringing the crop down on the tender flesh between Kahara's splayed legs. Kahara arched off the table in agony and screamed behind her gag.

Suddenly, the room was filled with what sounded like Rah's deep voice. "Let the Surrogate fuck you, why do you think we brought you here? You don't really expect Rom and I to service you forever do you? You disgust us."

After three more vicious blows to Kahara's throbbing core, Frank-Felecia rubbed the crop over her delicate nub.

"Let's see if Rupert can lick it all better for you."

"Yes, hopefully the Surrogate can teach you a thing or two, you are such a pitiful fuck."

It sounded like Rom's voice this time. Kahara shook her head violently.

"What are you saving yourself for – your precious lords? They hate you. Why else do you think they are paying us to do this? See the camera above you? They are getting off watching you writhe," Frank-Felecia sneered while delivering several more agonizing lashes. Rom and Rah's laughter filled the air.

"Now let Rupert have a taste. Surrogates are blood suckers, did you know that? Why else do you think we service your kind?"

Rupert obediently showed her his fangs as he ran his long tongue over one sharp tip. Then he fell on her, sinking them into the vein where her leg met her crotch. Kahara screamed in pain and disbelief as obscene sucking noises ensued.

"Are you sure you are not ready to have him fuck you instead? You are bound to run out of blood soon," Frank-Felecia warned.

Rupert released her vein and latched onto her clit, sinking his long tongue into her sheath. Drugged, bound, and helpless, Kahara writhed. Though her body was responding, her heart did not. She was sure she would vomit behind her gag. She was so repulsed by the Surrogate's touch he had no hope of bringing her to completion.

"You are pathetic," Rah's voice sneered. "You can't even come for the expert we had to pay to fuck you."

"Looks like we need more stimulation. Up her dosage and bring in Tom and Tim," Frank-Felecia ordered after Rupert had at her for some time.

"There we are," she cooed when two more slithering Surrogates entered. "A tit for each of you boys."

They wasted no time falling on her, sinking their fangs into the blue vein in each of her breasts and feeding noisily. Next they turned their attention to suckling and biting her nipples.

"Give her another shot of drugs," Frank-Felecia ordered. A Drone complied.

As he injected her IV, Kahara felt the drug hit her already reeling system, and fought her bonds with renewed vigor.

"You will take it and you will like it," Frank-Felecia commanded, bringing the crop down on her soft inner thighs before turning it on her breasts and belly.

One of the Surrogates relinquished a breast for Frank-Felecia to crop, turning his fangs on her throat instead, while his partner freed her other breast, sinking his fangs into her underarm.

"Surrogate food, now there is a use for you," Rom's voice sneered. "We should just let them suck you dry."

She couldn't hold out much longer. In her heart she knew the voices of her mates were synthesized but the drugs in her system were overpowering her. She could feel something in herself breaking. She was vaguely aware of another Surrogate sinking his fangs into her inner thigh. Kahara knew she didn't have long to live as her heart stuttered on the rapidly diminishing blood supply.

"Kahara, lady, we are on our way." It was Rom's mental voice on their private channel. She almost missed it as she had been trying to block the hurtful synthesized voices.

"Rom is that truly you?"

Gods she sounded awful. Rom feared for her.

"It is me, little one, hold on, we will be there soon."

"I tried to hold out Rom, but something broke. I am sorry. I love you both. Tell Rah I love you both. I never believed them."

Then silence – nothing more than a terrible silence – where his lady's mental touch had been.

~

210

Nothing could have prepared Rom and Rah for the unholy sight that met their anguished eyes as Drone Kane and his followers broke down the door to get to Kahara. Surrogates were swarming like vermin over her bound, gagged and ravaged body.

Rah's berserker broke free.

"Mine!" he roared, as he tore off arms and legs with his bare hands and ripped out jugulars with his fangs.

"Mine!" he bellowed, as he lifted Rupert from between her legs and slammed him into the stone wall. The Surrogate's head exploded on impact.

"Mine," he raged, as he tore open his pants, releasing his torrid erection, and sank it into her in one brutal thrust.

"Rah, no!" Rom screamed, to no avail. *"Kahara, forgive him, his berserker is loose, he has lost all control."*

"Mine," Rah sobbed, as he helplessly pounded into her limp body.

Kahara's eyes opened for a moment, meeting his anguished molten silver ones.

"Yes, Rah, beloved, I am yours."

"Mine," he wailed, burying his fists in her blood soaked hair before losing consciousness, as Rom injected him with a powerful sedative.

Rom covered his entwined brother and mate with his cloak, wrapped his arms around them both and openly wept.

~

Lights flickered in the room before going out altogether, indicating Rah's special ops team had disabled planetary security. Soon explosions could be heard as the fighters moved in, destroying all planet side resistance.

Kane and several other Drones helped Rom extract Rah and Kahara from the ruined building and to a waiting transport. Explosions roared and debris rained around them as Rah's forces battled the Surrogates'.

"Rah is out of commission. You are in charge of the troops," Rom informed Marc over his throat com.

"Understood, my lord, we have the situation mostly contained and your path to the transport is secured," the head of special ops responded.

"Take every last one of those Surrogates from the training facility into custody before destroying it. Make sure this entire planet is disabled, all interstellar transport and communications taken out," Rom further instructed.

"It shall be as you command, my lord."

Rom had no doubt it would be. Marc was the best of the best next to Rah. The man was thorough and exacting. The Surrogate planet was about to be thrust back into the dark ages – all modern technology totally disabled.

Let the scheming, exploitive, cloned bastards reinvent the wheel, Rom thought with grim satisfaction. As for the ones directly responsible for the torture of his mate – the bowels of hell would be a vacation spot when compared to their fate.

~

When Rom and the landing party arrived on the flagship, everything was in a flurry of activity. Lord Jarl and Chief Medical officer Saul met them in the docking port with healing chambers for Kahara and Rah.

Lord Jarl was a fearsome sight. Hackles standing straight on end, his eyes glowed yellow and his muzzle rippled where his lips were pulled back in a feral snarl, white fangs flashing.

"I have come to offer my protection. With your permission I will accompany your brother and our lady shaman to the medical ship," Jarl sent to Rom.

"Though I know I have a fleet to command and a war to fight, I cannot bring myself to let either one of them out of my sight. Your company as well as your counsel would be greatly appreciated," Rom informed the distraught wolf.

"It is my honor to serve, Lord Rom," Jarl assured him, falling in behind the healing chamber containing his lady shaman.

Everyone gave the procession wide berth as anyone having the misfortune of being too close to the lady's healing chamber received a cold glare from Lord Rom and a savage snarl from the formidable enraged wolf.

~

"What of our lady? How extensive is the damage?" Rom demanded of Saul as soon as he had finished running the diagnostics through the healing chamber.

"With her unusual makeup I really don't know what to expect. Physically she should mend in a couple of days but the mental and emotional trauma will take longer. I suggest we plan on keeping her in the chamber at least two weeks," Saul responded.

"Our lady shaman will not respond well to any drugs. I strongly advise they be kept to a minimum," Jarl advised Rom.

"Lord Jarl recommends she not be drugged," Rom shared with Saul.

"Her system has already been flooded with numerous drugs from hallucinogenics to aphrodisiacs. I will need to administer antidotes," Saul protested, wondering what the wolf would know about the lady's needs.

"Lord Jarl is a shaman as well as an ambassador," Rom informed the medical officer seeing his confusion. "Our lady is a shaman as

213

well. He will have a much better idea about her needs than we. Keep the drugs to an absolute minimum and monitor her very closely. I want no one near her but you, Lord Jarl, my brother and myself. One of us will be guarding her at all times."

"Yes, sir," Saul responded.

Once seeing to their lady, Chief Medical Officer Saul attempted to revive Rah, only to have to immediately put him under again.

"His berserker is still in the forefront, Lord Rom. I don't dare wake him least he tear the entire facility apart looking for your lady and those who harmed her," Saul apologized.

"We can't just leave him sedated indefinitely," Rom protested.

"No, but a couple hours in a healing chamber should rebalance his hormones and brain chemistry enough for him to regain rationality."

"I need him functional as soon as possible. The situation is beyond dire." Rom ran his hand through his already wild black hair in distress.

"Lord Jarl, will you take first watch and protect our lady? I need to call an emergency meeting of the council. I will keep my mind open to you and would welcome any input or suggestions you may have. My brother is the Commander and Chief and I the Head of State. Your formidable tactical knowledge will be invaluable to me during his absence."

"It will be my honor," Jarl replied before accompanying the doctor to the stasis hall where Kahara would be secured for the duration of her healing.

~ *Chapter 20* ~

"From what we saw at the facility and surrounding compound on Amon, this has been going on for years. The implications are that the entire planet is corrupt," Marc, the head of the special ops team reported to the council.

"It is unknown how many other planets in the United Alliance of Surrogate Planets are involved in the conspiracy, but by all intelligence reports coming in, things look pretty grim," Rom informed them. "It is my hope that by falsifying a medical quarantine and communications blackout on Amon, we can buy time to investigate the situation and decide on a course of action before the other planets in the Surrogate Alliance are any the wiser. However, we will have to move quickly. Commander and Chief Rah will not be available until later today. He ordered military backup before we left for the planet. Several armed fleets are en route to our location from various members of the Daguronian Coalition. Unfortunately, it will be a full week before any can reach us."

"Why wait for backup? I have evaluated their arms and am assured we are fully capable of subjugating the entire planet with our fighters alone," Zeb, Rah's scout, inquired.

"I am in full agreement with you, Lord Rom. This is more widespread than we know. It will not serve us to appear to be aware what is going on until we have a better idea of what we are up against," Jarl sent on their private channel.

"The corruption may be farther reaching than the United Alliance of Surrogate Planets. Amazon Lieutenant Zana has been exposed as a traitor. There were alien forces shadowing us to Taron. As you know their mission was to assassinate the lords of the Daguronian Sector and take our lady.

"We have been unable to discern who Zana was working for as she managed to poison herself before questioning. Nor do we yet know what sector the aliens are from or who they are affiliated with. It is best not to alert the enemy factions that we are aware of the conspiracy before we have a better idea of who is involved," Rom stated.

"We were able to disable all communications planet wide before Amon knew we were alerted to their treachery. As far as anyone from the outside can tell, we are still in orbit of Amon while our lady chooses her Surrogate and our lords conduct business of state. We were scheduled to be here for two weeks. I concur with Lord Rom, it is best to keep our knowledge a secret for now," Tactician Kev agreed.

"As far as my brother and I are concerned, the complete military takeover of planet Amon is a foregone conclusion. The treatment of our lady mate and the reports of the Drones now in our service made it clear the corruption runs deep rather than involving only a few factions of the operation. We fully intend to find the head of this abomination, even though it may involve forgoing the pleasure of the immediate retaliation we all crave."

"Might I suggest you establish Drone Kane and his followers as allies before the council? It could serve as advantageous to seek their knowledge in future council meetings," Jarl sent to Rom.

"You have read him and found him trustworthy?" Rom asked the ambassador.

"I read him when Lord Rah chose him to protect your lady. I would not have otherwise suggested it," he responded pragmatically.

"After Drone Kane's invaluable assistance in rescuing our lady from Amon, he and his followers defected from the Alliance. I would like to invite them to join the Coalition of the Daguronian

Sector. If it is approved I will assign Drone Kane as head of the newly formed Allied Drone Unit," Rom announced to the gathering.

"I vote yes. He is totally responsible for our lady having been found in time to save her life. He served her and us at great risk to his life," Marc spoke up.

"I second it," Kev agreed.

After a unanimous vote to invite the Drones into the Coalition, the Allied Drone Unit was officially formed.

~

That evening, after Rah had finally been successfully revived without loss of life or property, the two brothers were in their chambers going over the situation. Marc had pulled information from the Surrogate training facility before turning into so much rubble.

The torture of their mate had been recorded. As they watched the hologram of her being ravaged and heard the hurtful words broadcast in their own voices, tears ran down their faces.

When Kane had unbound Kahara's arms, her last conscious act had been to tenderly wrap them around Rah's sedated body.

"I am forever shamed. Through all she endured, she never doubted us as I did her. Even after I raped her poor, ravaged, bound body, her last act was one of love and acceptance. You should have put me down brother. I do not deserve to live having wronged her so."

Rah was clearly in agony. Rom had no idea how to ease him, his own pain overwhelming.

"She will be out of the chamber in two weeks. I will let her kill you herself if that is her wish." Rom attempted humor, but it fell flat for them both.

~

Kahara silently sat in their quarters, watching the fish in the wall tank. She had been sitting there quite some time, unmoving, while the concerned brothers watched her. She appeared serene and lovely in her dressing gown and unbound hair.

They were not fooled. She had not spoken since her release from the healing chamber three days before, nor had she eaten. The only deviation was when one of the giant men would forget themselves and move too fast. Kahara would become paralyzed into a beautiful marble statue, no breath visible under her lovely breasts. She would not meet their eyes, and openly flinched if either of them spoke.

The chamber had healed her body but, due to her unique shamanic makeup, it had been unable to remove all the drugs from her overloaded system. Neither had it been able to mend her tortured mind and heart.

Something in her had indeed broken, leaving the two powerful men feeling helpless.

The door slid open and Jarl padded into the room.

"You must return her to my planet. Otherwise you will lose her," he addressed the brothers.

"What can your people do for her there?" Rom queried.

"She has lost her soul and is trapped deep in her body. She wishes to rejoin you but cannot. My great-great grandsire, Belinu, the revered shaman of my people, is the only one that can help her now."

"How can you know this?" Rah asked.

"As your brother can attest, Lord Rah, I have some shamanic gift. That is why I am able to commune with you, why I was chosen by my people as ambassador. I have been able to contact her, but alone I have not the skills to heal her."

"I will set course for Taron." Rah quickly stood, glad to finally have action to take.

Kahara froze into statue mode.

"Sorry, little scrapper, I forgot, I just – forgot."

His discomfort and regret were painful to see but she could do nothing to ease him. She was free floating, forever in an agony of drug induced lust and abuse driven trauma.

"It is I that am broken."

It was a mere mental shadow but all three males caught it.

"Oh Gods, little one, we will do whatever it takes to mend you," Rom whispered.

~ *Chapter 21* ~

They had been traveling toward Taron for several days when Jarl approached Rom asking to speak with him. The wolf seemed uncharacteristically hesitant in his communication.

"Lord Rom, there is something I must ask of you. Rest assured I will assist you and Lord Rah in finding our shaman and procuring the healing of your lady regardless of your answer."

"What is it you require, Lord Jarl?"

"As you know, I had been guarding over your lady's healing cylinder while she was in it."

"Yes, my brother and I greatly appreciate your vigilant loyalty."

"When I was checking the premise to be sure it was secure before you brought Lady Kahara from the transport, I was drawn to another cylinder not far from hers."

"Yes?"

"I – well, would you accompany me to the stasis corridor. There is something I must show you," Jarl finally managed.

As Rom followed the Taronion wolf to the corridor, he could not help marveling at the size and grace of the lupine warrior turned ambassador. When they arrived, Jarl approached a particular chamber and sat in front of it on his haunches.

Floating in its fluids was a petite, honey-haired human female. Rom recognized her immediately. It was the woman he and his twin had found buried in the rubble with Kahara. They had taken them both from Earth.

"This female is my destined mate," Jarl stated. *"What must I do to obtain her?"*

"Mate? But you are lupine, not humanoid. How can she be your mate?"

Rom was perplexed. He had never heard of the Taronion wolves taking human mates. The thought was not an overly pleasant one.

"I am unusual among my kind. I will trust you to keep my secret."

With a shimmering of form the wolf shifted before Rom's astonished eyes, becoming a formidable, naked, six foot seven, humanoid male with long, silver-tipped black hair and yellow eyes.

"Why would you keep such an amazing thing secret?"

"People tend to fear what they do not understand. My kind has been hunted to near extinction. I am not anxious to be parted from my pelt," Jarl answered in a droll mental tone. *"The Taronian race gave our few survivors sanctuary three thousand years ago."*

"Why do you still speak to me on our mental path?"

"I regret, while in this form I am like you in most ways but I have no voice."

"You cannot speak?"

"Howl, growl and snarl only." Humor laced Jarl's mental tone. *"Not to appear impatient, but about my lady mate…"*

Rom reached for the touch pad on the stasis chamber.

"Her name is Rhiannon. She is from Earth, the same planet as Lady Kahara. She was rescued from the same earthquake. We found them together. I believe they were friends. Rhiannon is as yet unclaimed and was en route to the Surrogate planet for training and eventual placement with a mate. Needless to say, after we discovered their treachery, we did not transport her or any of the other females we gathered there."

"Is there a way I may claim her? I will gladly pay any price. I have many resources."

"She is under our protection so yes, there is a chance you may claim her but we do not sell these women. It must be a true mating with the lady in full agreement."

"I had hoped to obtain her and then over time earn her trust and agreement. I cannot even speak to her. How am I to gain her agreement first?" Jarl worried.

"I fear you face many complications with this mating. Her home planet has no shifters, she will be totally unfamiliar with the concept. She has not been revived since leaving her planet so she is not experienced with space travel or life from other worlds.

"If you are unwilling to expose yourself as shifter, with the scarcity of fertile females, there will also be protest over my allowing a Taronian wolf to mate a fertile human female with no hope of impregnating her. I could go on but I am sure you have the picture."

"Yet, she is my mate, my very nature demands I claim her."

"I said there were complications, not impossibilities. My brother and I would not have survived had Kahara not accepted us. I do understand your position. I know you to be a great warrior and honorable male, Ambassador, rest assured I will do all I can to aid you in this."

Rom picked up the touch pad again and keyed into it. "For now, she will be listed as being claimed by one Ambassador Lyall pending her acceptance. We will consult with my brother and lady mate as how to best proceed – once Kahara is herself again."

"I have no words to express my gratitude, Lord Rom." Jarl placed his massive fist over his heart and bowed his head. *"I am deeply indebted to you. We will see to the safety and healing of your lady before I request mine revived. It is a great relief to me to know she will not be given to another in the interim."*

Jarl resumed his wolf form and sat down in front of Rhiannon's stasis chamber, his lupine longing palatable in the air. Rah silently left the corridor, granting the ambassador privacy. He knew he needed to share the latest development involving Ambassador Jarl with Rah, sooner rather than later.

"Brother, what is your location?" Rom sent to his twin.

"I am on the bridge," Rah's immediate response sounded in Rom's head.

"Can you break away? I need to speak with you."

This was a discussion Rom wanted to have in person with his brother rather than telepathically. He was sure Rah would not be pleased with the ambassador's shifter status given his closeness to their lady.

"Yes, where are you?"

"The conference room, come alone. We need to speak privately." Rom headed down the corridor to the conference room in question.

~

"That damned wolf has been sleeping at the foot of our lady's bed all this time and it is a humanoid male? I am going to kill him!" Rah roared.

"Shifters do not desire any female but their mate. He saw no conflict in his protection of Kahara during our absences. He considers it his duty as a warrior and guardian to protect, as he calls her, his Lady Shaman," Rom tried to soothe his enraged brother.

"She is not his lady anything," Rah continued to rage.

"He rarely takes human form and would not now, except he has discovered his mate to be human. She is also our lady's friend. We picked them up at the same site."

After some time and many soothing words, Rah finally cooled off enough to hear reason. Rah agreed with Rom's choice of giving Lord Jarl first opportunity to claim Rhiannon as his lady. They were also in full agreement the wolf would no longer be sleeping in, or even allowed near, Kahara's chamber.

~

It took Rah quite some time to be civil after discovering Jarl was a shifter. Not that Rah was prejudiced against shifters, but he could not tolerate Jarl, in male humanoid form, around Kahara given their closeness. He just could not get past his possessive jealousy.

Fortunately, while en route to Taron, Rom suggested Rah and Jarl collaborate to further establish a working mental link. All three males agreed they would need it to protect Kahara.

Rom was very adept at telepathic communication with other gifted races as he used the skill often in his role as ambassador. Rah, on the other hand, mostly limited his telepathic communications to his twin. He was just beginning to trust his innermost being with his mate, so he found opening up to the Taronion shifter a little disconcerting.

"It will be more comfortable when you learn to block your private thoughts and only project your communications. Until then, I will be vigilant in filtering your inner thoughts and pay attention only to those you project," Jarl kindly reassured Rah during one of their practice sessions.

"That is downright human of you, Lord Jarl," Rah quipped.

"It is only courteous. This being my major form of communication, I am understandably more adept. I am honored you are willing to take the time to learn to share it with me."

True to lupine nature, Jarl took Rom literally, missing the cynicism altogether.

"I can also field your telepathic communications so that others do not have access while you master the skill. I will set up a private channel between the two of us, much like you enjoy with your mate and brother. They will not be blocked from our conversations but none other will have access."

"You can actually be that specific?" Rah was impressed in spite of himself.

"Yes, as can your brother and your mate. They are very gifted for humanoids. You have much potential as well. You have simply not taken the time to refine your natural skill."

"I can see where this will be very useful. Thank you for taking the time."

Rah was sincerely grateful to the shifter. The wellbeing of his mate rested in Jarl's willingness and ability to get her to his revered ancestor for healing. He had assured both brothers he would do all he could to help Kahara, regardless of their decision concerning his own mate.

Rah was loathe to admit it, but there was actually a building respect and budding friendship between the two warriors as they worked together to orchestrate the mission. They were also planning to set up long distance coordination between Rah's and Jarl's troops while on planet. With their races being allies, the war against the Surrogate planets could well prove a threat to Taron. Jarl's planet, shunning technology, was unarmed and could be in need of military protection. On the other hand, they were great tacticians with many unknown skills that would, no doubt, prove useful to Rah's race in exchange. If Jarl's race offered nothing more than the healing of Kahara, Rah would consider it more than fair.

~

The brothers carefully piloted the craft to the surface. Rather than improving, Kahara's condition had worsened. Any additional stimulation or movement caused her great discomfort. She sat stoic and silent in one of the seats behind the brothers.

Jarl was in wolf form, curled up at her feet. His proximity seemed less distressing to her than that of her mates. Jarl had indicated that it was in Kahara's best interest that she not be confronted with him in human form until after her healing. The wisdom of that was becoming increasingly clear.

Rom had tried to explain to her the necessity for the trip back to the ice planet but if she heard, she made no indication. Beyond the subtle leaning away from him if he got too close or cringing if he moved too fast, she did not respond at all.

Once the shuttle had safely landed on Taron, Rah approached Kahara with warm outer gear for her to wear. She continued to look down at her hands, clasped together in her lap, as if he were not standing before her.

"Kahara, love, you will need to wear these for our trip to the healer." She did not respond.

"I am not sure what to do here, brother, I am afraid to touch her in order to get gear on her," Rah beseeched his brother.

Rom crossed over to her seat and squatted down in front of her trying to make eye contact, but she kept her green eyes veiled with her lashes.

"Her maid has been the one to dress and groom her. We should have brought her along," Rom replied.

"The maid is clearly ill suited for the tundra. She would probably have been more hindrance than help."

227

"Will you allow one of us to help you into the jump suit and parka, little one?" Rom ventured.

Kahara visibly tightened, a shudder running through her small frame.

"Let's wrap her up in thermal blankets and a fur, and bundle her into the sled. I am unwilling to cause her the discomfort of attempting to dress her," Rom communicated to Rah.

"Here, Kahara, just let me put this on to protect your head," Rom continued in a soothing tone as he carefully and very slowly took a fur lined white hood from Rah, put it on her head and fastened it beneath her chin.

Kahara shuddered so violently her teeth rattled. Rah put the rest of the gear in a pack and brought blankets from the supply compartments. Rom helped her to her feet while Rah gently bundled her. By the time they were done, she was shaking and whimpering. When Rah lifted her into his arms to carry her out of the shuttle to the sled, she moaned in terror. Rah looked to his brother's pain filled eyes in anguish.

Jarl was looking on, his heart breaking for the Triad.

"Belinu, my great-great grandsire, is in contact with me. He thanks you for your willingness to leave all technology at the landing site and assures us our transport and escort will arrive shortly," he informed the brothers on their common channel.

As they stepped out of the shuttle into the frigid tundra night, a pack of oversized wolves was already approaching. The pack waited patiently as Kahara was secured into the sled.

A huge grey approached to be hitched to the sled while two others offered their backs for the brothers to mount. A black female came up to the sled, touching Kahara's face with her muzzle.

"What ails our lady shaman?" she demanded of Jarl.

"Betrayers used poison and cruelty to break her soul. Her mates and I have brought her for Belinu to heal," Jarl readily informed the alpha female.

"Then you have our alliance against the betrayers. She shall be avenged."

"The alpha female has pledged her pack's alliance against the Surrogates," Jarl informed Rah and Rom.

"What did you tell her?" Rom inquired.

"I spoke of their crimes against Lady Kahara. She is much loved by the Taronians. They wish to see her avenged," Jarl replied.

The trip to Shaman Belinu's den took most of the day. Rom and Rah rode wolf-back on either side of Kahara's sled while Jarl flanked it. By the time they arrived, the three moons were setting, casting the already dark night into deeper darkness.

Upon their arrival, Jarl introduced the brothers to his great-great grand sire, Belinu, an impressive pure white, blue eyed wolf. Jarl and he were much the same size and build. It was impossible to tell one was much older than the other.

Thanks to Jarl's lessons with Rah, both Rom and Rah communicated easily with the shaman. Kahara remained unresponsive and silent. The other wolves said their goodbyes and loped off into the dark arctic night to return to their den.

"We have brought a gift for your willingness to help our mate," Rom said, respectfully setting a small box down in front of the elder. *"We realize you do not use or condone technology but this will serve you well in that regard."*

Removing the device from its box, Rom indicated a button on the otherwise smooth metal surface.

"If you depress this button, all technology on or approaching your planet will be rendered useless. We designed it to be operated by either hand or paw. Any craft, communications or

weaponry in your atmosphere or on land will be affected. It will afford you much protection from anyone not honoring the no-technology treaty set up between our peoples. We have taken the liberty of placing a small drone satellite in Taron's orbit to relay the signal planet wide. Should you choose not to accept the gift we will remove the satellite post haste. "

"Normally I would refuse such a gift but you are correct, it will prove most useful in the times to come. I receive it with gratitude," Belinu responded formally. *"I will endeavor not to use it to drop you out of the sky."*

The elder had a sense of humor, Rom realized, detecting irony in his mental tone and the distinctive lupine smile on his muzzle.

Belinu directed the brothers to set up residence in a small private chamber off of his cave den. There was a vent hole for a fire. Like the den Rah and Kahara been sheltered in on their prior visit, there was geothermal heat providing a relatively comfortable environment if one happened to sport thick fur. Light was provided by glowing crystals.

After a light meal, of which Kahara ate very little, Rom and Rah settled her down on the sleeping chamber's pallet and covered her with a warm fur. They were careful not to crowd her, but for their own sanity, needed to lie down on either side of her, keeping her close and protected.

Belinu had told them to rest well as he would begin Kahara's healing upon their next rising. Both he and Jarl warned the brothers it would be intense and arduous requiring much energy from all of them.

~

Kahara floated in a haze of pain and despair. The drugs had not left her system, rendering every touch an exercise in torture – forcing her to use all of her energy to contain her agony. It had been all she could do to endure the trip. She was aware that her mates had brought her back to the ice planet – to a shaman – her only hope, as she knew it would take a very gifted healer to repair her shattered soul. She longed to return to the mates she would live and die for. Sleep was long in coming, disturbed by nightmares from her ordeal at the hands of the Surrogates.

~

After eight hours rest, Jarl sent a mental call to the brothers, instructing them to leave Kahara to her sleep while he and Belinu debriefed Rom and Rah on what the healing would involve. Jarl had spoken at length with Belinu about Kahara and his own findings. Both healers agreed the only way out for her was through. She and her mates would have to process out the drug through sexual intimacy before Jarl and Belinu could repair the damage to her heart, mind and soul. The drug in her system was taking all her strength and focus to control. She lacked the energy necessary to process any healing beyond what the healing cylinder had been able to provide her physical body.

"You have got to be kidding me!" Rah raged. "She can't stand to be touched. We will probably have to restrain her. It will be like her having to endure the torture all over again. There has to be another way."

"Isn't there an antidote?" Rom asked, running his hand through his long black hair in frustration.

"The shamanically gifted are not like other beings. The drug almost destroyed her delicate system as it is. To attempt an antidote would be fighting fire with fire. She would most likely be reduced to a vegetative state if she survived at all," Jarl explained.

"There is another chamber deeper in this cave that has a hot mineral pool. The water will aid in detoxifying as you both help her work the poisons out of her system. Jarl will help you set up for her healing there. Be prepared to spend several days in this phase after which Jarl and I will be able to call back her soul. It is the only way to save your mate. Given her gift, there simply is no other choice," Belinu instructed.

~

Kahara woke to Rah lifting and carrying her to another chamber in the den. Though she tried to avoid flinching from his touch, she failed.

"Gods, little scrapper, I am so sorry. This will get much worse before it gets better," Rah's agonized voice informed her. His obvious pain was a lance to her heart.

Rom met them in the chamber, rising up from where he was preparing a large, soft pallet of furs. The hot mineral pool warmed the chamber, filling it with steam and the soothing sound of running water. Jarl had given Rom numerous earthen jars of salves which Rom had placed near the pallet next to a supply of food and drinking water.

Rah carefully placed Kahara in the center of the large pallet. Both brothers sat down on either side of her. Rom placed one large finger beneath her chin, forcing her head up until her eyes finally met his.

"I need you to hear me, Kahara. The healer has informed us the only way to bring you back is by working the drugs out of your system through intercourse." Kahara's eyes flared. "Ah lady, if there were any other way we would not put you through this, believe me."

She shook her head back and forth in denial, eyes filling with fear.

"Know that we do this in love. You are our heart."

Kahara scuttled backward on the pallet trying to distance herself from Rom only to back into the warm, already naked body of Rah. She recoiled but had no place left to go that wasn't full of massive warrior. Rah gently wrapped his big scarred hands on her upper arms to steady her, while Rom carefully undid the fastening of her gown, letting it slowly slip from her shoulders.

Just the soft silk fabric, brushing down her overly sensitized nipples, was agonizing. Kahara whimpered in distress.

Rom's hands shook in response.

Rah closed his eyes in pain.

"Please, if you love me, just let me walk into the night." Her first communication with them was a plea for death. It was devastating to both men.

"If you choose to leave this world, we will follow, but Rah and I must at least try to bring you back to us. Please trust us one more time, little one."

Rom took his knife from the scabbard at his hip and cut the rest of her gown from her, rather than drag it against her overly sensitized flesh. Kahara shook in fear, eyes wild and dilated. She couldn't do this, not even for them. There was just too much pain. She threw herself forward trying to impale herself on the sharp blade. It was only Rom's finely honed warrior instincts that saved her tender flesh.

"Dear gods in heaven, Kahara," Rah shouted, pulling her back against his bare muscled chest, "No, lady no!"

"Jarl, she is trying to destroy herself rather than endure our touch," Rah called out to Jarl in desperation on their private channel.

"She is so hyper sensitized that she doesn't realize it is lust. All she knows is the pain. She is a wild animal caught in a trap only you can spring. You are going to have to force her until you can bring enough relief to ease her," Jarl responded. *"Do you need me to come do it? I can perform with none other than my mate, but I could provide some oral relief if you cannot bring yourselves to do it,"* Jarl offered, knowing full well what the suggestion would do to both males.

"HELL NO!" came through loud and clear from both warriors.

"That was manipulative, grandson," Belinu observed on their private path, humor in his mental tone.

"At this point, whatever it takes. We cannot afford to lose the Triad. They are the prophesized salvation of the entire sector," Jarl reminded his great grandsire.

"Remember, it is their very strength as a Triad that will bring that salvation. They will make it through this and be all the more bonded for it," Belinu assured Jarl.

~ *Chapter 22* ~

"You hold her down, brother, I will do this thing," Rah said, full of resolve. Rom took her into his embrace pulling her between his legs with her back resting against his chest.

The soft silk of his shirt was agony. Kahara hissed between her teeth as if burned.

"My clothing is furthering her discomfort. You hold her, Rah." Rom handed her back to Rah who pulled her between his legs, resting her back against his chest and massive erection.

"I'm not sure this is an improvement," Rah gritted out between his teeth as Kahara struggled, trying to pull away from his torrid member.

"Are you two sure you don't need my help?" Jarl prodded.

"Get out of my brain, beagle breath, before I hunt down your mangy ass and castrate you," Rah snarled.

"Testy," Jarl could not help but respond.

"Beagle breath? He calls the second most powerful shaman in the sector beagle breath?" Belinu observed, incredulous.

"Vindicating circumstances. I will let it slide this time," Jarl chuckled.

Rah held Kahara facing away from him and hooked her shapely bare legs over his, spreading them apart, affording his brother access to her tender core. It was drenched and glistening in the soft light. Still fully dressed and touching her nowhere else, Rom tentatively inserted a long callused finger into her inflamed folds.

Kahara screamed and arched into Rah, writhing in an attempt to get away from the intrusion. Her stomach muscles clenched and her entire body shook.

"Hold her still. I don't want to hurt her," Rom pleaded with Rah.

"For the love of the gods, don't drag it out. Just latch onto her and bring her over already," Rah gritted out as Kahara's hips ground against his member in her attempts to escape his brother, desperate screams still echoing in the chamber.

Rom lowered his head, closed his lips over her erect little bundle of nerves and sucked it into his mouth as he drove his finger deeper into her. He flicked it with his tongue once, twice and on the third she exploded into his mouth. It took all of Rah's strength hold her writhing body. Her agonized screams were painful to hear.

Kahara fought like a woman possessed. She repeatedly kicked Rom in the head before turning in Rah's lap to rain blows on his chest and face.

He did nothing to stop her. Stoically, Rah took the beating without flinching. She raked her nails down his cheek and chest drawing blood, and still he did nothing. She finally exhausted herself beating him and collapsed. He took her bruised hands into his, drew them to his mouth and licked his blood from them. He retrieved a jar of salve and gently applied it to her bruised knuckles.

Rom sat with his head in his hands, tears running down his strong jaw. Causing their lady such suffering was killing him.

"This is no time to rest, gentlemen, keep the releases coming. You can't afford to get behind the power curve," Jarl prodded them.

Rah could see he was right. Already Kahara's body was heating and squirming in discomfort.

"Come here, little scrapper, let me love you," Rah whispered into her ear.

"No, don't touch me. God, I can't stand to be touched, I really can't," she pleaded.

Rah pulled her diminutive body under his and held her down with one massive shoulder over her abdomen. He covered her wet slit with his mouth and sank his tongue into her trembling core.

Rom rallied and leaned over her, drawing one peaked nipple into his hot mouth while he plucked the other between his fingers. Rah sank one forefinger into her anus to the first knuckle. The burning penetration sent her crashing over the edge. Her screams filled the air and the beatings commenced.

When she collapsed in exhaustion from bludgeoning the brothers, Rom lay on his back, pulled her up to straddle his face and sank his teeth into her tender nub. He held it captive and flicked it with his tongue while pulling on her nipples with the fingers of both hands.

Coming up behind her, Rah pressed her shoulders into the pallet above Rom's head. Restraining her by a hand between her shoulder blades, he thrust three long fingers of his other hand into her core.

Another devastating release ravaged her body.

Hours later, Rom and Rah were in agony. Their cocks so hard they were near bursting. Repeatedly loving their mate without release was taking its toll. Rom was still in control – barely, but Rah was definitely the worse for wear. His eyes were beginning to show signs of the berserker. Kahara was shuddering beneath them in yet another shattering release. She had finally quit beating them, but still fought for her freedom.

In a weak moment, when the brothers relaxed their guard, Kahara, aided by her sweat dampened skin, slipped out of their grasp and bolted for the chamber entrance. The berserker broke free and Rah was on her instantly.

He drove her to the chamber floor on her hands and knees, mounted and entered her with a roar and one savage penetrating thrust. Sinking his teeth into her shoulder, he pounded into her with deep, brutal thrusts.

"Mine. You are mine. Never run from me. I will never let you go. Mine," he raged mindlessly over their Triad connection.

Rom was struggling to pull his brother off of their tiny mate when she suddenly broke free and turned in Rah's arms. She grabbed him by his long flying hair. Savagely pulling him to her, she stared into his eyes and screamed into his face.

"You really want a piece of this? Fuck me, fuck me deep!" Her hips thrusting up to meet his savage pounding thrusts, her claws raking his back, she continued to stare into his eyes, every bit as crazed as he. "I'm almost there, damn you, harder. I want to feel you so deep you will never find your way free of me."

Rom stopped trying to drag Rah off of her. This was an interesting development. He was undecided if it was a good sign. *"Jarl, she just went berserk on my berserker brother. Is this a good thing or no?"*

"Who is winning that battle?" Jarl wanted to know.

"I think she is, she is using him hard," Rom reported after watching her lock her legs behind his brother's driving flank, sinking her nails into his back.

"Finally! Now she can move through the backed up lust. Just do whatever she wants for as long as you can manage. You might try taking turns with your brother for a while to conserve your strength. You will need all you can muster," Jarl advised.

Rom's attention was drawn back to his brother and mate by Rah's bellowing roar and Kahara's scream of completion. Rah had no sooner rolled off of her so as to not crush her under his weight when her fevered green eyes lit on Rom.

"I want you inside me, Rom."

Her voice was sultry and demanding as she writhed on the floor reaching for him. It was his undoing. Rom fell on her like a man possessed. Kahara wrapped her long slender legs around his hips and, digging her heels in, met his every carnal thrust. Her sharp little nails raked his muscled back, drawing blood. His tight flank flexed under her heels as he labored over her, driving into her endlessly as she screamed for more, deeper, harder.

Rah lay next to the rutting couple trying desperately to regain his equilibrium and strength. What the hell just happened to their little mate? Who stole her and replaced her with this wanton wildcat? Not that he was complaining – he had just had the holy shit fucked out of him while in the middle of a berserker driven lust. Even his berserker had finally found its match in Kahara. He could still see her passion crazed green eyes as she looked into his, ripping at his hair and demanding he fuck her.

Now she was having her way with his brother and it was a sight to behold. He could feel his cock growing hard again as he watched Rom pound into her as she drew blood. At their thundering release Rom rolled off of her and she mounted Rah, impaling herself, as she sank down on him in one fluid movement. Her hips churned, drawing him deeper as her nails sank into his chest. Her head was thrown back as her glorious hair flowed down past her hips and grazed his balls.

"God almighty, I want you in my womb!" she screamed as they both blew up. His scalding seed pumped into her but instead of collapsing, she crawled off of him and stalked his still recuperating brother on all fours.

"Gods, lady, give me a second," Rom pleaded with her as she grabbed his semi erect cock and wrapped her mouth around it. She fondled Rom's sack as she thrust him in and out of her mouth, humming her delight. Unable to stand it another second, Rah approached her kneeling body from behind and took her rear. She arched her back and came undone for him as he pounded to release.

Rom had just pulled free from her mouth in time to be jumped again. She shoved him onto his back, straddled him, sank her tongue into his mouth and sank down onto him.

"I want your seed pumping inside me. Fuck me deep and come." Rom threw his head back, black hair flying, and with an agonized roar, complied.

Hours later, all three lay in an exhausted heap, the only movement – the occasional post orgasmic shudder. Finally, Rah rallied enough to lift Kahara and carry her to the hot pool of mineral water. Rom managed to crawl over and join them not too long afterward. They all soaked in silence. Both men held onto their mate in exhausted desperation as she appeared to sleep, suspended in the warm spring.

"Now what?" Rah inquired of the shifter.

"Sleep. When she awakens, bring her to us and we will complete her healing," Jarl responded.

~

"What in the hell happened to you two?" Kahara's shouted question brought both brothers out of a dead sleep. All three were back on the large pallet where they had collapsed after the mineral soak.

Rom looked at Rah. Both brothers were scratched, battered and bruised. Rom sported a black eye where Kahara's heel had landed while Rah's face and chest were covered with bloody scratches. Both men's backs and buttocks looked as if they had a run in with a wildcat – which they had.

Kahara, on the other hand, was unharmed. Aside from a bite mark on her shoulder, not so much as a bruise marked her perfect skin. She felt relaxed and sated with a delicious soreness in her rear and between her legs.

"*You* happened to us, little scrapper," Rah answered her. "Do you remember any of the last few days?"

"I thought I dreamt we made the most incredible love…It wasn't a dream, was it?"

"No, little one, it was only too real. It was the only way to relieve you of the drug," Rom assured her. "Can you find it in yourself to forgive us?"

"I might be persuaded," she said, gently pushing Rom onto his back, mounting his massive naked frame and taking his full lips in an ardent kiss. He became instantly hard.

"You are the most beautiful men imaginable," she whispered, sinking down and impaling herself on Rom's huge erection in one slow agonizing thrust.

"Oh gods, lady, gods," he gasped at the feel of her stretching to accommodate him.

"Rah, you have some making up to do as well, mister," she ordered, looking over her shoulder at him, wiggling her shapely bare bottom in invitation. "Mount up and get to it."

"Holy gods, lady, you take my breath," Rah gasped as he joined them. Mindful of how sore she must be, slowly he sank his torrid cock into her tight rear with a groan.

Rom could feel his brother enter their mate from behind and it was all he could do to hold still. It was unimaginable to him how badly he could want her again when he could hardly move from the rigorous two day orgy they had just shared.

Rah took her beautiful full breasts into his hands from behind and rolled her erect nipples between his thumbs and forefingers as he started to gently thrust in and out. Kahara began moving up and down on Rom in tandem to Rah's thrusts. Rolling her hips back she impaled her rear with Rah – forward, she took Rom into her core.

As their pace increased, Rom rubbed her swollen clitoris with his long fingers. Kahara threw her head back and wailed her orgasm, inner muscles spasming, causing both brothers to explode. They filled her to overflowing with their massive cocks and scalding seed.

Kahara burst out into tears as her mates roared their simultaneous releases.

"What is it, little one, did we hurt you?" Rom was aghast at the possibility.

"No, I just love you both so much," she sobbed.

~

The brothers took her back to the mineral pool and gently bathed her but she continued to cry, not speaking to them again. She would cling to one or the other of them and sob as her two concerned mates worked as a team to bathe and dress her.

"Jarl, she won't stop crying," Rah sent his concerned mental call to his shifter friend.

"This may not be a bad thing," Jarl responded. *"All is prepared for her healing. Bring her to us."*

When the Triad arrived at the healer's chamber, they were shocked to see two massive, handsome men instead of two wolves sitting around the fire. They were dressed in loin cloths with their hair wild and free about their shoulders. Jarl's distinctive, silver-tipped, black mane identified him. The other man had a wild mass of white hair hanging half way down his muscular back and looked more like Jarl's brother than his great-great grandsire.

There was a pallet arranged next to the fire where Jarl indicated they should place Kahara. Rah, having carried her from their chamber, gently laid her down with obvious reluctance.

Jarl instructed her mates to sit on either side of the pallet while he went to her feet. Belinu went to kneel by her head, took up an ancient rattle made from animal hide and bird feathers, and shook it over Kahara. He howled an eerie tone, raising the hair on the back of the brothers' necks. Jarl added his purposefully discordant cry.

Rom could literally feel the notes reverberate off of each other, setting up first a dissonance, then a resonance of great power, as harmonies tumbled around the stone walls of the chamber. The sound went on and on without either shifter seeming to pause for breath.

Kahara started to shake uncontrollably. Still sobbing, her shaking became convulsions and her cries a lament. Her voice blended with the shifters howls with such impact it seemed to take all the air from the chamber.

Belinu fell down next to Kahara and convulsed as well, his body movements perfectly mirroring hers. His mouth opened in a silent scream as Kahara bewailed her pain. Jarl continued his howl, having taken up the rattle when Belinu went into trance.

"What is he doing to her? He is hurting her! I cannot stand her pain. I am going to put a stop to this," Rah raged.

"Do not interfere or you will cause deep damage. He is helping her purge the pain she carries in order to bring back her soul," Jarl informed him. *"She knows you are here with her. Stand strong for her."*

"Kahara, let it move lady, we are with you," Rom encouraged her while his eyes met his brother's, willing him to lend his power to her healing.

After what seemed like forever, Kahara stilled. Belinu returned to himself and sat up. The chamber was silent but for the occasional crackle of the dying fire.

"Your woman's soul has been returned to her body. She now needs to sleep that they may merge and heal." Belinu spoke on their common mental path for the first time since the ritual had begun. Looking exhausted and spent, he came up on all fours and with a swirling of air, shifted, returning to his lupine form before padding out of the chamber.

"Take your lady back to the healing pool, bathe her and find your rest," Jarl instructed the brothers. *"I will stand guard while you recover."*

"Jarl?" Rom addressed the obviously exhausted shifter.

"Lord Rom?" Jarl responded.

"There are no words to thank you."

"It is my honor and pleasure to serve," Jarl assured him before shifting into his formidable lupine form to better guard the Triad.

~ *Chapter 23* ~

The trip to the ice planet Taron had been strenuous but successful. Though she had little memory of the process, Kahara was fully recovered, thanks to the steadfast support and guidance from Jarl and the formidable shamanic skill of his great-great grandfather, Belinu.

Kahara was sufficiently recovered to be approached with Lord Jarl's request regarding her friend, Rhiannon. Rom accompanied the Taronian wolf to their quarters to face the music.

"Kahara, Ambassador Jarl has a favor to ask and a confession to make," Rom stated as they entered the sitting room where she was seated before the fire, playing chess with Rah.

"Ah yes, and the flee-bitten cur can't have one without the other," Rah said with a smirk. He was still not pleased with Jarl's failure to expose his humanoid side before growing close to their mate.

Kahara could swear the wolf looked nervous as she looked at Rah in confusion, surprised by his caustic attitude toward the ambassador.

"Jarl, I owe you my life several times over. Surely you know I will help you with anything you need," Kahara assured Jarl on their mental path.

"I am a shifter and I require your friend Rhiannon as my mate." Jarl, true to his lupine nature, was direct and to the point. Kahara just sat and blinked at him.

"Rhiannon *is human, Jarl, she can't be your mate…what is a shifter?"*

"A demonstration is worth a thousand words," Rah chuckled, throwing his brother the blanket from the back of the couch.

"Okay wolf-man, I have you covered, let 'er rip," Rom snickered, as he stood ready to hold the blanket up in front of Jarl's lower half.

"I do not find this nearly as humorous as it appears the two of you do," Jarl replied, as he obediently let the shift begin.

The air whirled around him as he dematerialized into a toroidal field only to rematerialize as a man, leaving Jarl standing before Kahara in humanoid form.

Kahara sat, stunned, blinking her eyes. Slowly the shock wore off and realization hit.

"Why, you son of a bitch!" she heatedly exclaimed.

"Yes, my mother whelped me," Jarl readily admitted.

"I let you put your head in my lap – I even scratched your ears!" Her voice rose with her escalating anger.

"I like having my ears scratched," Jarl defended, lupine reflexes serving him well as he ducked the vase Kahara had hurled at his poor head.

"I ran around half dressed while you were in my room! You slept at the foot of my damn bed, you mangy cur!" she screamed at the hapless shifter.

"My kind does not pay attention to nudity. I was protecting you while your mates were not present to do so." Jarl dodged another flying missile, a large bust from the mantle. *"I do not, nor have I ever had, mange."* He managed to sound offended as he ducked the wine bottle that followed the bust.

"Just as a suggestion – I would shift back and slink on out of here. She clearly needs time to cool off," Rah chuckled.

Jarl did so, flinching when he heard something shattering against the door that had just closed behind his hasty retreat.

~

"I can't believe he hid it from me all this time," Kahara agonized to her mates later that evening as they discussed the latest development.

"Lady, need I remind, you kept your shamanic nature hidden from your mates?" Rom gently inserted, hoping to offer some prospective.

"I was afraid you would reject me."

"Lord Jarl told me his kind was so feared and hated they were hunted to near extinction before he and Belinu found sanctuary among the wolves on Taron. They became refugees hundreds of years ago. To my knowledge, he has not taken human form since."

"I was enraged when I first discovered he could take human form and had been in such close contact with you. Yet, after working with him and coming to know him better, I do not believe it was his intention to deceive. Lupines are direct and honest to a fault," Rah added in an uncharacteristic show of support for the shifter. "Like you, it had just become ingrained in him not to show that side of his nature to others."

"I see your point," Kahara conceded.

"I have no doubt Rhiannon is his mate. I have seen him mooning over her stasis chamber for hours on end. He is really pining for her," Rom shared with them.

"I feel his pain." Rah looked at Kahara meaningfully. "This mating business can really bring a male to his knees."

Kahara wondered at his meaning. She could not imagine anything ever taking the powerful warrior to his knees, least of all her.

"What do you suggest?" Kahara asked her mates.

"I promised Ambassador Jarl he could have first claim on Rhiannon, conditional upon the lady accepting him," Rom informed her.

"I think we should revive her and give him the chance to win her," Rah added.

"We are unsure how to proceed. We were hoping you might have some suggestions and would be willing to aid him," Rom continued.

"In all reality, Jarl has been a loyal friend and defender. Have him return tomorrow evening and maybe the four of us can work out the best way to move forward."

~

The next evening, Jarl showed up at their door, fully dressed and in humanoid form. He was carrying fresh cut flowers procured from the ship's greenhouse as a peace offering and looked uncertain of his reception.

"Has she taken chill yet?" he asked Rom, as the male opened the door.

"The earth expression is 'cooled off' and yes, somewhat. Come in," Rom replied as Jarl looked carefully around the door jamb before slinking inside like the lupine he was.

"Yes, do come in," Kahara encouraged from across the room where she stood, arms folded over her chest. "At least you showed up as human rather than trying to win me over with your puppy dog eyes."

"My eyes are the same in either form," Jarl responded, perplexed.

"Talk to me out loud, Jarl," Kahara reprimanded, hands on hips. "I would really like to be able to hear your apology."

"I cannot, Lady Kahara, I am mute."

"I'm so sorry, Jarl, I didn't know."

"I am a much better wolf than human, lady. I have not mastered the finer points of human interaction. That is why I mostly reside in wolf form, yet now I have found my mate and she is human. Could you find it in your heart to help me win her?"

"This could be an uphill battle. Rhiannon has not been treated well by the men in her life and has little trust of them. She is particularly terrified of large men and you are nearly as large as my mates, Jarl."

"A male has dared mistreat my mate?" Jarl's mental voice was a fierce growl.

"I'm afraid so. Her father was a huge, vicious man that beat her unmercifully from the time she was a small child," Kahara regretfully replied. "To my knowledge, she has never taken a man to her bed. Also, she has not been debriefed or trained, and after spending so long in stasis, has a long recovery ahead of her.

"We have kept her suspended, fearing she would come into season before she was ready to take a mate. Your being a shifter is beyond her experience. I almost fainted when you shifted and I have had time to adjust to the seemingly impossible. She is not even aware there is life on other worlds much less space travel."

"I have waited my lifetime to find her. I will give her all the gentleness and understanding she may require, but claim her I must – or, like your mates, die trying. In this we are the same."

"We may not have much time. Earth females cycle monthly, not annually," Kahara warned him. "We can put it off for several months but not beyond that without the risk of interfering with her fertility."

"So, I only have a few months to convince her to mate with an animal that cannot even speak to her," Jarl's mental voice was full of self-loathing.

"I will have to earn her trust first, Lord Jarl. I have not been forthright either," Kahara confessed. "She knew me when I was under cover as a Japanese woman. She will not even recognize me. Given her history and our close friendship I am sure she will feel betrayed."

"What is Japanese?" Jarl wanted to know.

Kahara sent him a mental image of the woman she had been when Rhiannon knew her.

"So we all have inadvertently misled each other through omission," Jarl stated, knowing full well that Kahara's mates were still not aware of the extent of her capabilities, nor she of theirs.

"Yes, I guess we have," the Triad agreed in unison, before looking at each other in surprise.

"My mates and I discussed your dilemma and will assist you in any way we can. Rom has instructed Chief Medical Officer Saul to revive her. She should be ready to come out of stasis and begin her rehabilitation day after tomorrow. It is probably best I work with her first and regain her trust. When we see how she adjusts we will have a much better idea how to move forward with your courtship. I will keep you informed of our progress and naturally, as her mate, you will have final say in all that we do," Kahara told the shifter.

"There are no words that can express my gratitude." Jarl bowed to the Triad. *"It is my understanding I have no rights as her mate until she accepts me,"* he added to Kahara, perplexed at her offer to give him final say in Rhiannon's care.

"I know you are the only one that can truly heal my friend, and the only one with any hope of winning her as mate. I also have 'seen' that, should you accomplish this thing, you, Rhiannon and my Triad will work together as allies and friends for centuries to come to the mutual benefit of all our peoples."

The three massive warriors looked at Kahara in shocked silence. None of them missed the prophetic nature of her statement or the altered state she was in when she uttered it. Her eyes had glazed over and glowed emerald from within. Suddenly she seemed to shake herself and return to normal.

"What did you say, Jarl?" she asked, seeming disoriented.

"I was expressing my gratitude, lady," he simply responded, earning a questioning look from the twin brothers.

"While your lady has always been somewhat precognizant, she is now becoming an unconscious channel. The shamanic healing she received from Belinu further opened her natural gifts. To draw her attention to it at this time would not serve her. She is still delicate from her ordeal and may prove to be somewhat volatile," he shared with the brothers on their private channel.

"We have a meeting of the Council tomorrow at first bell to discuss the situation with the United Alliance of Surrogate Planets and their treason," Rom informed Jarl, wisely changing the subject. "Would you do us the honor of serving on the Council and taking up your rightful place as Ambassador? Your wisdom and knowledge will be greatly appreciated."

"It is my honor to serve," Jarl responded.

"Why don't you show up in human form? These people all know and respect you and will not be put off by your gifts. There is no time like the present to start getting used to relating as a human," Kahara encouraged him.

"I fully trust you to know the best way to proceed, lady."

"This is a good place to start," Rom agreed. "It will establish you in our midst as humanoid before you meet your lady mate."

"Until then, may your Triad be blessed with knowledge and comforted with love." Turning on his heel he quietly left the staterooms.

"What did he mean by that?" Rah wanted to know.

"I don't know, but I have a really bad feeling we will find out before long," his brother answered him thoughtfully.

~

Kahara's volatility reared its ugly head the very next morning.

The ruling Triad of the Daguronian Sector, Lords Rom and Rah Andor and their mate Lady Kahara, had been in the war room on the Karinian flagship discussing their response to the treachery of the United Alliance of Surrogate Planets. Among those present were Chief Medical Officer Saul, Head Tactician Kev, Head of Recon Zeb, Head of Special Ops Marc, Ambassador of Taron Lord Jarl Lyall (in all his humanoid glory) and the newly appointed Head of the Allied Drone Unit, Drone Kane.

The morning had been going better than Rah expected. While the Council was at first surprised at the humanoid appearance of the Taronian shifter, they settled into the knowledge with relative ease. Many of them had heard of such a race and, to a male, had learned to trust and respect Lord Jarl in wolf form.

They had been discussing ways to correct the situation without losing the vital service of the Surrogate planets when Lady Kahara stood up to her full diminutive height, a good foot and a half shorter than her mates, and addressed the council. What she lacked in stature, she more than made up for in sheer feminine outrage.

"We are not going to merely reprimand, then police the Alliance. We will break this by god monopoly and heal the brutalized women," Kahara dictated. "We will also put an end to the piracy and slave trade. Furthermore, I have been trained by the biggest badass bastards in the business to be a by god, assassin. I will *not* sit on the sidelines like one of your pampered fertile ninnies. We *will* operate as the Triad we were born to be and right this horrific wrong together."

A shocked silence ensued in the wake of Kahara's outburst. Her mates noticed her eyes were glowing emerald – again.

"Trained as an assassin? Our lady was trained as an assassin?" Rah exclaimed in horrified disbelief to his brother over their private channel.

"But lady, consider your value to us and your safety…," Rah began.

"My safety and my value lie in the breaking of this abhorrent exploitation of men and women alike. Were it not for this vile system in place, there would be no need to treat me or any other woman as if we were subhuman. We were designed to be partners, helpmates, not incubators and useless burdensome chattel."

"Our lady shaman speaks true," Jarl offered.

"Shut up, beagle breath, I will not willingly endanger her," Rah raged at him on their private channel.

"It is this system that endangers me and all other women," Kahara declared, hearing the exchange between the shifter and her mate. "I *will* be part of the solution – not part of the problem. You expect me to sit aside and watch my mates endanger themselves without me? Would you offer me the same? Would you let me go to war unsupported by all you can offer?" she challenged both of her mates.

"You must admit, she has a valid point," Jarl pointed out.

"Damn it, wolf, your pelt will grace my hearth if you do not shut up," Rah warned the shifter.

"Lord Rom, you fought with my pack, you participated in an empathic Triad with me and your lady mate. You saw our males

*and females work as a combined force. How many causalities did
we sustain?"* Jarl challenged.

"None, we vanquished an entire unit of technologically armed
enemy without breaking the treaty ourselves or suffering a single
casualty on our side," Rom responded honestly after relaying
Jarl's question to the council members. He carefully watched his
brother's response.

*"Had we not taken up the Triad, how many of us would have
survived?"* Jarl pressed and Rom relayed.

"Best case scenario, Lady Kahara and the alphas but in all
probability – no one."

*"Once the Triad was established, how much danger was your
lady mate in?"* Jarl continued his line of questioning.

"Virtually none."

*"How would you rate your lady's value and effectiveness in the
Triad?"*

"Without her and her unique skills bonded with ours, we would
all have died on the tundra."

*"I do not lightly interfere in your affairs, yet I am shaman and as
such I have my gifts and my sworn duties. I know the prophesies.
Your lady is the predestined hope of all our peoples. To shelter
her from her destiny will destroy not only your Triad but the
future of the entire sector. She is what she is. Honor her, protect
her, but do not stifle or underestimate her. She – your Triad – is
our only hope."* That said, the Taronian ambassador silently
turned and exited the conference chamber.

Rom relayed the shifter's powerful declaration to the council
before adding, "It looks to me like we will just have to be the first
ruling Triad in recorded history to go to war as a team."

"What are you thinking, brother? I will not have it! She is a gentle lady to be protected. She has not the size or skills to be a warrior," Rah protested.

"*She* is standing right next to you and more than capable of speaking for herself," Kahara snapped. "And if that is what you think, *mate*, then you don't know me at all. I would strongly suggest you make a concerted effort to correct that little oversight in the very near future," Kahara all but snarled, before following Lord Jarl out of the war room in a swirl of skirts.

Her departure was followed by shocked silence.

"Because this meeting cannot go on without all the required, and I might add, most valuable members, we will disperse and come together again tomorrow morning after first bell," Rom dictated. Though Rom, as usual, was calm and formal, Rah could swear his brother was hiding a smile.

~ *Chapter 24* ~

"This was supposed to be simple; find our mate, procure her, protect her, and breed her. What the hell happened?" a disgruntled Rah asked his brother as they walked together down the corridor on the way to their staterooms.

"Kahara happened," Rom answered as they entered their quarters.

"I have nothing I want to hear from you and less I want to say," Kahara told the two men the moment they stepped through the door. "I will see *you* in the training facility," she informed Rah, pushing one small forefinger into his massive chest to emphasize her demand before stomping out, wearing a form fitting black leather jumpsuit and matching boots. Her long hair was in a tight French braid that swayed on her back with her angry steps.

"Did you see what she was wearing?" Rah was incredulous.

"Yes, how could I miss it? The leather pants conform to her sweet little backside in a most pleasing fashion," Rom observed, looking longingly at the door she had slammed in her wake.

"*And* she just walked out, unescorted, into the common area of a ship full of warriors!" Rah shouted at his brother.

Both men hastened to follow her. When they reached the training facility, Kahara was standing, arms crossed, tapping her small, boot-clad foot in agitation.

All the warriors had stopped training, frozen in shock.

"I asked for a sword and short knives. What about that is so difficult to understand, Commander Marc?" she said in a deceptively soft voice.

"Lady, I do not think we have anything in your size," Marc tried to defend himself.

"Then come as close as you can and correct the deplorable lack at your earliest opportunity."

"Yes, ma'am," Marc said, looking over her shoulder at her mates that had, thankfully, just arrived.

"And, Commander Marc?"

"Yes, ma'am?"

"Feel free to look at me when you talk to me, not my mates."

"Yes, ma'am," Marc responded, quickly heading to the weaponry room to do her bidding.

When Marc returned with the requested sword, knives and scabbards, Rom rescued him by stepping forward and adjusting the belts to his mate's small frame. He was careful to be impersonal and efficient as he tended his lady, fully aware she was in no mood to be coddled or patronized. Marc hastened across the room to join his men.

"Do you prefer your sword on your left hip for a cross draw, your right hip for direct draw or on your back?" Rom asked. His tone was the same as he would have used to address any other warrior he was setting up with weaponry.

"Cross draw," she responded.

"Short knives on calf or thigh?"

"Left calf, right thigh."

Rom was impressed with her choices. The overly long sword would have impeded her ability to reach a short knife on her left thigh. By having one short knife on her calf and one on her thigh she insured their availability in a number of stances. Her diminutive size left her in a good position for throwing her opponent in a takedown. By not putting the sword on her back she was free to do so. The longer range of motion afforded by the cross draw position gave her more room to maneuver the long blade with her shorter arms while not opening up her protective fighting stance to do so.

Rom walked over to the locker that held his personal gear and withdrew his wrist bands. They were made of Tantanium – a living blue-black metal that would adjust to her smaller wrists. The bands would support her delicate bone structure and carpel joints while she wielded the heavy weapons.

Returning, he fastened them to her wrists and watched them adjust. Kahara heard the warriors across the room murmur amongst themselves at his action.

"Why do I get the feeling there is special significance to these bands?" she challenged.

"By placing my wrist bands on your wrists, I have committed myself to apprentice you in the wielding way. It is not a commitment taken lightly or often extended. Only the most skilled of apprentices are ever offered and never by a member of the ruling class."

"And you have offered this to me why?" she asked, suspicious and fully prepared to refuse if he was doing it simply because she was his mate.

"Because I deem you a worthy warrior, lady, and because you are a member of the ruling Triad. Only an equal may train you," Rom formally informed her. "Do you accept?"

"I am honored to do so, Lord Rom," she said, taking a step back, placing her right fist over her heart and bending slightly at the waist, surprising him with the appropriate response.

"Brother, what in the holy world of the gods are you doing?" Rah asked him on their private channel.

"Offering our lady her due. It is inevitable and I would have her well trained. I trust only you or me to do so and, though you are the superior warrior, unless I am mistaken, it is your ass she is preparing to kick. For you to offer would be a conflict of interests," Rom answered his brother, wry humor dripping off of every mental word.

"She cannot hope to take me on!"

"That, brother mine, remains to be seen."

To Rah's utter amazement, their petite mate walked over to the training mat in smooth determined strides. The warriors still gathered there evacuated posthaste. Turning, she crooked her forefinger at him in invitation.

"Lady, do you not think it wise to at least let Rom train you first?" he inquired.

"Lord, don't you think it wise to at least weapon up first?" she responded.

A pin drop could have been heard in the training room.

"I insist you be trained before meeting me," Rah arrogantly dictated.

"And what leads you to believe I have not been?" Kahara replied in equal arrogance. "It has been my experience that it serves well for warriors to demonstrate their current skills in order to establish the appropriate starting place for further training. Am I not correct Commander Marc?" she addressed the head of special ops, never taking her eyes off of Rah.

"Yes, ma'am, that is the accepted approach."

"I fear hurting you, lady," Rah protested in desperation.

"Do you doubt your control then?" Kahara challenged his skills.

"No, it is your weaker gender, childlike size, small bones and lack of skill that has me concerned," he insulted her in a raised voice.

"Fine, then call Saul in with a healing chamber on the off chance I break a nail," she hissed.

Rom could be heard calling Saul on his throat com while Rah stomped over to his locker and donned his sword, short knives and wrist bands in total exasperation.

This should take about a nanosecond – he was thinking, as he stepped up to his tiny mate on the training mat, curtly bowed and assumed the traditional fighting stance.

Kahara surprised him by returning his bow and taking up a stance of her own. It was not one he was familiar with but looked balanced and effective.

Rah sprang into action. With a lightning fast move, he whirled on Kahara intending to gently pin her and be done with it. It was a great strategy, except she was no longer there. To his utter disbelief, her sword *was* – seemingly suspended in thin air, the disembodied sword slapped him on the ass with the flat of the blade on his way by.

Kahara shimmered back into view on the other side of the mat. Rah crouched and turned toward her only to have her sword smack him again from behind, her image across from him fading out of existence.

He whirled back around just in time to be the recipient of a well-placed high kick to the bottom of his chin. He was too big and she too small for it to have knocked him down but he shook his head – swaying on his feet and seeing stars. He lunged at her. She dropped and rolled under his grasping arms, taking a chunk out of his leather pants with one of her short blades on her way by. She continued the roll and regained her feet across from him, dangling the severed leather between two delicate fingers and regarded him with a raised eyebrow. She had not even broken a sweat.

Rah returned to a fighting stance to regroup. Kahara courteously did the same. Rah dropped into a low crouch and swept at her legs with one of his in an attempt to take her off her feet. She jumped, knees high, and his sweeping kick passed harmlessly under her. She landed, immediately sprang into the air again, delivering a flying kick to the side of his head as he attempted to spin back around, resulting in more stars and headshaking on his part.

Before he could regain his equilibrium, she dropped and rolled between his widely braced legs, and came to her feet behind him in one smooth motion. This time she had one of *his* short blades and a sizeable chunk of the crotch of his pants in her hands.

He was learning to hate that little raised eyebrow of hers, he decided, hand going to his empty leg scabbard. Yup, as he feared, it *was* his knife in her delicate little fist. He had a strong suspicion it could just as well have been his balls in her other hand where the remains of his pants now resided.

Kahara irreverently threw both items over her shoulder with a casual toss before resuming her strange fighting stance.

Enough! Pulling out all the stops he charged her, planning to use his mass to bowl her over before she managed to hurt herself. Kahara held her ground until the last second when she spun with all the grace of a ballerina and planted her shapely hip into one of his. Dropping low, she took one of his massive arms and threw him over her back on her way around, using his momentum to slam him down on the mat. The entire facility shook with the impact of his three hundred pounds as he landed flat on his back.

All was still.

The entire room held its breath in utter amazement. Not one of the males present had ever put Commander and Chief Lord Rah Andor on his back. Yet, standing over him, with her sword pressed against his throat, his tiny mate seemed to have expected no other outcome.

"Yield the match?" she asked in a soft voice, speaking for the first time since the match began.

"I yield," he whispered, his eyes raking over her from his prone position.

"Damn, broke a nail," she hissed, examining the fingers of her free hand. She re-sheathed her sword, bowed to the prone Rah and left the room full of astonished warriors.

"How did you let her do that and have it look so convincing?" Marc wanted to know.

"I would never dishonor a warrior so," Rah responded, finally climbing back to his feet and proudly standing to his full seven foot stature. "I did not throw the match. It was fairly won by our lady." In so saying, he granted her equal status in the world of warriors. "If you gentlemen will excuse me, I will go see to our lady's broken nail."

"As you were." Rom ordered the speechless warriors back to their training as if nothing noteworthy had taken place. Casually gripping his wrist behind his back, he calmly followed his brother out of the facility.

"I will not allow you to reprimand her," Rom warned his silent brooding brother on the way to their staterooms.

"Reprimand her – hell, I fully intend to drop before her on my knees and beg her to train me," Rah ground out.

"Before or after you see to your exposed balls?" Rom inquired, eying Rah's ruined uniform pants and earning himself a caustic glare.

When he and his brother entered their rooms, Rah walked up to a wary Kahara, took her left hand and examined it.

"Just as I suspected," he exclaimed.

"What?" Kahara and Rom asked in unison.

"She lied. Lady Badass did not so much as break a nail."

~

"I will leave you two to debrief," Rom stated as he watched his brother and their mate regard each other in wary silence.

"Would you be willing to have Saul check you for damage?" Rah ventured in a soft voice, after the door closed behind his brother.

"Why? You never touched me," Kahara pointed out in confusion.

"I want to be sure you did not hurt yourself on me, little scrapper. You threw me, for the sake of the gods. Your smaller frame could have been damaged bearing my weight."

"It isn't as if I lifted you, Rah, I just helped you get where you were going, taking myself out of the equation. I'm fine."

Again they regarded each other in silence. Finally she dropped her eyes to the floor.

"I'm sorry, Rah, I lost my temper. I should never have shamed you in front of your warriors. I was totally in the wrong," she apologized in a small voice.

Rah walked over to her. Putting one large finger under her chin, he forced her head back until she looked into his eyes. His huge frame dwarfed her, his body heat crowded her and his scent raised havoc with her libido.

"You hurt my pride in the council and again when you called me weaker, childlike and lacking skill in front of your warriors. I just lost it. You are my mate. I should never have embarrassed you in such a way," Kahara went on.

"You are my pride, Kahara, not my shame. As the formidable warrior you are, you were fully in your rights to put me in my place."

"How can I possibly be your pride? I intentionally took advantage of your unwillingness to hurt me and made you look foolish," she agonized.

"How can I look foolish when your very skill shows my worth?"

"I don't understand?"

"The gods must consider me an exceptional warrior to have gifted me with a mate such as you. You are my pride, you have not shamed me," he reiterated.

"You're not mad at me?" she asked, searching his eyes.

"No, are you mad at me?" he countered.

"No, not any more. I was, though."

"You said, I do not know you," he reminded her of her earlier charge.

"I was mad, I had no right to say that either," she apologized.

"But there was truth to your statement. I have been so busy hiding from you in shame of my carnal nature that I have not allowed myself to truly know you. I judged you by what you are, a Fertile, rather than whom you are. I have misjudged you and underestimated you at every turn. There can be no excuse for this. You deserve better."

"I understand, Rah. It has not been easy for any of us. So much has happened so fast."

"I am a man of action, not a man of words. For you, I will try to deepen my communication skills. I want to know you, Kahara. I want to know the remarkable woman you are," he said, bringing his scarred warrior's hand to her soft face and running his callused thumb across her full lower lip.

"I love you, Rah," she stated, looking into his molten eyes as she nuzzled her face into his hand.

"How can you say this when I have not let you know me?"

"I cheated," she said, smiling. "I have read you. I know the measure of the man you are and I love that man, Rah, I love you where you have not even seen yourself."

He crushed her to his broad chest, overtaken by emotion. Somehow he knew what she said was true. He felt her in his very soul. She resided in a part of him he had not even visited.

Bending down, he covered her mouth with his and forced his tongue between her lips. She opened for him willingly. Their tongues dueled as he plundered the dark delicious recesses. As she opened her mouth to him he opened his mind to her. He let her see his pride in her, his desire of her. He let her see his fear of his love for her, fear of the weakness he thought it created. He showed her the deep shame he felt at what he viewed as his repeated failure to protect her, his doubt she had any need of him at all, given her own strength and fighting ability.

In return, she poured her love and acceptance into his mind and heart. She showed him her deep respect of him and his strength, his deep value as a leader, warrior and mate. She let him see how she trusted him with her mind, heart, body and soul. Then she shared her desire of him, how watching him fly the transport or command his men made her wet for him. How fighting him, full out, as he took care not to hurt her, had turned her on like no other.

Soon they found themselves on the carpet of the living room, tearing at each other's clothes, seeking the skin beneath and the ultimate intimacy to be found there. In no time they were naked, coming together in a frantic quest for union on all levels.

"Gods, lady, how I want you!" Rah exclaimed as he mantled over her, bracing his considerable weight on his powerful arms.

"Fill me, Rah, fill me with all that you are," she pleaded.

And fill her he did. Slowly, relentlessly, he sank his massive erection into her welcoming depths, stretching her impossibly as she wrapped her long legs around his hips, allowing him full access. He plunged deep, then slowly withdrew, allowing her to feel the passage of every ridge, until only the fat head remained inside. He held still, pausing ever so briefly, before slowly sinking into her again.

She opened her mind to him, allowing him to experience the glory of his possession. He reciprocated and she felt the devastation of her inner muscles gripping him like a fist. The shared sensations had them moaning in unison. The pace quickened until he was pounding into her uncontrollably, but he did not have to call his brother to protect her. Their mental bond had him fully apprised of the pleasure she knew in their joining.

Their coming together grew ever deeper, harder, and more violent until they both erupted. His roar and her screams blended in a celebration of their total union. Rah collapsed over her, barely able to brace his weight on his elbows, as he repeatedly sipped at her lips.

"So nice to see the two of you have kissed and made up," Rom stated from the doorway. "I could have forgone losing myself in my uniform while discussing weaponry with Marc, however. We are, after all, one in all things," he teasingly reminded. "Shall we share a bath before dinner? I am sure, at this point, we could all use one, and in my case, a change of pants as well."

"Rom, are you well? Should I send Saul to your quarters?" Marc's worried voice came over the com.

"I am fine, why ever would you ask?" Rom innocently inquired, looking down at his mate and brother still entwined on the floor in sardonic humor.

"Your eyes lost focus, you moaned in distress, convulsed repeatedly before running from the room in the middle of making a weapons order. Surely, my lord, you can imagine why I might be concerned," Marc replied.

"Oh, that. It must be a bug I picked up planet side. I will see Saul if I have reoccurring episodes," Rom promised before breaking the connection. "About that bath?" he asked the other members of his beloved Triad, arching one dark brow – silver eyes twinkling.

~ Chapter 25 ~

Immediately following Kahara's rescue from the Surrogate facility on Amon, Rah had ordered the planet put in quarantine and all communications jammed. It was unknown how many others in the United Alliance of Surrogate Planets were involved in the conspiracy, but according to intelligence reports coming in, things looked pretty grim.

It was the Council's hope that by enforcing a medical quarantine and communications blackout, they could investigate the situation and decide on a course of action before the other planets in the Alliance were any the wiser. For this to work, however, they were going to have to move quickly. Rah had ordered military backup, and several armed fleets from various members of the Daguronian Coalition were en route to their location.

As far as Rom and Rah were concerned, the complete military takeover of planet Amon was a foregone conclusion. The treatment of their mate, coupled with the reports of the Drones now in their service, made it clear the corruption ran deep rather than involving just a few factions of the operation.

While Rom, Rah, and Jarl, with a substantial escort of fighters, had accompanied Kahara to Taron for healing, the remainder of the fleet had stayed orbiting Amon and assuring its isolation and containment. Backup was due to arrive the next day and the council was hammering out final battle plans to overtake the planet.

~

"While I agree that we must first focus on the military takeover of Amon, I don't believe for a moment it is the head of the beast. I also see the necessity of simultaneously making moves to obtain control of the fertile population. If we do not set up provision for mates, we will not get the long term support we need from the members of the Coalition. As long as the Surrogate Alliance controls all the fertile population, they control the sector. In short, they have you all by the balls," Kahara addressed the council.

"Aptly put, Lady Kahara. Until we replace their services, we can never hope to conquer the Alliance," Head Tactician Kev agreed.

The meeting had been underway for several days during which time Rom, Rah and every other member of the council had become increasingly impressed with their lady's insights, grasp of the situation, and brilliant tactical skills. She was unorthodox in her approach and well versed in the rudiments of combat.

"Do you have any suggestions, Lady Kahara?" Commander Marc wanted to know.

"All of you know the situation much better than I, but from my perspective, we should set up a facility for fertile refugees and redirect all gathering missions to deliver there rather than the Surrogate planets. This facility should be prepared to perform numerous functions: deprogramming and rehabilitation of Fertiles rescued from the existing Surrogate system, reviving and training new Fertiles arriving from the gathering missions and placement of Fertiles with their mates."

"Who would you propose to head this project? This has been handled by the Surrogate Alliance for millennia. We have no one qualified to attempt such an operation," Chief Medical Officer Saul worried.

"Actually, I have been giving that some thought. My friend Rhiannon has a doctorate degree in social work and much experience in setting up shelters for battered women and Planned Parenthood clinics. She has been a women's advocate for years and has dedicated her life to just this sort of thing. She is being rehabilitated from stasis as we speak and will be in need of a place to redirect her gifts and passion," Kahara shared.

"Ambassador Jarl, what is your take on our lady's suggestion? You may speak freely as everything shared in council is held in the strictest confidence," Rom asked the shifter.

"I cannot speak for my lady Rhiannon as she does not know she is my mate, nor have I won her. There are many variables involved. Looking into it shamanically as a possible future event, I see it as a viable possibility and mutually beneficial outworking. Should the lady choose to accept me, I would be willing to help her head the project and contribute my healing skills to the facility to help deprogram and heal the refugees from the Surrogate planets. I am also adequately trained to serve as liaison with your forces and head security for the facility," Jarl spoke on their telepathic channel and Rom relayed to the council.

"How soon do you think Rhiannon can be approached with the proposal?" Rom ventured.

"She has yet to meet me in human form," Jarl replied in alarm.

"Not *that* proposal, Ambassador Jarl – that is between the lady and yourself. I refer to the job proposal," Rom clarified, hiding a smile.

"Naturally, Chief Medical Officer Saul has the last say, but I think she is ready now. It would give her something to look forward to. She is at loose ends, having lost her past life and not found her new one," Kahara stated.

"Saul?" Rom invited the doctor's input.

"I see no reason why not. She is physically strong enough."

"Then I will leave it to you, Lady Kahara, to address it with her," Rom instructed with a warm smile.

"We have not yet addressed the issue of providing Surrogates for the Fertiles," Drone Kane brought up. The twin brothers suddenly looked panicked as they simultaneously glanced at their mate.

"This meeting is adjourned until first bell tomorrow morning. The issue of Surrogates will be the first item on the docket." Rom and his brother quickly gathered their startled mate and evacuated the room.

~

"Come sit with us, little one. We need to talk," Rom ventured.

"Did I say something wrong in the meeting?"

"No, lady, everything you offered was not only appropriate but held great value," Rah hastened to assure her, glancing at his brother with worried eyes.

"It is about the issue of the Surrogates," Rom pressed forward. "There is additional information you will need about them before addressing it tomorrow."

"I thought we had all agreed to eliminate them from the program." Kahara was confused.

"No, they cannot be eliminated, lady," Rah said grimly.

"I don't see why not. The military can train and provide household guards, and nannies can also be trained. On earth most of the couples bring up their own children. I don't see why that can't be an option as well."

"Surrogates also perform the function of carrying the children." Rom flinched in anticipation of her response.

"Carrying as in how?"

"As in their womb. They carry and deliver all of our children. That is how and why they change gender," Rom clarified.

"Not our children, they won't! *I* will carry our children," Kahara firmly stated.

"No, lady, you will not," Rah dictated.

"What do you mean I will not? It is *my* choice." Her voice was starting to rise.

"Kahara, little one," Rom pleaded for understanding as he took her hand in his, "our children will be twin boys. They gestate close to two years. Each weighing twenty five pounds at birth. You physically cannot carry our children. None of the Fertiles can. That is why we have to have Surrogates."

"And you kept this from me *why*?" Kahara raged, pulling her hand out of his.

"It was in the educational material Zana failed to provide. By the time we realized you had not been debriefed, you were in your season and Rom in Satra," Rah informed her. "We were going to fill you in on all the particulars during our stay on Amon, but you were taken from us before we could."

"Oh god," Kahara moaned, burying her face in her hands. "I know I'm going to regret asking this, but just how do we get the babies in the Surrogate – with a damn test tube?"

"No, lady, once you are impregnated with our children, the transfer is made through natural intercourse," Rom explained.

"*Natural* intercourse?"

"With the Surrogate, Kahara. You have intercourse with your Surrogate. How else?" Rah snapped, not in the least happy with the prospect himself.

"I think I want to be alone with this for a while," Kahara whispered to her mates, not trusting herself.

"Kahara…"

"Now. Alone now. Leave!" she screamed at them.

Both men wisely complied.

~

"Lord Rah, your lady has called me to your quarters. Is she ill?" Chief Medical Officer Saul's worried voice came over the brother's com as they were walking down the corridor after evacuating their stateroom.

"Lady, are you well?" Rom immediately asked her over their Triad telepathic link.

"Just peachy. Leave me alone," was the curt reply, causing both brothers to flinch at the frigid response.

"She will probably be asking you to give her information on the medical function of Surrogates," Rah informed the doctor.

"Oh yes, that is first thing on the docket in the morning. I have to say, your lady is well prepared and well informed – a real asset to the council," the doctor complimented.

The brothers looked at each other and groaned.

"Should we warn him?" Rom asked Rah.

"No, he is on his own," Rah growled.

"Lord Rah, your lady has asked I come to your quarters. Is there a problem?" Drone Kane on the com this time.

Rah raised an eyebrow at his brother.

Rom put his hands to either side, palms up, and shrugged.

"She probably wants to consult with you on the function of Surrogates in preparation for tomorrow's meeting," Rom told the drone.

"I will be pleased to assist your lady in any way. She is a brilliant strategist, invaluable to our cause," Kane complimented.

Rom pleaded to heaven with his eyes.

"Lord Rah, Kev here, your lady has requested my presence in your chambers. Is there something I need to know?"

"She is gathering information for tomorrow's meeting."

"A most worthy mate you have in our lady, sir. Her brilliance continues to amaze me."

"Lords, your lady mate has requested my presence in your quarters..." Jarl began on their telepathic channel.

"Yes, we have a problem here," Rah snapped, drawing a startled look from Rom. *"We just had to inform our heretofore ignorant mate of the true function of a Surrogate and how the embryonic transfer is accomplished."*

"She did not know?"

"Zana left it out of her education."

"This could be bad."

"Tell us about it," Rah agreed. *"Will you be sleeping in your lady's quarters as wolf tonight?"* Rah queried.

"Yes, I would leave her protection to no other."

"My brother and I may have need of your stateroom tonight. Would you mind if we use it?"

"That bad?"

"Yes, every bit that bad," Rah assured him.

"By all means, make yourselves at home. You may find you need to turn up the temperature as it is set for an arctic wolf. What do you wish for me to share with your lady?"

"We will leave that to your discernment. As her healer and friend we totally trust your judgment. Well," Rah amended, "share anything other than this conversation."

~

As Rom called the meeting to order the next morning, he watched their lady mate out of the corner of his eye where she sat between his brother and him at the head of the council table. She looked elegant and refreshed in a mint green confection that left her creamy shoulders bare. He considered the fact she wore the emerald Triad pendant and earrings as a good sign. Her expression was serene, her bearing confident – no one could tell she had a worry in the world.

He and his brother had spent a cold restless night sharing Jarl's huge, low pallet-bed. They would no sooner drift off when one or the other of them would reach for their soft mate and encounter a gnarly grumpy brother instead. They would blow apart and take up opposite sides of the bed just to suffer a reoccurrence in a couple of hours. The night had not been restful nor had it been pleasant.

"The first item on the docket this morning is the issue of making provision for Surrogate service." Rom cringed inwardly.

"I have taken the liberty of consulting with the authorities and have some findings I would like to share with the council," Kahara announced in the wake of Rom's opening statement.

"By all means, lady, you have the floor."

"Upon consulting with medical authorities, I have discovered that approximately ninety-eight percent of the few Fertiles remaining in the Daguronian Sector are incapable of carrying their own children. From information gathered through shamanic divination, Lord Jarl and I have ascertained that these limitations were intentionally bred into the species, as was the sterile condition of the majority of the native females. While it may be possible to reverse this dysfunction, correction will not take place on a wide scale until generations into the future.

"Consultation with our local authority on Surrogates, Drone Kane, brings to light the importance of Surrogates being in close proximity to the Fertile in order to align with her frequency. This enables the Surrogate to provide an intrauterine environment attuned to that of the natural mother. However, it is not necessary to have sexual relations to achieve this. That particular practice was developed by the Surrogate planets to better market their services and alienate the Fertiles from their mates. Normal day to day social interaction and occasional ingestion of the mother's blood is more than adequate to provide the alignment needed.

"Passing the fertilized eggs from the mother to the Surrogate is largely unsuccessful when attempted by artificial means. The exchange is best made body to body. However, Drone Kane also informs me that the aping of intercourse during the procedure was also developed for exploitive purposes. The process was originally a highly sacred ceremony shared with both the mother and father or fathers present. The current practices are considered an abomination by the traditionalists among the Drone population.

"Drone Kane has also shared the origins of the Surrogates. The race was initially cloned to provide an alternative to pregnancy and delivery for the very rich and pampered females of your race. Over the years, the Alliance of Surrogate Planets manipulated the DNA of the embryos the Surrogates carried to produce the situation we now have. Apparently it was a well-executed, long term plan to gain monopoly of a necessity they created.

"Tactician Kev informs me that, given the scope of this long term conspiracy, and in light of the sophisticated programming techniques used on me in their facility, this is not an isolated incident. He calculates the probability of deep corruption in every member of The United Alliance of Surrogate Planets is in the ninety-ninth percentile.

"Our Chief Medical Officer Saul has assured me you have the technology and knowledge to reproduce the cloning procedure using the DNA donated by our Drone allies. By using Drone DNA rather than Surrogate DNA, we will revert back to the pure form of the race. The original Surrogates, now referred to as Drones, change from male to female during pregnancy but, unlike the current Surrogates, revert back to male after delivery. This allows them to surrogate more than one child. We all believe the Drones to be much better suited to the need at hand.

"Our Drone allies have indicated their willingness to provide the DNA and head the project. We should have the next generation of Drones available to carry children in seven years. Drone Kane believes he and his men can obtain enough Drones from the Traditionalist Underground on the Surrogate planets to provide not only a wide cross-section of DNA, but an adequate number of Drone/Surrogates for our Fertiles until the new generation becomes available."

One could almost hear the shattering of former realities amongst the members of the council as a result of their lady's report. To a male they were shocked speechless.

"What do you see as our next steps?" Marc asked after a long, pregnant silence in the council chamber.

"That, I feel I must defer to my mates, Lords Rom and Rah Andor as rulers of the Daguronian Sector, and to their most competent council members. I have only four additional items I would draw attention to at this time:

"One, it may be wise to maintain quarantine and communications blackout but not attack Amon. We can use fabricated reports of solar flares to explain loss of communication, and the resulting radiation poisoning could be the reason for quarantine. We should draw back our fleets in order to not draw attention until Drone Kane has the opportunity to contact the other Traditionalist Underground members in the Alliance.

"Two, in order to not prematurely alert the Alliance that we are aware of their activities, it would probably be best to slow down – but not altogether stop – deliveries made by gathering operations.

Instead, we could recruit loyal, hopefully petite Amazons – if such beings exist – and use those deliveries as Trojan horses.

"Three, in the future, gathering and placement of Fertiles, and Surrogate services should be kept as totally separate operations to prevent the reoccurrence of this monopoly.

"Four, I would ask that Drone Kane conduct his duties remotely."

"What is a Trojan?" Rah asked.

"A wonderful Earth legend I will share in its entirety tonight by the fire if you like but, in short, a way of infiltrating the enemy camp."

"What prompts your request for Drone Kane serving remotely?" Rom wanted to know.

"That would be another fireside story," she answered him, smiling serenely.

~

"There is the fire, we are sitting beside it, I would hear this story of the Trojans," Rah informed his mate as she sat between him and his twin on the oversized couch.

"First I want to hear about Drone Kane," Rom argued.

"Okay, first Drone Kane and then the Trojan Horse," Kahara conceded.

"After intensive research I have concurred with my mates' opinion that I do indeed need a Surrogate. I have considered my options and decided that Drone Kane would be the best choice. I have not approached him as I wanted to seek the consultation of my mates. If you both agree that he is the best option, we will approach him with the request. Should he be willing to serve in that capacity, he will most likely be pregnant with our offspring in the not so distant future. In order to keep him safe and still on active duty providing his formidable knowledge and connections, remote direction of the operation would be the best option."

"Perfect, pristine and infallible logic, lady mate," Rah complemented in amazement.

"I have my moments."

"You were absolutely unbelievable in council today, little one. The entire Daguronian Sector will forever be in your debt," Rom praised, running his knuckles down her velvet cheek in a loving caress.

Not knowing how to respond to the compliment, Kahara began the promised tale, eyes twinkling, as both giant warriors gave her their undivided attention like a couple of small boys.

"Once upon a time, on ancient Earth, there raged a war between two powerful races – the Greeks and the Trojans. Seeking to gain entrance into the well-armed and sealed city of Troy, an inventive Greek warrior ordered a large wooden horse to be built. Its insides were to be hollow so that soldiers could hide within it.

"During the night, they built the statue and their warriors climbed inside. The next day the Greek fleet sailed away, leaving the giant horse behind.

"The Trojans came to the shoreline, wondering at the huge construction left on the beach after the departure of the Greeks. The Trojans celebrated what they thought was their victory, and dragged the wooden horse through the gates into Troy as spoils of war.

"That night, after most of Troy was asleep or in a drunken stupor, the Greek warriors came out from the horse, and slaughtered the Trojans."

~ *Chapter 26* ~

"As Head Tactician, I must point out that the Triad must be impeccable as it will not only be the ruling entity for the entire Daguronian Sector, but it will also serve as *the* model for our future," Kev stated when given the floor at the council meeting the following morning.

"Your point being?" Rah challenged.

"The Chalice of the Karinian Triad must be legally bonded to her mates as soon as possible. The legitimacy of the Triad must be above reproach," Kev announced, shocking the entire council.

"Who is he talking about?" Kahara whispered to Rom.

"You, lady, he is talking about you. You are the Chalice," Rom answered, clearly upset by the turn the meeting had taken.

"As head of security might I remind you, during the current situation with the Alliance of Surrogate Planets, to take our lady to a Presentation Gala in order to enter into prenuptial negotiations would be to put her at great risk," Rah informed Kev, every bit the Commander and Chief of the Daguronian forces.

"Nonetheless, negotiations must be concluded, documents signed and the bonding ceremony completed in order to solidify the Triad and secure the Chalice. Until that has taken place, she will be at risk of abduction and the Triad subject to invalidation," Kev insisted.

"Given the subject involves the personal lives of the members of the Triad, I request we adjourn, allowing them time for a private discussion," Rom stated, no less agitated than his twin. "This meeting will resume first bell tomorrow morning."

~

"I will not allow the council to dictate our private lives," Rah raged while pacing the floor of their staterooms.

"I don't think Kev intended to dictate to us, but rather to indicate what you have to admit is a valid point," Rom replied.

"Valid point or not, she deserves more time. I will not have her pressured into this," Rah countered. "Nor will I compromise her safety to satisfy a bunch of politicians."

"Once again, she is standing right here and she has some questions, if the two of you don't mind." Kahara's irritation was clear in her voice.

"My apologies. We have discussed things just between the two of us all of our lives. It is not our intent to exclude you. Old habits tend to die hard," Rah apologized. "What are your questions?"

"Well, I have built up quite a few: What is a Chalice? What is a Presentation Gala? What are prenuptial negotiations? What did Zeb mean by legally bonded? Why do I need more time? And lastly, what am I being pressured into?"

The brothers looked at each other helplessly.

"The Chalice is the destined and bonded mate of the ruling mirror twin brothers of Dagur. A Presentation Gala is a formal ball where Fertiles are first presented to the public in search of their mate. Prenuptial negotiations are where we form a legal agreement as to what you demand in exchange for your bonding with us and giving us exclusive rights to sire your children. Legally bonded is much like your Earth concept of marriage but it is for life. We have no divorce.

"We had hoped to give you more time to get to know us better and better understand what arrangements you prefer in the prenuptial agreement. I do not want you pressured into finalizing our bonding. I want you to do it because it is your desire to join with us once you fully understand what all it implies," Rah answered.

"In that case, I see no need for a gala as I have already found my mates. We did discuss prenuptials and I told you I am very comfortable working things out as we go. As my mates, you will naturally sire our children – I thought that was covered in the ceremony of the red goblet. As far as I am concerned, I am already bonded to you both so there is no pressure involved. I don't need more time to know what I want. I love you – it is you I want – end of story. So as I see it, all we need is a legal binding marriage ceremony. Is there something I'm missing here?"

The brothers looked at each other again. Rom shrugged. Rah pinched the bridge of his nose. Kahara looked from one to the other in growing concern. What if they had changed their minds? Maybe they wanted out. Were they the ones being pressured into something *they* were unsure of?

"Don't you want to be bonded to me?" Kahara asked in a worried voice at their continued silence.

"That is our utmost, driving desire, little one. We just want to insure you are safe and fairly treated," Rom assured her. "The way this was supposed to go was for us to acquire you from Earth, deliver you to the Surrogate planet for training and matching with your Surrogate. Then we would have courted you, offered for you at a gala. Had you accepted us, we would have worked out the prenuptial agreement and had a bonding ceremony. You then would have taken up residence at your chosen resort until your season, at which point the bonding would have been consummated."

"I can only thank god that things did not go according to plan," Kahara stated dryly.

"On that we are in full agreement, though we both would have gladly died to prevent the damage we caused you during your cycle and your abduction," Rah stated.

"Surely, we can find a way to satisfy the requirements even though, given the vindicating circumstances, we can't be expected to fulfill them in the traditional ways," Kahara suggested.

"As we are their rulers, the people will expect to witness our formal bonding. You deserve the finest ceremony we can provide. Yet to expose you to the masses is to risk you," Rah worried.

"We also have to be sure all the legal requirements are met to satisfy the dictates of our station as ruling Triad," Rom added.

"Why can't we hold a formal ceremony on the flagship and broadcast it? Couldn't we also import whatever officiates we need to satisfy the legal requirements?" Kahara asked.

"Excellent idea, little scrapper, I will get intelligence working on a legal, viable solution," Rah stated before leaving to set things into motion. He could hardly contain his joy – their lady mate had just granted them the final bonding. He hadn't realized how terrified he had been that she would not. True, he had not wanted to pressure her, but ultimately he feared her rejection. He had no illusions – he had handled her like a bumbling brute from the very beginning.

Rom turned to Kahara in the wake of his brother's departure and pulled her into his arms, stroking her hair.

"Thank you, lady, I don't know what we did to deserve you," he said, knowing he spoke for his brother as well. He could feel Rah's joy adding to his own overflowing heart.

~

That night Kahara was surprised when the brothers informed her that they had arranged a special meal to be delivered to their stateroom rather than go to the formal dinner in the captain's dining room.

"How did you know I have enjoyed about all the assemblies I can stand?" she asked her mates.

"I think we are all sick of council and negotiations, little one, but we are dining in to share an intimate evening with our lady." Rom walked up to her, gently taking her by the shoulders to pull her into his embrace. He kissed the top of her head before releasing her for his brother to greet. Rah surprised her by lifting her off of her feet in a bear hug. He took her mouth in a short, devastating kiss before setting her back on her feet.

"Wow!" Kahara gasped, fanning herself. "What did I do to deserve *that*?"

Rah cast a devilish grin over his shoulder on his way into the master suite to change out of his uniform.

"You have transformed my brother, Kahara. I have never seen him so happy," Rom told her before going to change as well.

Deciding to lose her formal dress, Kahara went to her dressing room and shed the heavy garment.

"What I wouldn't give for a set of sweats and a pizza," she murmured to herself, scanning her closet for something comfortable. She settled on a scooped-neck sheath in soft shades of amber silk. At least it was light and loose fitting, unlike the yards of heavy fabric that comprised most of her gowns.

"What are these sweats and pizza you so lust after?" Rah's mental voice caressed her mind. She sent him a mental image in response. *"The garments are hideous and the food looks like something's flattened innards!"* he declared in disgust. She giggled.

When she returned to the sitting room, both brothers stood from their chairs to greet her. They were dressed in black leather pants and silk shirts opened at the throat. With their molten silver eyes, long black hair tied back at their napes and muscles rippling with their movements, they took her breath away.

"You are a vision, lady. I so prefer that lovely dress to the despicable, unsightly rags you projected to me. Would you truly enjoy donning such an abomination?" Rah inquired.

"Don't knock it till you try it. They make them for men, too," she smiled up into his face as he took her arm and guided her to the dining room where a veritable feast awaited.

The table was intimately and formally set for three with linen, porcelain, crystal and candlelight. The side board held numerous covered dishes, and wait staff stood in attendance. As soon as Rah sat her in her chair and Rom positioned it under the table, a waiter placed a crisp linen napkin in her lap. Another poured them wine.

Dinner was delicious and relaxing, even with the formal staff attending. Throughout the evening the brothers watched her closely, admiring her with identical molten mercury eyes. When dessert had been consumed, the staff cleaned up and cleared out with efficient grace. The Triad retired to the living room with small crystal glasses filled with a delicious cordial.

"Come, lady, sit with us," Rom invited. The three of them settled into the comfortable oversized sofa with Kahara in the middle. "We have been studying Earth customs," he continued.

"Why?" Kahara asked in surprise.

"We want to do right by you according to both our ways and yours," Rah answered for his brother.

She loved that about them. They truly were one in all things – totally complimenting each other like two mirror halves of a whole.

They stood up at the same time, each coming down on one knee in front of her. Rah took her by the left hand while Rom reached into his pocket, drew out a ring and held it up to her. It was made of two bands, one silver, the other gold – woven together forming an intricate Celtic knot. The weave parted slightly to surround a sizeable, brilliant blue diamond.

"Lady Kahara, would you do us the honor of becoming our wife?" they asked in unison, looking into her eyes. She could feel Rah's fear of rejection and Rom's solid enfoldment.

"Understand, lady, in our way – in this marriage – there will be no divorce," Rah warned in a gruff voice before she could answer.

"No," she firmly stated. Both brothers braced themselves for the ultimate devastation. "No, there will be no divorce, and yes, I will marry you. You are the love of my life. I will gladly tie myself to you both for all time."

Rah held her hand up while Rom slid the beautiful ring onto her finger. It was done with a deliberate, if gentle, finality.

"You have just granted us our deepest desire, little one. We both want this to be perfect for you," Rom said, taking her into his arms and holding her against his trembling frame. "We understand it is no small thing to take on not one, but two mates and the responsibility of co-ruling an entire sector."

"We will dedicate our lives to making sure you never regret your trust in us," Rah assured, coming up behind, pulling her long hair aside and kissing her neck.

"Rah has seen to all the arrangements for our bonding ceremony to take place in two days' time. The officials will be here by then, and that gives us opportunity to write up the prenuptial agreement for them to approve."

"But I said I don't need one…," Kahara began.

"We know, little scrapper, and we appreciate your trust, but legally there must be one in place before the bonding can be completed. Rom and I thought the three of us could draw something up that is mutually acceptable."

"This brings us to another subject – your Surrogate. Do you feel prepared to ask Drone Kane?" Rom asked.

"Yes, the sooner the better," she responded.

"I have looked into the archives and there is ceremony involved in the old ways that you need to be aware of." Rom searched her eyes.

"What ceremony?" Rah and Kahara asked in unison.

"Once the Surrogate is chosen, there needs to be an exchange of blood to complete the Surrogate's attunement to the parents. It is a sacred ceremony involving much reverence and tenderness among the participants. Intercourse is not required nor is it necessarily ruled out, but nudity is involved."

"Is this really necessary?" Rah growled.

"The attunement is necessary for the Surrogate to safely carry the fetus. The ceremony is to honor and accept Drone Kane. Given all he has done and will be to us, I think it is our duty to honor his ancient traditions," Rom answered.

Kahara nodded. "I agree. As ruling Triad we need to set precedence. The Drones hold fast to tradition and that needs to be honored, given all they are willing to provide."

"Though I like it not, I have to bow to your infallible logic and integrity, lady," Rah agreed. He spoke into his throat com. "Drone Kane, could you come to our quarters?"

"Yes, my lord," Kane immediately answered.

"He is on his way," Rah informed his brother and their mate, just before the door chime sounded announcing the Drone's arrival.

"My lords and lady," Kane addressed them, placing a fist over his heart and bowing respectfully. "How can I serve?"

"Thanks for coming so promptly, Drone Kane. Please have a seat and share a glass of cordial with us. I have something I wish to ask of you," Kahara addressed him.

"As you wish my lady," Kane responded, taking the indicated chair.

Rom handed him a glass before sitting across from him on the couch with Rah and Kahara. They sipped in silence for a while before Kahara, realizing the choice of Surrogate was hers to make, took the initiative.

"Drone Kane, I want you to know there will be no hard feelings should you refuse my request."

"Lady, I can think of nothing I would deny you," he responded, somewhat perplexed.

"Would you do me the honor of being my Surrogate?"

Kane looked like a giant fish out of water as his mouth worked but no sound came. Kahara had begun to fear he would refuse when he stood from his chair and knelt before her, fist over his heart.

"Lady, you do me the greatest of honors. Never did I think, coarse beast that I am, I would ever have the privilege of serving as Surrogate, much less to the ruling Triad. I most gratefully accept."

"Rom has researched the archives and found there is an ancient bonding ceremony that was held between Surrogates and their prospective families. Is this ceremony part of the old ways that you hold to?" Kahara asked the Drone.

"Yes, lady, but I would not expect you to submit to it. I can probably manage with a small taste of your blood."

"Is there a more complete attunement achieved with the ceremony?"

"Yes, lady."

"My mates and I have chosen to honor your ways by holding to the sacred rites of your race."

"You honor me and all my kind. There are no words."

"We see no need to wait, Drone Kane. Are you prepared to move forward?" Rah asked.

"Yes, my lord."

"Where is the best location for the ceremony?" Rom inquired.

"In ancient times there were temples with ceremonial quarters. Lacking that, I would respectfully suggest a bedroom, my lord. But first, our lady needs to ingest the blood of her mates to finalize their genetic bond and grant her immortality."

"Immortality?" Kahara questioned.

"Yes, little one, once we have completed the final bonding we would have given you our blood. Once accepted you will be granted the same life span as your mates."

"And you live how long?"

"Unless we are divested of our head or heart, or obtain damage the healing chamber cannot correct in time, we are virtually an immortal race. For example, when Rah broke his leg in the crash and succumbed to infection, without the intervention of a healing chamber, he would have been lost to us," Rom explained.

Rah poured a glass of wine and brought it to his brother. Rom let his fangs down, ripped his own wrist open and allowed his blood flow into the wine. After a short time he ran his tongue over the wound, sealing it. Rah took the glass and repeated the same procedure.

Rah and Rom stood in front of their lady, both men holding the glass to her lips.

"Drink of the red goblet once more that we may become as one for eternity," they whispered in unison.

Looking deeply into the eyes of her beloved mates, Kahara drank as they bid her without question. Her trust of and dedication to them was clearly demonstrated by the act.

They all adjourned to the huge master. The soft lighting, flickering fire, and glowing fish tank lent a surreal quality to the environment. All three men disrobed. Kahara was overwhelmed with the combined male beauty as they surrounded her where she stood before the fireplace.

Rom approached her and gently unfastened her gown, sliding it off of her shoulders to pool on the floor. She was left standing in nothing but her lace thong. Rom stood back and Kane approached, his electric blue eyes searching hers from under a lock of his long, thick blonde hair.

"Lady, you were greatly mistreated by my race. I have no wish to further traumatize you. Are you sure you are up to this?" he quietly asked.

"Yes, Kane, I am fully recovered. Lord Jarl saw to my healing and I totally trust all three of you," she responded without hesitation.

Kane reached up and gently framed her face with his huge hands, brushing his full lips over hers in a tender caress. Rah embraced her from behind and Rom came up behind Kane.

Kane deepened the kiss, slanting his warm mouth over hers and delving inside. She returned his kiss without hesitation while Rah pressed his torso into her from behind, sealing her breasts to Kane's broad chest. She felt Kane shudder at the contact.

Rom reached around Kane and took Kahara's hips, pulling her flush with Kane's raging erection, and the kiss became more carnal. Kahara put her arms around the big Drone's neck and participated fully. Kane shook with passion.

Rah's huge member was up against the small of her back and he began to rub it along her spine. He kissed her neck and fondled the sides of her breasts where they were crushed against Kane's hair roughened chest. Rom filled both of his hands with her rear, pulling her tighter against the Drone and rubbed her against Kane's erection.

Kane pulled back from the kiss and looked into Kahara's eyes. He was shaking uncontrollably. His irises had become slit like a cat's, eyes glowing neon blue, and fangs peeking out from beneath his full upper lip.

"I commit my life to your sacred Triad and to your children," he formally stated, then sank his fangs into Kahara's throat. She arched in shock and pain just before ecstasy took her. Kane drank at her vein while convulsing against her belly in orgasmic rapture. Rom and Rah embraced them tightly and sank their fangs into either side of the Drone's neck, drinking deeply.

The Triad mental link now included Kane and they all shared in his unending climax until Kahara became overwhelmed and lost consciousness, sagging between them. Kane sealed her vein with a swipe of his tongue. Rah lifted her and took her to their bed, reverently covering her.

"Have I harmed your lady?" Kane asked in concern. "I tried to be mindful not to hold her too tightly or take too much."

"She is well, just temporarily overcome," Rah assured him, still linked with the Triad.

"It was my understanding the kiss and the taking of the lady's blood was just for the combination of the Triad's DNA. I mistakenly assumed the rapture was just a myth. Had I known, I would have had you restrain me," Kane agonized.

"Be at ease, you showed amazing restraint, Drone Kane," Rom assured him. See, she is already waking." He indicated the bed where Kahara regarded them with sleepy emerald eyes.

"Damn, what a rush!" she whispered before closing her eyes again.

The men were sitting in the living room discussing the Drone's requirements for proximity to Kahara in order to maintain the attunement when she emerged from the bedroom wearing her silk shift.

"My lady, are you well?" Kane anxiously inquired, immediately standing in her presence.

"Yes, I'm fine. Thanks for your concern."

"Come sit, little one, we were just preparing a contract and discussing Drone Kane's needs," Rom greeted her. "All that is required is your signature," he continued, indicating the port on the coffee table. "This makes Kane officially your Drone. With his amazing ability to return to male after delivering our child, he can be your only Surrogate should you so choose."

"Drone Kane, would you be willing to serve as my sole Surrogate should I have more than one pregnancy?" Kahara asked.

"My life is in service to you, lady. I will surrogate all of your children and guard you and them until I draw my last breath," he formally accepted.

"What would you like in exchange for your services?" Rom asked again, indicating the port where he was writing up the contract.

"Nothing beyond the amazing privilege you have granted me," Kane responded, taken aback by the offer.

"I would request that you retain your position as head of the Allied Drone Unit," Rom stated. "I trust no other with the position."

"I am honored! Never had I hoped to aspire to such a station, much less keep it upon becoming Surrogate to the Triad," Kane acknowledged the magnitude of Rah's offering.

"As Surrogate to the Royal Triad, all of your needs will be met. Should you desire anything at all for your health or comfort, it will be provided. We will start with adjoining quarters to us in each of our residences, including this ship. You will have uniforms suitable to your military station and custom made weapons," Rom continued. "I will indicate this in the contract and the four of us will sign it, establishing a new precedent for the treatment of Surrogates. No longer will you be bought and sold. You will have equal rights, your services negotiated for and your interests protected by contractual agreement."

And so the new order began. The ruling Triad transformed the very fabric of the former exploitative system with one of loyalty, synergy and mutual respect among species.

~ Epilogue ~

The Royal Triad stood together, one huge brother on either side of their diminutive mate. The Chalice was dressed in a pearl incrusted, pure white gown complete with veil and train in the way of her home world. The Mirror twins wore formal black uniforms with sashes crossing their impressive chests, one gold, the other silver, attached at the hip in common with their lady. The bonding was dully officiated and broadcast across the galaxies from the banquet room on the flag ship of the Daguronian Fleet.

"It is done. The Triad is legally bonded. The prophecy is fulfilled and the tide of change has begun!" Ambassador Lord Jarl Lyall sent to Shaman Belinu on his home world.

"I am complete," his great-great grandfather's distant reply.

About the Author

Having been brought up overseas and living with local families in many cultures, Cahira O'Donnell has a rich history to draw upon. Throughout her life and her travels she has been a dedicated student of shamanism and an explorer of the esoteric realms. Being psychic herself, Cahira's real-life experiences with the supernatural infuses her paranormal romance writing with profound accuracy.

Armed with her history, combined with a degree in Psychology and a deep understanding of human nature, Cahira creates stories that are engaging, dynamic, realistic and boldly erotic.

Cahira now lives in the beautiful mountains of Colorado where she enjoys a quiet home, beautiful scenery and immersing herself in the art of storytelling.

To learn more about Cahira and her novels visit:
www.cahiraodonnell.com

Read on for a look at

THE ORACLE
OF VIDAR

THE DAGURONIAN
CHRONICLES

BOOK 2

By Cahira O'Donnell

COMING SOON!

From Dark River Publishing

CAHIRA O'DONNELL

THE ORACLE
OF VIDAR

THE DAGURONIAN
CHRONICLES BOOK TWO

THE ORACLE OF VIDAR

By Cahira O'Donnell

~ *Chapter 1* ~

Taken from her bed and abducted by aliens was about the last way Michelle expected to spend Monday morning. She had gone to sleep the night before like any other night, fully planning to get up with her alarm, brew some coffee and grab a power bar on her way out the door to work.

Instead, at about 2:00 am she'd been awakened by a huge hand over her mouth and brilliant, moss-green eyes staring down at her from behind long hanks of black hair. The male hulking over her in silence was close to seven foot tall, dark skinned and deeply muscled.

She froze, looking up at him with shocked amber eyes. His cheek bones were high, his nose straight, mouth full and sensual. He searched her eyes, nostrils flaring as he inhaled, taking in her scent.

She realized he was alien as his eyes shifted, glowing brilliant florescent green. His irises became oval like a cat. He pulled back his generous lips in a silent snarl, exposing sharp canines.

It was as close to wetting the bed Michelle had come in her adult life.

Shaking uncontrollably, she whimpered from behind his hand. He tightened his grip, pinning her head to the bed, and pulled the covers down to her waist. She was horrified.

In the summer she slept in the nude and her full breasts were suddenly exposed. The cool air caused her nipples to pucker, drawing his unearthly gaze. His eyes grew unbearably brighter, his canines lengthened as he leaned down, sinking his teeth into her neck where it met her shoulder. His other hand wrapped around her breast, the thumb teasing her nipple.

Michelle had grabbed him by his long thick hair with both hands, trying to force him away when she felt his teeth penetrate. She fully expected him to rip her throat out or at least drain her dry, but he simply held on with his teeth, running his tongue over her skin in languid strokes. At first it was painful, but pain soon gave way to sensuality as his tongue caressed her sensitive neck and his rough thumb stimulated her erect nipple.

What was wrong with her? Accosted in her own bed by an alien monster and she was becoming aroused? Feeling herself increasingly impaired, she realized he was actually injecting her with some sort of poison rather than drinking from her. Soon her body was no longer her own. She couldn't lift a finger to protect herself. A surreal lethargy overtook her and her arms fell helplessly back to the bed.

After releasing his bite, he ran his warm, rough tongue over the wound before sitting back on his haunches. All she could do was watch him with hooded eyes as he took his hand from her mouth. He leaned into her again and nibbled at the corner of her bruised lips, running the tip of his tongue over them in a soothing caress. His breath was sweet and spicy, his scent alien, yet masculine and clean.

He stood and pulled her covers the rest of the way off. She was defenseless. Like a cat held by the nape, her muscles refused to respond. He pulled the top sheet free and gently wrapped it around her before lifting her into his arms as if she weighed no more than a child.

Powerful, long legged strides took him from her small house into the back yard. She felt his muscles bunch as he leapt straight into the air, easily clearing the six foot fence and landing in an empty lot just as sirens started to go off. By the time he reached the center of the vacant property, she could hear a tornado approaching like a freight train.

Michelle couldn't move her head to see where the twister was coming from, but she could see straight above where a silent black craft suddenly appeared. A sling was lowered and her captor strapped her into it. He hung on to the strapping with casual strength as they were lifted into the craft.

Large hands reached for her to pull them into the open door, but her captor snarled at the other males. They took his outstretched arm instead, pulling them both on board. Huge doors slid shut silently, completely blocking out the sound of the approaching tornado.

The alien lifted her from the sling and carried her to a seat where he lowered himself and arranged her on his lap. Restraints automatically dropped over them, securing them in place. Michelle could feel her stomach drop to the floor as the silent craft sped away.

No more than thirty minutes had passed when she felt the craft bank and slow. As she looked up at the alien who held her in his lap, she noticed his long hair lifting to float around his head. Her scalp prickled as hers did the same.

When the restraints suddenly released, their bodies literally floated out of the seat. The man held her to his muscular chest with one arm while pulling them along using handholds located on the wall of the craft.

As they reached a door, he waited until it slid open before drifting through a tube into a much larger craft. Other men moved as if to follow, but her captor warned them off with a snarl and a show of canines.

When they entered the second vessel, her somersaulting stomach was grateful to feel gravity slowly return. He carried her down a long corridor, gravity increasing with every step until it felt almost normal. His long black hair lifted and fell with his strides, his bright green eyes returning to her face often as if assessing her condition.

They entered a large sterile looking room furnished in metal. He gently placed her on a gurney and proceeded to undress. Taking off his black jumpsuit with efficient movements, he placed it in a lidded container.

She was shocked by the sheer size and beauty of his naked body. Bronze skin covered massive musculature. His chest was hairless, wide and deeply muscled. His abdomen rippled with an impressive six pack. He had long powerful arms and legs, but what caught and held her attention was the thick, fully erect member that reached above his navel.

At seeing her eyes lock onto his manhood and widen, his full sensual lips lifted ever so slightly. He leaned over her, his long thick hair brushing her face. To her utter embarrassment he removed her sheet and placed it in the same container as he had his jumpsuit. He lifted her into his arms against his naked chest. With her body still not responding, she had no choice but to remain compliant against his warm, powerful form.

He carried her to a large vertical cylinder set into the wall that slid open upon his approach. After stepping inside, the cylinder promptly shut them in. They were bathed in a blue light that made her skin tingle. The back of the cylinder slid open, letting them out into another room with a bathing pool filled in clear liquid, steps leading down into it.

He entered the pool. She could feel the warm, thick liquid covering her body as he went deeper. His eyes met hers as if trying to communicate something before slowly lowering them both until their heads were entirely submerged. She managed to grab a breath of air at the last minute when she finally understood his intent.

He carried her out of the pool and into another cylinder in the opposite wall. This time they were blasted with air that dried their skin and hair before being let out into another room. The gurney he placed her on was padded – much more comfortable than the first one which had been cold hard metal. He wrapped her in a soft blanket, crossed over to a locker and pulled out a charcoal uniform, dressing quickly.

He came back to the gurney, a door opened and another man, clad in a light blue jumpsuit, entered. The newcomer approached, but stopped in seeming surprise when he looked at her. He pulled the blanket from her shoulders and looked at the bite mark on her neck.

Her captor snarled viciously, pulling his lips back and showing long canines. He let out a terrifying hiss and grabbed the second man's wrist. They froze, looking at each other over her prone body.

"You did not sedate her."

"No."

"You have marked her, she is in Thrall."

"Yes, as is my right."

"She is the one then?"

"Yes, she is the one that is mine."

Michelle was oblivious to the telepathic communication between the two men. To her they appeared to be frozen over her, staring into each other's eyes. Her captor's lips rippled in challenge while the other looked at him questioningly. They seemed to come to a silent understanding as her captor slowly released the smaller man's wrist.

The newcomer lifted a small device, running it just above her body. He approached a screen and studied it for a while before turning, silently regarding her abductor.

"She appears perfectly healthy and her body has yielded, Majesty. I see no reason you cannot proceed with the Claiming."

"Her body yielded but her fear beats at me. I must first earn her trust and ignite her desire. To claim her now would be little better than rape."

"It is a dangerous time. As an Alpha with your mate in Thrall, you will not be able to tolerate another close to her. Until you have made her yours, you will be extremely volatile and prone to violence."

"This I have noticed."

"She will remain in Thrall until you mate her. Her race is not telepathic nor are they empathic. You will not be able to communicate with her until after you are bonded. The longer you wait to take her, the more feral you will become. I am sure your Animal emerging will not further endear you to her."

"Yet I will not rape any woman, least of all my mate. What would you suggest I do?"

"Take her to your quarters and gentle her but do not take overly long. Neither of you will be able to eat or drink until the mating is complete. The longer you wait, the weaker she will become and the more violent the mating."

Lord Lann Ramos, Alpha and ruler of planet Vidar, lifted his helpless, terrified mate into his arms and headed to the door.

"Congratulations on finding the one that is yours, Majesty," Dr. Fenton said silently.

Lann paused without turning, nodded in response and left the room.

~

As the monster carried her out of the room and down another hall, an armed military guard in grey uniforms fell in behind them in silence. The only sound – boot heels striking the floor. While they were all giants, her captor towered over the other men by several inches. She could tell he was being treated with deference and guessed he must be someone important in the scheme of things.

They rounded a corner and stopped in front of a door. Two of the guards drew weapons and entered the chamber. Returning after a short time, they nodded to the man holding her. The men bowed to her captor as he entered the quarters. Two of them stood guard outside the door just before it slid shut.

Lann passed through a richly appointed living room into a large master suite. He placed her unresponsive body on a huge bed, pulled back the covers to draw them over her. He left briefly, returning with a hairbrush, of all things, and sat next to her.

Starting at the ends, he brushed the tangles out of her long reddish-brown hair. His hands were gentle and steady as he worked at the intimate task. Once her hair was tangle free, he carefully arranged it on the soft pillow and sat back to admire his work. His moss green eyes were proprietary. He ran the backs of his fingers down her soft cheek in a gentle caress.

Michelle closed her eyes in despair. She was still unable to move a muscle. She had no idea who he was or where they were but was relatively sure they were no longer on earth. He terrified her, yet she felt strangely drawn to him. Beyond her depth, she was completely overwhelmed. A single tear leaked from one amber eye to flow across her temple. He leaned down and took it into his mouth with a kiss.

Seeing her exhaustion, he dimmed the lights and undressed. Lann climbed into bed next to her to draw her unresisting body into his arms. Her escalating fear slammed into him, breaking his heart.

When in Thrall, females of his race madly desired their mate, but also knew what was happening to them. Because few fertile Vidarian females remained, mating was a rare and sacred blessing. If fortunate enough to be the mate of an Alpha, Fertiles had been raised knowing his Animal would protect them with its life. The male would take only the greatest care in claiming her. When his canines extended and eyes glowed, it was seen as a sign of his growing ardor, attracting her further. Instead, his poor little mate no doubt saw him as a hideous monster bent on devouring her.

As he lay with her sweet body in his arms, his desire escalated. He was a large man and it became impossible to hide his growing erection. As it pressed against her hip, terror flowed from her in waves. He stroked her hair to sooth and reassure. After a while she seemed to settle. His erection, on the other hand, did not. If anything it grew in size and rigidity. He managed to hold perfectly still until she gave in to exhaustion and fell into a fitful sleep.

By all the stars in the heavens, he wanted her. Everything in him demanded he make her his in every way. Only an Alpha's true mate entered into the Thrall when he bit and injected her with his essence. Vidarians were beings of instinct. Once his mate was under his Thrall, every instinct dictated he take her. He literally shook with the effort to resist his very nature. Lann knew he was fighting a losing battle.

Michelle woke in the throes of a panic attack. She had dreamt she was paralyzed only to wake and find, in fact, she was – paralyzed – in the arms of the huge being that had taken her from her home.

He lay very still, but she could see glowing eyes in the dark indicating his wakefulness. His hot breath ruffled her hair, massive erection pressing against her hip. Occasionally, he would run his hand up and down her bare arm. He didn't speak and she could not, so they lay together in silence.

By morning, one could cut the tension with a knife. Lann was in an agony of lust, Michelle in heartrending terror. He knew he had to move forward. She was not calming and they were running out of time.

Carefully, he unwrapped her small body from the blanket and pulled her into him, skin to skin. He made no effort to hide his torrid member. She needed to get used to his body. Ignoring her fear, he leaned over and brushed her soft lips with his. He nuzzled her neck as he ran large hands over her back, pulling her more fully into his erection.

Michelle could feel him trembling. He was being gentle but it was clearly costing him. She knew enough about men's bodies to know he had wanted her all night but made no move to rape her.

His kiss was soft and undemanding. When he nuzzled her neck, goose bumps rose on her skin and her nipples peaked, pressing into his bare chest. She could tell he noticed her response as his cock twitched between them, but still he was unhurried. After holding her, nuzzling her neck and rubbing her back for quite some time, he pulled away.

He encircled her slender neck with a long fingered hand before sliding it down to cover her breast. Lann rolled the nipple between his thumb and forefinger. She felt lightning streak to her core, causing moisture to pool between her legs. He inhaled, taking in her scent with a slight smile while his eyes searched hers. He took the other breast into his hot mouth and suckled greedily before holding the nipple between his teeth and flicking it with his tongue. She became drenching wet. He spent a long time making love to her breasts. Her fear was slowly transformed to burning desire.

When she was sure she could stand no more, he ran his hand down her body to the juncture of her thighs and gently tested her readiness. Her clitoris was erect and throbbing, her core creaming copiously. He took his time circling the taught little nub with the pad of his finger until she nearly came undone.

Lann could feel and scent his lady's growing response – he was all but at the end of his control. He could feel the wildness rising in him, trying to overcome all gentleness. He had no choice but to take her to the next level.

Sliding down her body, he placed her long legs over his shoulders and took her core in a scalding, open mouthed kiss. He ran his tongue over her erect clitoris as he carefully sank one long, thick finger into her wet depths. Even though she was paralyzed in Thrall, her inner muscles gripped his fingers like a vice. He could feel her trembling from the inside out. Now, instead of fear, her passion washed over him, further straining his control.

Michelle had never been so hot, had never wanted anyone so much. His mouth, scorching and ravenous, devoured her. His finger stretched and burned yet left her craving more. It was absolute torture being unable to move – enduring sensual torment without lifting into him. She wanted to grab his long hair and hold his face to her. She wanted to pull him up her body and impale herself on his huge member.

Lann, totally attuned to his mate, knew the exact moment she was about to explode for him. It was now or never. If he waited until she came apart, he ran the risk of his Animal emerging and tearing into her with blind abandon, hurting and terrifying her in the process.

He rose over Michelle, pressed her legs further apart and settled the huge engorged head of his long, thick member at her wet entrance. Mantled over her, he captured her eyes with his. He knew his own were glowing bright green and would probably frighten his lady, but he had to watch her while he took her. He had to look into his mate's face while he breached her for the first time, making her forever his.

Slowly he pressed forward as her wet tissues yielded to his possession. He could feel her stretch to accommodate him. By the stars, she was petite, delicate and so tight he thought he would explode. He paused, trying to give Michelle time to adjust.

Her eyes were looking into his pleadingly, but pleading for what he did not know. Did she want him to stop? He would die for her but he could not stop. He simply had to make her his. The Claiming was upon him. Everything in him demanded it…

Other Books By
Cahira O'Donnell

The Long Dark Night

The Seven Sisters Series
Book One

Ghost Hawk

The Seven Sisters Series
Book Two
(Coming Soon)

To Taste You Again

The Daguronian Chronicles

(Coming Soon)

Oracle Of Vidar

The Daguronian Chronicles
Book Two
(Coming Soon)

Other Books By

Cahira O'Donnell

WITH ALL THAT I AM

THE DAGURONIAN CHRONICLES

(COMING SOON)

YOU ARE MY HEART

THE DAGURONIAN CHRONICLES

(COMING SOON)

THE KING'S DAGGER

THE DAGURONIAN CHRONICLES

(COMING SOON)

---

www.ingramcontent.com/pod-product-compliance
Lightning Source LLC
Chambersburg PA
CBHW060515180626
46817CB00002B/369